FATES ANOINTED

FATES ANOINTED

Alexander Webb

WILLIAM KIMBER · LONDON

First published in 1985 by
WILLIAM KIMBER & CO. LIMITED
100 Jermyn Street, London SW1Y 6EE

ISBN 0 7183 0578 7

Photoset in North Wales by
Derek Doyle & Associates Mold, Clwyd
and printed in Great Britain by
Biddles Limited, Guildford, Surrey

For my wife Kathleen

Contents

To a small boy who one day asked of his star – 'What is it, and where did you find it?' St Vincent replied, 'I found it upon the sea; and if you become a sailor, and search diligently, perhaps you may find just such another.'

I

Half Pay

Nelson was dead! Napoleon's 'grand design' to put a vast flotilla of flat-bottomed invasion craft across the Channel was in abeyance. Lieutenant Philip Masterman Naseby, newly commissioned and beached, was on half pay.

It was Christmas 1805. His Britannic Majesty's ship *Defiance* had been paid off less than a month and already life ashore had begun to rankle.

Staring morosely out over the rain-washed cobbles, Naseby, perhaps for the thousandth time in the past weeks, was forced to reflect on a fickle fate which had at one and the same time lifted a penniless midshipman, devoid both of family and influence, to the lordly position of officer and 'gentleman'. Only to then cast him adrift with little hope of appointment and hence minus the wherewithal to acquit himself as his new station demanded.

Packed off to sea as a volunteer first class – rated Captain's servant – at the tender age of thirteen by a now deceased uncle (a charitable act which had discharged, albeit grudgingly, that ageing kinsman's obligation to his lately orphaned nephew) Naseby's feet had been placed precariously upon the first rung of what could, with comfortable optimism, be looked upon as a ladder offering glittering prospects. Indeed, where better for a gangling misfit with little respect for his elders and a penchant for rough and tumble brawling!

That had been almost nine years ago now, February 1797. Nelson, as Commodore under Sir John Jervis, had been engaged in trouncing the Spanish off Cape St Vincent. An epic piece of maritime destruction which had been duly celebrated in the stern old Admiral's choice of a 'legend' on which to rest his elevation to an earldom. Old Jervey had until recently been First Lord of the Admiralty, having attained the post under Addington in 1801.

The necessary step from volunteer first class to midshipman had followed as, in the natural order of things, a timely accident had provided a vacancy, and the intervening years had seen the gangling youth become a sturdy six-footer with a shock of unruly black hair and a steady eye. A so-so navigator – mathematics had ever been a stumbling block – and an, at best, adequate seaman; two abysmal attempts to pass his examination for lieutenant had resulted in failure. With the result that midshipman Philip Naseby was doomed to remain just that – had not Villeneuve's clash with Nelson at Trafalgar provided an opportunity, eagerly seized, to demonstrate the one asset which he held in abundance – a reckless courage and unyielding ferocity such as possessed by few men – which naturally inspired lesser spirits to follow. 'Leadership,' Vice-Admiral Collingwood, commanding the lee column of which *Defiance* had been a part, had termed it. 'It' being sufficient following Collingwood's recommendation for the Lords of Admiralty to advance a 'valorous and deserving' young aspirant to lieutenant. Unfortunately for Naseby, however, one of many.

At least as a midshipman he had been certain of a berth; while now, as a decidedly junior lieutenant lacking the necessary influence at court or in Admiralty – competing with the offspring of nobility – his chances of employment would seem, at best, slim.

Turning away from the tiny rain-flecked window, Naseby gazed gloomily around him. The drab little room: bed, fireplace and solitary wooden chair. Decidedly utilitarian. 'Hardly an adequate reward for gallantry!' he muttered to himself, only to lapse grudgingly into a self-derisory smile as his natural humour asserted itself. He would be twenty-two in a fortnight. Nelson had been a post captain at that age! But then, Nelson was dead. While it was extremely unlikely, mused Naseby, sobering somewhat, that he would ever manage to put himself in the way of being made post – there being none to aid him in this.

Outside – nay, downstairs in this very lodging house – it was Christmas Day. Throughout this great nation in a million homes people were keeping Christmas according to their lights. He, Philip Naseby, was alone. Well, it had ever been thus.

Abruptly he snatched up his pea-jacket and headed for the door.

It was bitterly cold outside with the beginnings of a driving sleet that, sink his chin resolutely beneath the folds of his muffler though he did, managed nevertheless to find its way inside his clothing, icy tentacles snaking and slithering against protesting goose-fleshed skin. Setting his teeth, he forged grimly out of the alley and headed towards Broad Street, bitterly mindful of his aloneness and the rapidly gathering twilight. At any event, he was not going to spend this evening fretting in that squalid lodging house.

From a shadowed doorway off to his right a plaintive voice momentarily arrested his attention. 'Fourpence, dearie, fourpence for a gobble. No teef, dearie. Only fourpence?' His flesh revolting, Naseby hurried on, shutting his mind to the scab-encrusted crone who beckoned lewdly from the shadows. Fourpence! The price of a basic meal at one of Portsmouth's baser eating houses. God! And men fought and died for this misbegotten island! He shivered involuntarily. Well, not, he told himself forcefully, Philip Naseby Esquire. If he fought it was because fighting, in all its many and varied forms, was what he was best at. And if he wore the King's coat when doing so, why, then, that was simply due to an accident of birth. Had he been born a Frenchman, it would have been Napoleon's coat in which he waged war. Nothing more nor less than that. Philip Naseby, now a lieutenant in His Britannic Majesty's Navy, was, ever had been, and always would be, primarily an opportunist. A soldier of fortune in the strictest sense. A mercenary, if you will. And as such fought, aye and right well, for Philip Naseby, for advancement, and, should the prevailing fates decree it, for the chance of prize money. Which golden opportunity those same fates had not as yet seen fit to vouchsafe him.

Such line of thought, of course, brought him full circle back to a necessarily desultory assessment of his chances of future employment. Mentally he changed tack, considering instead the two shillings and ninepence which he had with reckless abandon decided he could afford to spend on his forthcoming evening's entertainment. Little enough in all conscience, but to a half pay naval officer with over four weeks to go before his next visit to the clerk of the cheque, a tidy outlay. Pulling up short in his tracks, he realised that he had almost charged, unseeing, past his destination, so absorbed had he been in his scowling assessment of his meagre resources.

Retracing his steps, and stamping loudly in the low doorway, Naseby ducked his six feet and entered the eating house, his footfalls becoming suddenly silent as they fell on the thick layer of sawdust covering the flagstoned floor. The place stank of burnt tallow from the smoking lamps, heavily intermingled with the reek of boiled cabbage. The whole was overlaid with the pungent aroma of cheap tobacco rising contentedly from a dozen long-stemmed clay pipes. The proprietor, a patch-eyed veteran, bobbed before him, knuckling his forehead and grunting unintelligibly. Naseby ordered the fourpenny ordinary and a tankard of ale, taking a seat at one of the rough oak tables farthest from the doorway. It was a rare enough event, he realised, in the mundane affairs of the eating house to have to cater to the tastes of such a lordly personage as a naval lieutenant, even a half pay one like himself. Especially on such a night as this.

A buxom woman in a soiled apron brought his meal across, greasily unkempt hair falling distastefully across the plate as she bent to serve him. Naseby shut his eyes. Not that a happening so commonplace as this could serve to steal his appetite. Not after some nine years at sea, the greater part of which had been spent in a ravenous appreciation of the delicacy of the biscuit-fed rat! Life in the gunroom mess even in 1805 had not yet progressed sufficiently for starvation not to be the natural order of things.

Hungrily he addressed his plate, wondering at the same time how wardroom fare would taste; if, that was, he ever got the chance to find out. Despite his mood the boiled mutton proved palatable enough, at least when helped down by liberal gulpings of ale, and Naseby found himself somewhat enjoying the meal. At a corner table a one-legged seaman hoisted his tankard in good-natured salutation:

'Good on 'ee, Cap'n! An' a right Merry Christmas to 'ee!'

Naseby returned the sentiment, draining his tankard and signalling for a refill. 'Will yer 'ave the puddin', zur – it's duff, with currants an' sultanas?' enquired the woman, smiling shyly. Naseby assented and then, feeling recklessly expansive, decided also on a bottle of port to see it off. She dropped him a curtsey, then hurried off to obey the jovially given order.

Outside in the night it would be cold and lonely. But within the eating house it was warm and friendly. Naseby felt a deal more at peace with the world and the next hour and a half went by pleasantly enough. By the time he left the eating house, the previous stinging sleet had given way to softly falling flakes of snow which seemed to blossom luminescently in the muted glow from nearby buildings. Tugging up the deep collar of his pea-jacket, he turned his footsteps towards the dockyard area and the Keppel's Head. What wind there was now drove the white, swirling snowflakes whistling about his ears as he trekked towards the cheerfully beckoning public house, his spirits restless, and conscious in his bones of the urgent yearning to get to sea again.

The main taproom was packed to the rafters, with everywhere a liberal smattering of blue coats, not a few of which were decked out in gold lace, the festive illumination reflecting dazzlingly off the heavy bullion-fringed epaulettes sported by their owners. Naseby was acutely conscious of his lack of a lieutenant's full dress coat with the smart white lapels and cuffs, instead of the rather plain undress one with its spartan piping which he had decided was all that his stinted finances could stand. Swallowing his qualms in a defiant determination to put a brave face upon it, he imperiously cleared himself a path to the bar, senses quickened by the fragrant waftings of cigar smoke from the cramped cluster of side tables to his right.

His refreshment secured, he allowed himself to be drifted in the general direction of those same tables by the slowly milling crowd, at one of which a glittering array of senior post captains were avidly discussing the forthcoming state funeral of the nation's latest hero and martyr in St Paul's Cathedral. They passed on naturally enough from this to a highly optimistic assessment of the possibilities of the war drawing to a successful conclusion over the next twelve months. Naseby shut his ears to such arrant windbaggery and shuffled instead over to a momentarily vacant window space, his thoughts growing introspective despite the merry din which assaulted him from all sides. Reaching the window and gazing unseeingly at the already banking snow against its thickly leaded panes, it was with a sharply pleasant and heartwarming sensation of surprise that he felt a friendly hand descend upon his shoulder and turned to look bemusedly into the ruddy-complexioned face of someone whom he had not set eyes on since the turn of the century.

'Siras, Siras Blount!' he stammered, taken all aback, his senses reeling and his mind groping back over the long years of separation to the time that they had spent together as midshipmen before the lad who had perhaps at that time constituted his sole friend in all the world, although senior to him by some four years, had passed his examination for lieutenant and been posted to a frigate.

'Aye, Philip, aye,' chuckled the other, literally bursting with good humour and clasping a proprietary arm about Naseby's imposing breadth of shoulder. 'A lieutenant, no less,' he beamed appreciatively. 'Managed to sort out the jolly old spherical trigonometry, then?' Naseby managed to nod non-committally. As he remembered, Siras had ever been the leading light in those awful classes in navigational problems and the taking of daily sightings conducted by the peppery old sailing master Mister Glassforth. 'And yourself, Siras. Why, you've hardly changed at all,' he said, skilfully diverting the topic of conversation from his own sad lack of academic accomplishment. At which utterance Blount, feigning indignation, withdrew a pace, or at least as far as the gaily milling throng would allow, retorting, 'Then what would you be expecting, me lad, long white side whiskers and a cane for walking? Faith, man, I'm but a brace or two of summers riper than you!' He sobered, casting his tawny thatched head on one side, and ran a discerning eye up and down Naseby's rugged six feet, then let go an almost wistful sigh: 'But, then I can't rightly say the same of yourself, Philip.' A smile, so warm it seemed to light up his whole face, while making a dull pang of loneliness to kindle deep within the breast of its recipient. 'What in the world do they feed to midshipmen these days to make them grow into such sturdily flanked thoroughbreds as the one which I now see before me. For I'll warrant, you've not been a lieutenant overlong?'

Naseby laughed, falling easily into the spirit of the thing. 'Well, in answer to your first question, it's biscuit-fed rat, at a farthing each, when you can get 'em! As for your second, I'll have you to know, Senior Lieutenant Siras Blount, that I've been both an officer and a gentleman – mind a 'gentleman', I say – ' He repeated the word so as to lay special emphasis on the descriptive accolade, 'these past three weeks!' adding whimsically, 'In fact, I've already drawn my first month's half pay as such.'

At this point Naseby could well have expected to be experiencing a certain inevitable discomfiture at his rather evident pecuniary embarrassment. Blount, he had already noted, was arrayed in immaculate full dress of a cut and quality which could only have come from one of the more superior naval outfitters such as Messrs Thomas Allen of Bond Street in London. While if those hose weren't from Threshers in the Strand and the gold buckles which adorned his shoes from Yardleys, then he, Naseby, was a Dutchman! Yet somehow, gazing into that same well remembered ruddily complexioned face, positively alive with genuine and heartfelt joy at their so chance meeting, he could feel no wit of such churlish reserve.

His train of thought must, however, have been mirrored on his face, for looking studiously into his eyes, Blount said slowly, 'I've been uncommon lucky in the matter of prize money, Philip, Providence having seen fit to throw a nice fat merchantman or two in our way, so to speak!' He grinned a little self-consciously, adding, 'Besides which, as you will remember, my father left me a little when he died.'

Naseby nodded absently, conscious once again of wishing to change the subject.

The snow was falling more heavily still when at last the two parted company, albeit reluctantly on the part of Philip

Naseby, outside the Keppel's Head, to go their separate ways. Which in Naseby's case meant back to the squalid little lodging house and its even more squalid attic room, devoid of all warmth and cheer, to huddle once more morosely beneath the frayed blankets and dream of prize money and action, and of the sea! Still, the pair had promised to meet the following day, Boxing Day, and pass the evening together. This prospect it was that warmed him and sustained his flagging spirits on the lonely trudge through the snow back to Cobbs Alley.

His way led him past the Long Rooms, one of the better haunts of the nobility, in search of a diverting way to part with some small quantity of their wealth. Perhaps at roulette or one of the numerous other games of chance which the establishment offered. It was around ten thirty, early as yet for any of its elegant patrons to be disgorging into the night. Which was why, perhaps, the thoroughly bored and obviously numb with cold young whore engaged in patiently awaiting an opportunity to ply her trade, fixed on Naseby. True indeed, even hidden beneath muffler and pea-jacket and with his one shabby cocked hat pulled low about his ears, his height and bearing were such as to warrant a second look. Perhaps even a third. But even the necessarily heavy clothing and freshly acquired layering of snow would hardly have served to pass him off as a member of 'carriage trade'. Be that as it may, it was to Naseby that she made her pitch, opening her cloak and throwing off her hood, the better that he might assay her charms and perchance feel encouraged to sample her wares.

'A shilling'll do it, dearie. My place ain't far, an' you c'n stay the night.' She was a handsome wench, right enough; there was no denying that, thought Naseby. While the forlorn prospect of spending another night, tonight of all nights, shivering alone in that attic was, to put it mildly, an abomination. Against that was the fact that, what with the polite necessity of standing round for round of drinks with Blount in the Keppel's Head, he had already spent far more of his pitiful subsistence money than was prudent. Thus he hesitated, while the softly fluttering flakes of snow fell silent and fluffy against the girl's partially exposed bosom. 'Well, make up yer mind, dearie, afore I catches me death o' cold an' is no use ta yer!' Deftly she shrugged one heavy breast completely free of its restraining bodice, tilting back her head seductively. 'Right you are, m'girl!' decided Naseby, taking her by the arm. After all, he mused, what was a shilling?

True to her word, the silently beckoning house to which she led Naseby was but a stone's throw from the Long Rooms – along a snow-blanketed alleyway and up a shallow flight of narrow stone steps which would doubtless prove treacherous when the dawn chill had turned the powdered snow to ice. Passing through a low entrance way and across a small courtyard, walled in on all sides, Naseby found himself confronted by a sudden turn of circumstances which perhaps he should have already been expecting.

As if growing from the loftily confining walls which hemmed him in to right and left, sprang several figures, wraithlike in the illuminating snow. A clasping hand found his shoulder, its owner attempting to spin him for the cudgel's blow. Instantly alive to his danger and to the folly of trying to break free only to be struck down from his unengaged flank, Naseby shoulder-charged his assailant. He was rewarded by a sharp explosion of rancid breath in his face and a startled oath. Something glanced off the back of his head, divesting him of his precious cocked hat, and he span tangle-footed to plant a brine-hardened fist squarely against a softly yielding moon face.

He had the measure of the place now, while his eyes already accustomed to the semi-dark had taken the number of his enemies. Added to this, the instinct of the natural born fighting man had succeeded in putting a wall firmly at his back. There were four of them, at least two with cudgels, while he fancied that out of the tail of one eye he had caught the momentary reflection of a knife in someone's hand. Of the young whore there was nothing to be seen. Foolishly as it now seemed, Naseby had left his lodging house without benefit of, or indeed thought for, his sword. A rather plain affair, it was true, but much to be desired at this moment.

Something flickered briefly towards his body, causing him to throw up a defensive left arm, the deflected blade falling with a dull rasp in the snow. That got rid of the knife, anyway. He hoped that there was not another. Then there was no more time to think, only to sell his life dearly, as in a desperate rush his ragged assailants were upon him, gouging and grappling. Furiously seeking hands, their owners grown mindless in their singleness of purpose, intertwined hopelessly in the folds of his clothing, rending and tearing at the heavy cloth in a frantic, near maniacal effort to bear him down into the snow of the yard. There to lie helpless while the life-quenching rain of blows could extort their toll of him.

Snarling like an enraged beast Naseby, with a convulsive effort opened his shoulders, spilling his assailants to right and left, lashing out with all the controlled power of his solidly muscled thirteen stone. At least they would find the meagre coinage about his person little enough payment for the harsh outlay of blood and gristle which had been necessary for its securing. His right knee rammed jarringly into the crotch of a particularly lanky individual, while with his left forearm he warded off a sweeping blow from the cudgel. A thumb strove for his unguarded right eye and he viciously chopped with the horny palm of his open land at the man's windpipe, eliciting a gurgling sound as the fellow tumbled lifeless to the ground. Someone was rasping a hoarse command and at once he was free, the breath coming noisily in his throat, with only a fleeting moment in which to plant a wickedly arcing boot into the small of the back of a fleeing man. The unfortunate straggler let out a yelp of pain and half crawled, half shambled, off into the night.

Drawing himself up to his full height, Naseby drew deeply of the night air, feeling its soothing chill invade his lungs and start in to cool the passions of his fighting blood. Typical of the town of Portsmouth in the year 1805, the desperately fought brawl had summoned forth not a single curious soul, despite the fact that the little snow-layered courtyard was ringed on three sides by densely populated dwelling houses. At least one of the ruffians would roll no more unsuspecting customers. The man, a raggedly clothed seaman complete with heavily tarred pigtail and earring, was lying prostrate in the snow, his head at an unnatural angle; a splotch of thickly congealing blood at his gaping mouth shone blackly in the night.

Most likely some poor bastard of a deserter from one of the several men-of-war in from the Channel Fleet. No captain or first lieutenant in his right mind would allow on shore pressed men, who would immediately proceed to run. But there were always a few who managed to slip away from a victualling party or who somehow stole over the side at night. Even should the fellow's reason for being on shore be a legitimate one, a niggardly Admiralty paid them little enough. If at all. And then only in scrip. Useless paper, which some treacherous longshore shark would contrive to steal the lion's share of.

It was a shameful system and one which Naseby as a born liberal and secret radical could abhor. Abhor but not change, as numerous bouts of 'kissing the gunner's daughter' bent over the breech of a gun with the stinging bite of the rattan-cane wielded by some burly bo'sun's mate playing spitefully across his bared buttocks had taught him. This was a jungle, whether aboard ship or on shore. A jungle as mindlessly evil and rottenly corrupt as any which he had seen on the southern continent of America in '98. The name of the game was survival of the fittest. Every man for himself. Whichever way you wanted to put it. And the only course open to a sensible man, was to go in wholeheartedly. Play them at their own game, only on your own account, and as far as it was possible, according to your own set of rules; or perhaps lack of same.

Leaving the slowly whitening corpse, Naseby made his way thoughtfully back to the road, footsteps crunching comfortingly in the snow, heavy flakes of which were still falling caressingly about his head and shoulders. The ruin of his only cocked hat was underneath his arm. (Some heavy-footed oaf among his assailants had jumped on it in the scuffle.) His pea-jacket had taken some rough usage, too. While the one vastly comforting factor to be borne in mind was that at least his generously calved legs had been snugly tucked into soft leather Hessian boots rather than his one pair of white silk stockings and pinchbeck buckled shoes. Reserved only, he had firmly resolved, for the most formal of occasions. Although truth to tell, what singularly mundane occurrence in the life of a half pay lieutenant could conceivably constitute a requirement for the stately formality of silken hose, would be difficult to imagine.

There was no sign of the heavy-breasted young whore outside the Long Rooms. Not that this was any real surprise. The Cobbs Alley lodging house was in darkness when he reached it, which again came as no surprise. In answer to persistent hammerings, the wizened old landlady Mrs Porter drew open the door, scowling darkly at being roused out of her bed at so ungodly an hour, and Naseby was in due course allowed to escape the crone's shrewish tongue in the dubious sanctuary afforded by his unwelcoming attic room.

Treating himself to the luxury of a candle, he peered ruefully at his slightly battered features in the cracked and cloudy looking glass over the mantel. A pair of steady brown eyes stared whimsically back at him from out of a full, almost square, face, noticing the smidgen of claret that had leaked from the perhaps over-broad nose onto one side of his generous-lipped mouth. Stifling a yawn he ran a tentative hand over his bruised jawline, then grinned; it would take a heftily wielded belaying pin to crack that solid-looking mass of bone, he knew.

The thought crossed his mind to mount a sortie downstairs in search of a bowl of water with which to bathe his face. But he decided against this for fear of once again rousing the wizened demon of a landlady from its lair. He made do instead with a gob of spittle and a corner of his handkerchief.

Vacantly he wondered what the morrow would bring. Fancy bumping into Siras of all people! After all these years. Perhaps it was not so strange, really. Such chance encounters interspersed with lengthy separations were very much a feature of navy life and as such, something which the men of the fighting service grew philosophically to accept.

Whistling softly, he divested himself of his clothes and crawled gratefully beneath the covers, remembering at the last moment to extinguish the precious candle, which had already burned down a measurable amount.

Siras had been looking well, there was no denying that. And indeed, why not?

Kester on the West Indian station had promised him a step to commander on his rejoining the squadron in the New Year, having the jealously guarded authority to do so as Commander in Chief of a station outside of home waters. Naseby told himself that he should be envious of his long lost friend's good fortune, and supposed that in truth he was. But for the life of him, he could not find it in his heart of hearts to countenance anything other than a genuine feeling of joy and good fellowship towards the hugely likable Blount.

With which lofty and uncharacteristically selfless thoughts, Lieutenant Philip Naseby closed his eyes and composed himself for sleep. It was scarce four hours till dawn in any case, he told himself sleepily. Well, there had been many occasions over the last nine years when the unutterable luxury of so much uninterrupted sleep would have been something which he would have given half a year's pay for. Life at sea was far from being an easy one. There was no denying that!

II

The Christmas Present

Roused from sleep by the habit of years a few minutes before dawn and tumbling out of bed in a brave effort to ignore the biting cold which nipped at his bare feet from the naked floorboards of the attic, Naseby was at once prey to a strange presentiment that somehow his position in the scheme of things had in some as yet undisclosed way altered since the previous evening. It was a sensation at once eerie while yet benign to which he was by far from being a stranger. Crossing at once to the frost-glazed window, inured now to the cold, he was in time to both witness the first pale gleam of dawn above the picturesquely luminescent rooftops and the slithering arrival at the lodging house of a precariously mounted messenger, coat tails flying. Still in the grip of his strange awareness, Naseby set himself hastily to dressing.

Pulling on shirt and breeches, he was therefore not at all surprised to hear an urgent hammering on the downstairs door, followed by a muffled mention of his name as he finished tugging on his boots. The logical part of his brain was of course completely cognisant of the fact that subconsciously he may have been listening to the rapid approach of hoofbeats on the treacherous veneer of ice for some moments as he awoke from sleep, without being aware that he had done so.

From there it was none too great a stretch to realise that a peculiarly questing and imaginative mind such as Naseby knew himself to be possessed of – and yearning as he was for some intervening harbinger of destiny to propel him once more into the pre-ordained hurly-burly of events – was fertile soil from which could spring the natural merging of his own and the hurrying messenger's fates. Be that as it may, that self same intuitively imaginative mind, acknowledged free-thinker that he was, leaned strongly towards the improbable. Instinctively accepting the unacceptable. 'There are stranger things in heaven and earth, Horatio,' muttered Naseby to himself as he answered the sharp rap on the attic room door.

The messenger he saw was no more than a boy, perhaps not yet fourteen, and wearing the uniform of a midshipman. 'Lieutenant Philip Naseby, sir?' enquired the messenger in a reedy voice. Naseby replied in the affirmative, hoping as he did so that the wild flutterings in his breast were not making themselves evident on his face. 'With the compliments of Commander Blount, sir; and I was told to say that no reply was necessary, sir!'

Almost quivering with excitement, Naseby took the missive which was held out to him, barely managing a grunt as the midshipman tramped off down the narrow stairway, leaving him alone and thus safe to let out the exclamatory whoosh of breath which had risen in his chest at hearing his friend described as 'commander'.

Turning back into the room and back-heeling the door shut behind him, Naseby hurried to the window, while for no good reason that he could think of, starting to giggle in a way which was not only absurd in one of his physique and bearing, but totally at odds with the dignity of the uniform which he wore.

Slitting open the thin wafer with his thumbnail and unfolding the contents, he read, 'Lieutenant Philip Naseby, you are hereby requested and required – ' Naseby could not suppress a belly laugh at this, Siras's irreverent use of official naval phraseology in what a quickly scanning glance to the foot of the page had already told him was a private letter between friends. His sense of the march of events, be it supernatural or otherwise, had as he had known it would proved itself once more infallible.

Fumbling in the pocket of his waistcoat, which he had forgotten to don and which still lay draped across his solitary wooden chair, for his silver turnip watch, he saw that it was yet five minutes short of the hour. He had ample time, and to spare. His rendezvous with Siras at the dockyard gate was for eight o'clock.

The snow-packed cobbles underfoot were indeed treacherous, much of the snow having turned to ice overnight. The wind was keen and ideal for an offing as Naseby could now appreciate without experiencing an accompanying pang as a result.

At the dockyard Blount was waiting for him, his, if it were possible, even ruddier face wreathed in a welcoming smile which warmed Naseby to the very marrow.

'Siras! Er, I mean sir!' exclaimed Naseby, eagerly clasping the broad hand held out to him. Nonetheless, he could not help but comment on the gleaming object that took his eye. 'I see you had it ready, sir?' the use of the so necessary correct form of address falling more readily to his lips this time. His gaze indicated the heavy gold epaulette which the other wore on his left shoulder, denoting his rank as commander.

'Never hurts to be prepared!' chuckled Blount with more than a hint of pride. 'When it travels to the other side, then I'll know I've arrived!' The same gold symbol of rank when worn on the opposite, right, shoulder indicated its wearer had attained the immensity of being posted captain, with his feet planted securely on the ladder of seniority, which provided that he did not die first or manage to disgrace himself, would inexorably result in his gaining a similar adornment for his other, left, shoulder after three years should have expired from his date of being gazetted. While in the fullness of time that same inexorable and inflexible march up the gilded ladder of power would see him hoisting his flag as an admiral.

'It's a foregone conclusion though, sir,' rejoined Naseby – which he knew full well to be a comfortable enough prediction. From commander, who bore the full weight of responsibility and immense power, along with the title of captain when in command of a ship, to the established permanence of being made post was very much a giant step. The gap between these two was far greater in the naval scheme of things even than that between a lowly lieutenant and a lofty commander. Nevertheless, it was a step that could with all confidence expect to be taken. Siras Blount was on his way!

'Yes, that is, provided I don't get cut in half by a ball from some Frog broadside in the meantime!' stated the other matter of factly.

Naseby changed the subject with a question. 'The *Resolve*, sir, how many guns?'

'Eighteen,' replied Blount, and then went on, his boundless enthusiasm making itself evident in his tone of voice. 'She's a right trim little craft, Philip. I saw her once at the Nore in '83. Maynard was commanding her then.'

A momentary silence settled over the pair as they entered the dockyard. Maynard had fallen to a French musket ball a year later. Much as had Nelson at Trafalgar. It was left to Naseby to rekindle the conversation.

'You haven't told me yet, sir, the circumstances surrounding your promotion.'

'Yes. You could have knocked me down with a feather,' replied Blount, brightening visibly. 'I got back to the Feathers last night to find a most immediate summons awaiting me from Sir Charles Peregrine.' Peregrine, as Naseby knew, was currently the Rear Admiral in charge of the inshore squadron which had until recently been engaged in the blockading of Brest. 'Well, you'll recall that it was none too late when we parted company at the Keppel's Head, and since Sir Charles has rooms but a floor above mine at the Feathers – ' So, Siras's good fortune in the matter of prize money ran to his being able to afford a suite of rooms, mused Naseby, conscious despite himself at this stage in the proceedings of a slight twinge of envy. 'So you naturally felt able to answer his summons immediately, sir,' he supplied, blandly enough.

'As fast as my two knock-kneed legs could carry me!' affirmed Blount.

Yes, come to think of it, Siras did have knock-knees. It was something of a comfort to notice it now, and served completely to wipe away all trace of Naseby's bourgeoning feelings of inferiority at his friend's splendiferous style of living.

Over the next quarter of an hour Naseby was able to elicit from a comically self-satisfied Siras all the relevant details concerning that highly fortunate individual's midnight interview with Sir Charles Peregrine. While as he listened to his friend's at times almost pompous recounting of it, Naseby was for the life of him in very real danger of lapsing into disrespectful peals of laughter.

It had been decided by the Lords of Admiralty in their wisdom, under orders from the Cabinet, that in the light of recent events – the crushing blow inflicted on the combined French and Spanish fleets by Vice Admiral Lord Nelson at Trafalgar – the continuing war should now be pursued to a speedy and vigorous climax. A sentiment which Naseby vocally applauded, being at the same time astutely aware of its present impossibility of execution, as well as abhorring the merest suggestion that the war should be over before he might have a chance of distinguishing himself. 'Thank heaven for Bonaparte!' would have been his own private toast should a glass have been handy.

In order to expiate a proposed push by land forces, the decision had been taken to almost double the strength of the blockading squadrons. The determination in Whitehall being that never again should the naval presence of Napoleon Bonaparte be seen beyond the sanctuary of their own harbours. Accordingly, every vessel that would float and was capable of bearing ordnance was being ordered into the Channel. Among them was His Britannic Majesty's eighteen gun sloop of war *Resolve*. The early confirmation of Siras Blount's hitherto only promised step to commander was but one of many new appointments pushed through over the last few days. The Lords of Admiralty, it seemed, did not keep Christmas.

At least it was evidence, if such were needed, mused Naseby, of the urgency attached to the current situation in the Channel by their lordships!

'And so when Sir Charles offered me the chance of choosing one out of my two lieutenants, I naturally thought of you,' Blount was concluding, with perhaps the smallest trace of self-gratifying condescension.

'For which unwarranted kindness I shall forever be in your debt, sir,' applauded Naseby, and meant it.

'Tch, tch,' murmured Blount expansively, 'look on it as a somewhat belated Christmas present, my dear Philip, and say no more about it.'

'Aye, aye, sir!' responded Naseby, knuckling his forehead in a comic parody of the lower deck, and introducing a timely touch of levity into a threateningly maudlin turn in the conversation. Had he been surer of Commander Blount's political and patriotic leanings, or rather absence of same, Naseby might well have pointed out the unassailable fact – one which seemed by the way to have momentarily escaped their lordships in the prevailing mood of patriotic fervour sweeping the country – that while it was undoubtedly true that Britannia indeed ruled the waves, the Royal Navy being now virtually omnipotent at sea, the Emperor Napoleon was if anything even more omnipotent on land, holding the continent of Europe in a grip of iron, and with much of the rest of the world subservient to his will.

No matter what governmental propaganda might be handed out to the common herd, and even believed by certain of the more gullible amongst their more privileged 'betters', Naseby knew the truth to be otherwise. England stood alone, and largely had done since the inception of this epic war.

However, unsure as he was of the capability for independent thought possessed by his friend, who would in all likelihood reveal himself at the gentlest prompting as a confirmed dyed-in-the-wool pro-Establishment figure and ranting Tory to boot, Naseby deemed it wiser to keep his own counsel. An unfettered mental capacity was very much a rarity on the quarterdeck of a King's ship, as Naseby had often had occasion to bemoan during his formative years in the Service.

The rest of the conversation concerning the victualling and readying for sea of the sloop *Resolve* took up most of the morning and ended with Naseby being introduced to the ship's only other lieutenant, one Thomas Edwards, an undersized sprig of a man with a squint in one eye and whom Naseby was not at all surprised to find was vastly senior to himself. Well, no matter, he inwardly temporised, the fact of his regaining the sea at all was miracle enough, without expecting to be first lieutenant as well. Besides which, he was doubly fortunate in that appointed to a nimble-footed sloop as he was instead of a lumbering ship of the line with anything up to a possible eight lieutenants, he should have ample opportunity to distinguish himself. After all, there were only two men on the quarterdeck standing between him and overall command of the ship.

Perhaps it was indicative of the inherent harshness of the service at this time, and to the tawdry value which it attached to human life, even that of a friend, that Naseby could so lightly countenance the necessary suffering and death of two fellow officers which would be required to place him in the captain's cabin. It was also, perhaps, a useful insight into his character ...

*

The *Resolve* thrashed along with a brisk nor'easterly singing gustily in her rigging, the sloop's trim lines making light work of the mid-Channel turbulence. Balancing himself easily on the rhythmically undulating deck, Second Lieutenant Philip Naseby, who had the watch with the junior midshipman, a sandy-haired youngster by the oddly appropriate name of Fairley, took a confirmatory glance at the gently rocking compass card afloat in the lighted binnacle box before resuming his patient, rolling-gaited pacing up and down, back and forth, along the vacant weather side.

It was good to be walking a deck again with the refreshing tang of salt setting up the familiar tingling sensation on his skin, his Hessian-booted feet clumping comfortingly as he kept his onerous vigil.

There was yet an hour to go before dawn; before the eagle-eyed lookout could be posted aloft and the *Resolve* once again resound to the martial sound of the drum, as her people were beat to quarters. Ready to meet the new day, as in every ship of His Majesty's Navy at sea during war-time, able to meet any eventuality.

Resolve was under orders to join up with the inshore squadron before dusk on the 31st off Ushant. Her task over the next weeks and months: to set up a careful and all encompassing watch on the French naval base at Brest – Rear Admiral Peregrine's 'terrier at the foxhole', as it were – against the all too real danger of some straying segment of the blockaded enemy fleet managing to get to sea with conditions foul for the British.

It was a great responsibility for her newly promoted, and proud, commander, Siras Blount. One which, should he and his officers prove equal to the task, would doubtless result in his being made post in the forthcoming twelve to eighteen months. If not, should some mass breakout of French line-of-sail occur as a direct result of any lack of vigilance on the part of the *Resolve* or her people – then! But Naseby did not like to think about that possibility. Likely enough a court martial for her captain and a lifetime on the beach for her officers. Naseby suppressed a shudder.

The wind was veering; already in the past half an hour it had altered a full couple of points. Crossing to the binnacle, Naseby addressed a curt order to the diminutive midshipman: 'Mister Fairley, my compliments to the captain, and the wind's veered two points!' The midshipman disappeared below and Naseby addressed himself to the task of keeping a weather eye on the helmsman …

'Sail ho!' sang out the voice of the lookout from aloft.

'Where away?' bellowed Edwards, who had the watch, his voice booming surprisingly for so slight a man.

'One – two points – the starboard bow,' came the reply, the wind whipping at the lookout's words and making communication between masthead and deck difficult.

'Mister Peterson, take the bring-em-near and get up to the foretopmast head; as quickly as possible, Mister Peterson, if you please!' ordered the captain, newly arrived on deck and plainly doing his utmost to contain his impatience, and just as obviously losing the battle.

In addition to Fairley and a 1st class volunteer by the name of Anson, the *Resolve* had two other midshipmen, the senior of whom was Peterson, a lanky nineteen-year-old who was looking forward to his examination for lieutenant.

'What the devil's keeping that midshipman!' fumed Blount, almost dancing on the deck in his anxiety.

'A frigate, sir. She's almost hull up on the horizon now!' sang out Peterson from the masthead.

Snatching up a telescope from beside the wheel, Naseby took a perch in the mizzen shrouds, balancing precariously and doing his best to steady the glass to the rise and fall of the ship.

The frigate's foreroyals were visible from the deck now.

'What nationality is she?' demanded Blount of the lookout, but Peterson was down on the deck now and came running aft to report.

'Frigate's a Frenchman, sir!'

'Aye, she's a Frog all right,' confirmed Shelby, the master's mate. 'Or I'm a Dutchman, sir!'

Naseby had already reached that conclusion from the frigate's lines and sail configuration, but deemed it best to wait until he should be certain.

There were perhaps fifteen minutes left of the forenoon watch. The sky was grey with low scudding clouds which seemed to rake the loftily circling mastheads, and an urgently churning sea which had the little sloop pitching and tossing like a cork in a rain barrel.

'Very well. Clear for action, Mister Edwards! Have the guns loaded, but not run out until I give the word!' ordered Blount curtly, obviously coming to a decision.

The staccato roll of the single drum accompanied by myriad scurrying feet and the steady tramp of *Resolve*'s tiny complement of marines sent a thrill of anticipation coursing hotly through Naseby's veins. Under no circumstances could the frail scantlings and pop-gun armament of a sloop of war stand up to a broadside from an enemy frigate. Armed with anything from thirty-six to forty-four guns, and eighteen pounders to boot! Blount was merely going through the motions while intending to remain to windward of the enemy and if necessary show the frigate a clean pair of heels. A plan with which Naseby heartily concurred. *Resolve*'s duty was plain: use every artifice to keep the Frenchman in sight until such time as a British ship of comparable size should be encountered.

As number two, Naseby's place was at the guns. Accordingly he now stood, legs braced easily to the send of the deck, hands clasped behind his back and his narrowing gaze held firmly on the steadily nearing pyramid of French canvas. The sloop's deck had been sprayed with sand to prevent the feet of the gun crews slipping, and beside each gun was a tub of water over which sputtered a softly glowing length of slow match, against failure by the gun's flintlock firing mechanism. Each one of them also had its covering canvas hood so necessary to keep out spray.

In the magazine Hodgkins the gunner would be padding backwards and forwards in his list slippers, handing out serge cartridges through the heavily wetted blanket screen to the waiting line of powder monkeys, whose fleet-footed task it was to keep the *Resolve*'s armament supplied during battle. At each grey-shadowed companionway a grim-visaged marine sentry, bayonet fixed, stood ready, his orders to prevent anyone other than those with business below from seeking shelter beneath the waterline.

Apart from the ever present shipboard noises and the scarcely heeded play of the water overside, all were enveloped in a strangely silent world peopled by blandly waiting figures. Each in his own way was caught up in the eerie fascination provided by the ever nearing enemy frigate and a needful reappraisal of his own frail mortality.

'Larboard a point!' intoned the captain to the seemingly unconcerned bulk of the quartermaster at the wheel. 'Aye, aye, sir. Course sou'sou' west.'

In the past couple of hours the wind had continued to veer, blowing now from almost due east, and taking *Resolve* just abaft the beam.

'Frigate's hoisting her colours, sir,' observed Edwards the first lieutenant sombrely.

'Very well, we'll return the compliment, if you please!' replied the captain.

Casting a considering eye aft, Naseby was relieved to see that Siras had apparently managed at last to bring his tautly stretched nerves under control. It wasn't a matter of courage, of that he was sure. No one could ever accuse the ruddy-featured Siras of being lacking in physical courage. Moral courage, however – the cool-headed ability to make a decision and stick to it, to place his command and his reputation in the way of danger – was something else again. As Naseby well knew. Many an officer, capable of seamanship and promising of mien, would be found wanting when faced with a situation which required the throwing into the pot of his career prospects and future employment. The difference, perhaps, mused Naseby in a moment of insight, between an Admiral Byng and a Lord Nelson.

With the frigate tacking to intercept, the two ships ploughed along in a bluff east wind with the gap narrowing steadily between them to not quite long cannon shot. The hands had been sent to dinner, faring poorly on cold salt pork and ship's biscuit.

'She's beginning to head-reach on us, sir!' spoke up Edwards, telescope to eye. Naseby steadied his own glass. It was true: while *Resolve* was undeniably the faster ship, the greater spread of canvas which the frigate possessed was beginning to tell at this point of sailing. A thin plume of water rose up perhaps a cable's distance to starboard. The dull boom of the cannon came a moment later.

'She's trying a ranging shot at us, sir!' called out Naseby unnecessarily.

'No need to concern ourselves at present,' countered the captain shortly.

The choppy conditions of the Channel had long since given way to the long greyish green rollers of the Atlantic. If *Resolve* were to have any chance at all of leading her heavily armed pursuer onto the guns of a waiting British line-of-sail, Blount would have to make the decision to stand in for Ushant in the next half an hour or so.

To starboard several more lofty plumes of water, somewhat nearer this time, rose up as if to drive the point home more forcibly.

'If'n the Frog gets any nearer, mates, cap'n'll 'ave to 'aul 'is colours,' muttered an elderly gun captain matter of factly.

'Belay that kind of talk there!' rasped Naseby sourly, sending in the toe of his boot to add weight to the command; at the same time, however, having to admit privately that the fellow was right. Should the Frenchman once succeed in getting the frail little sloop under the full force of his broadside, the end would come swiftly indeed.

'Stand by to put the ship about, Mister Edwards!' commanded the captain, tersely, strain literally oozing from his words and adding to the sharp tension of his officers. At least the first lieutenant Edwards seemed steady enough,

Naseby found time to reflect thankfully. Throughout the ship, pipes shrilled as the hands ran to the braces, petty officers blistering the bare backs of the seamen with their knotted rope ends. The *Resolve* was turning.

'Let go and haul!' blared Edwards through the speaking trumpet.

Naseby cast an eye aloft as the sloop's yards came creaking round, the hands hauling mightily at the braces, her sails filling taut as *Resolve* heeled to the starboard tack. The rattle of blocks and squealing of shrouds set up a high-pitched cacophony of sound which endured until the sloop had settled comfortably on her new course.

'Keep her full and by!' ordered the captain, casting an anxious glance aft at the Frenchman.

For the next fifteen minutes *Resolve* made good her fleeting advantage as the frigate, her yards braced sharply round, struggled manfully to claw back the lost ground.

'Confound your innards!' railed Blount at the quartermaster, who in his wisdom remained philosophically indifferent to his captain's ill-humour. *Resolve* was making too much leeway. Lying this close to the wind the lighter sloop was finding it difficult to hold her weather station on the frigate. Her deck canted steeply over as she exposed her copper-sheathed hull to the elements. The Frenchman with his larger mass in the water would prove better able to avoid drifting to leeward. At the end of an hour *Resolve* tacked again.

Naseby set glass to eye. Once again the gap was narrowing; soon the frigate's guns would begin anew to churn up the intervening expanse of water with her carefully sighted ranging shots. On their present course they should sight Ushant within the hour, all being well – provided that was, that the wind didn't play them false. A freak wave swept over the lee rail, swilling grittily across the sanded deck planking and drenching the men crouching at the guns.

Close hauled, *Resolve*'s starboard battery would prove less than useless, aimed as it was into the swelling grey waters overside; that steep was the cant of her deck. Even, that was, should her pop-gun armament be capable of causing the Frenchman any mischief in the first place. While the gradually closing frigate was clearly not hampered on either account with her imposing port side battery of eighteen pounders rearing majestically out of the water.

'She'll be poppin' off at us any minute now,' remarked that same incautious gun captain. Naseby silently agreed. Her present tack and the relative position of the two ships would allow the Frenchman's skyward tilting guns maximum elevation; a chance not to be missed.

An odd whirring sound high overhead drew Naseby's eyes like a magnet. A raggedly gaping hole had appeared as if by magic in the *Resolve*'s tautly filled main topsail.

'He's got the range, mateys!'

Naseby didn't bother to heed the softly spoken words, his attention instead on the hazy fragments of smoke being whipped by the wind from the Frenchman's side. Quickly he darted a look aft. Blount was standing as if transfixed: chin jutting and hands clasped beneath upthrust coat tails, his gaze held firmly on the closing enemy frigate. Perhaps, thought Naseby uncharitably, at this moment he saw the inexorably approaching ruination of all his brightly gilted prospects of promotion.

Edwards the first lieutenant was, he saw, also casting a leery eye at his captain. In truth there was little enough at present that the *Resolve*'s commander could be doing appreciably to alter the situation, but nevertheless Blount's oddly unmoving attitude worried him in a way which Naseby himself could not quite define.

And it was doubly irritating to find that this same sense of something being not quite right on the quarterdeck had transmitted itself also to the veteran Mister Edwards.

III

Dashed Hopes

An eighteen pound ball came smashing through the *Resolve*'s starboard bulwark amidships, taking the head clean off an olive-skinned gun captain and scything straight on to dislodge a gun on the larboard side. For an instant only Naseby stared at the redly spouting corpse kneeling as in an attitude of prayer.

Keeping his tone even, he said, 'Mister Long, my compliments to the captain and respectfully submit that we might open fire to advantage now – and hurry!'

'Aye, aye, sir,' squeaked Long, gulping down his horror and going scurrying off along the deck.

The range was a bare two cables and closing fast, and while it was highly doubtful if *Resolve*'s small calibre armament could actually afford significant damage to the stouter timbers of the Frenchman, it would at least provide the men with the illusion that they were fighting back. Besides, there was always a chance, be it ever so slim, that a lucky shot might succeed in knocking off a spar!

Midshipman Long was at his elbow. 'The captain says for you to see what you can do, sir!'

Naseby snatched out his sword, opening his mouth to blare his orders. Suddenly the whole world shook and he found himself lying face down in a reeking pile of hotly steaming entrails. The deck was rocking as if perched atop an erupting volcano. All around a writhing red mass – all that remained of the starboard battery's decimated gun crew – seethed and struggled in an agony of violent death. The din was incredible. A second smashing broadside tore into the frail scantlings of the little sloop.

Something was across his legs, pinning him down, and he realised that it was part of the sloop's fallen maintopmast yard. Much of the rest of the mast had already disappeared over the side, and twisting his head as far as he was able, he could see that the foretop had been lost, too.

Soon he was aware of frenzied activity going on around him, but for what seemed like an eternity he lay prone, one side of his face pressed hard against the splintered deck timbers, and retched horribly.

When at last he was able to gather enough of his wits to attempt a look towards the quarterdeck it was to see Siras kneeling stupidly beside the shattered remnants of the wheel, his mouth agape, fishlike, while his fingers plucked ineffectually at a blackened shard of timber which seemed to have somehow erupted from the side of his face.

Of Edwards the first lieutenant there was nothing to be seen. Helplessly Naseby looked away. Someone was at his side now, rough hands tugging at his shoulders; gradually the terrible weight on his legs was being eased. A sudden spasm of pain – and then he was free.

'You'm orl roight now, Mister Naseby, zur,' purred a voice in his ear.

Weakly he tried to nod, but the movement caused a fountain of pain to start in his skull. This wouldn't do; he must take a grip on himself. There was a great deal to do. And, as if from far, far away, out of a dimly cherished memory, the thought occurred to him that he was almost certainly now in command. The knowledge brought nothing. At least he was on his feet, however.

'Frenchi's 'auled 'is wind, zur, we'm driftin' down to 'im.'

Aware vaguely that he was still more than a little stunned, Naseby took a cautious lungful of air. The acrid smoke from a blaze up forrad and the inhuman stench of death caused his stomach to revolt. Slowly the paroxysm passed. His sword was pushed roughly into his hand by an unseen seaman and then he was off, half stumbling, half running, along the deck, eyes heeding little of the dreadful carnage wreaked by the Frenchman's crushing broadsides.

Blount was dead. An almost comic expression lay on his

upturned face. Kneeling, Naseby could see where the razor-edged splinter had lanced through the back of his head.

His own head clear at last, he scanned the quarterdeck for the master's mate Shelby, locating him by the rail. In as cool a voice as he could muster, he rapped out his orders. There seemed little likelihood that the Frenchman would fire again. Why should he? The sloop was helpless, the more immediate danger being incineration from the raging blaze up forrad. Evidently a gun had exploded, sending a cascade of burning debris across the deck.

There was no hope of saving the sloop. Once let a hungry fire take hold in a vessel constructed of timber and tar and the result was inevitable. All too soon the flames would be seeking the powder magazine. There was very little time. Naseby hoped devoutly that the French captain would not be so put out at the loss of his easily won prize as to leave what pitiful few remained of her crew to their fate.

With nothing left aloft with which to signify surrender, he had a nearly white tablecloth suspended over the side, a dozen or so seamen striving valiantly to launch the one remaining ship's boat.

His first brief tenure of command, and he was surrendering! It was a bitter pill to swallow, but there wasn't time to think about that now. His legs buckling beneath him, he ran hastily below. Should the Frenchman capture the ship's log and signal books, it would be his last command ever; for that matter, he reflected, it probably was, anyway.

The sad sight of the death of the sloop *Resolve* was one which Philip Naseby knew he would carry with him to the grave. Watching, moist-eyed, from the gently heaving deck of the Frenchman, it seemed to him at that moment that his whole world had come to an end. As in a way, it had. For what indeed had he left to look forward to now. Captivity, certainly. Exchange, possibly, but unlikely for one with so little influence. And then not for some time to come. Bonaparte had had his nose bloodied all too recently for anything to be hoped for from that quarter yet. Besides which, in the overall scheme of things, he was but a decidedly junior officer.

What of the surrender of the sloop? True, the ship had since sunk. What, that was, hadn't been consumed by the flames prior to the sea holding sway. Strangely, the fire hadn't made it to the magazine after all. It was to be supposed that the sea had contrived to arrive there first.

The fact remained that he had surrendered. No mean crime in the harsh world of His Majesty's Navy. There would eventually have to be a court martial. With himself as the senior officer, and the one who had been responsible for ordering the surrender, on trial. Perhaps for his life. For a moment the dread spectre of the rope added its nightmare presence to Naseby's wild imaginings. Then he managed to throw such childish fears off. As the sloop's most junior lieutenant and finding himself abruptly in command of a lifeless, dismasted and already burning hulk, he could not reasonably be expected to have acted contrary. It followed from that that there was little that even a notoriously brutal service such as Naseby knew the Royal Navy to be, could in any justice do to him. In fact, he revised, any impartial bench of post captains might even go so far as to commend him for acting so speedily to save what was left of the *Resolve*'s people. Not to mention having had the presence of mind to carry out his duty regarding the ship's papers! Still, he mused as he was led below, it was hardly the stuff of which dreams were made. Nor careers moulded.

Of the *Resolve*'s complement of one hundred and fifteen officers, men and ship's boys, but a bare nineteen had been hauled aboard the French frigate. Which, as Naseby was informed, was the *Lorraine* 44, a newly launched tentacle of empire under the command of frigate captain Jacques Elmonde: a cold fish, if ever there was one!

Naseby's plain old sword had been snatched from his side before he had even had a chance to formally surrender it and after a few brief words, the *Resolve*'s senior surviving officer had been unceremoniously bundled below to be confined in unutterable squalor with the common herd. A state owed no doubt to the oft nobly expressed sentiments of *liberté, egalité, fraternité.* Thus he found himself, at least for the moment, become somewhat less of a radical. It stank like a cesspit down here, and so dark that you couldn't see a hand in front of you.

The wounded amongst the survivors, three in number, had been carted protestingly off to suffer the unimaginable attentions of the *Lorraine*'s surgeon.

Hastily Naseby turned his mind to other matters. That left sixteen in their cramped little prison, including himself. Sixteen English seamen on which the rats could feed. Something nudged him in the darkness and a hand settled hesitatingly on his arm.

'Is that you, Mister Naseby?' It was Shelby, the master's mate.

'Aye,' answered Naseby. 'Any ideas on our course?'

'East nor' east unless I miss my guess,' replied the other consideringly. 'Not that the night will see us very much further forward!'

It was a well known fact that the lubberly French preferred to lay hove to during the hours of darkness, as did also the Spanish. There was always the chance – a very real possibility, in fact – that so long as the *Lorraine* remained in Channel waters she might fall foul of a hunting British frigate.

Morning, however, was to bring no such fortunate occurrence, and it was with an exceedingly heavy heart that on the morning of the second day following, Naseby and his tattered little band were trooped ashore at Cherbourg; Shelby and the rest of the *Resolve*'s people to go one way and himself, as the sole surviving commissioned officer, to go another ...

*

It was one of those glorious early spring days. From his tiny turret room window overlooking the picturesque eastern battlements, Lieutenant Philip Naseby, late of His Britannic Majesty's eighteen gun sloop *Resolve*, could feel the enervating warmth of the midday sun gently teasing new life into the wasted inactivity of his sinews and by craning up to his full height on the balls of threadbare stockinged feet, just glimpse its welcoming golden radiance peeping at him from an almost cloudless pale blue sky.

A little over four months had passed since the sinking of the *Resolve*. Four long wearisome months, during which time he had slowly fretted himself into a state of near insanity. Down on the battlements some thirty feet below, the steady to and fro tramp of the sentry, heavily booted feet resounding solidly on the irregularly spaced flagstones, set up a correspondingly monotonous echo in his skull; jibing at dangerously frayed nerves in a way which threatened to leave him mindless.

Extend his parole, the fort's commander Major Chavalle had said in the loftily assumed manner of one gentleman to another, and there was no reason at all why the gallant lieutenant should not be permitted to enjoy the comparative freedom of the township some three quarters of a mile away. 'Under a token guard, of course.' Purely a formality; merely to allay the fears of the townspeople. Naseby would understand. Quite absurd, really. This last had been accompanied by a not quite disarming smile, and Naseby, never one to shun the all too seldom extended hand of Providence, had with as gracious a bow as he could muster, readily agreed.

Unfortunately, however, events thus far had unhappily contrived to rob him of any real chance to put vaguely formed plans for his escape into effect. On only two occasions had he been allowed to venture beyond his once-daily exercise along the battlements. The first time being an hour long excursion into the surrounding countryside in the ever watchful company of a trio of heavily armed gendarmes, and the second, but four days previous, an even shorter hike culminating in a visit to a strategically placed bordello just beyond the forward confines of the fort.

Today was a Friday, of that Naseby was sure, and early in May, though the actual date had managed to lose itself in the unutterable boredom of his day to day captivity. The heavy tramp of booted feet in the corridor immediately outside his door caused him to seek a hastily composed posture of feigned indifference on the room's crude wooden cot.

A key sounded in the lock, and the next instant the cumbersome oak door swung inward, revealing a blue and red-coated lieutenant and two gendarmes.

'If you would accompany me, please!' commanded the officer coolly.

Shrugging into his poorly patched lieutenant's coat, Naseby caught up his boots, falling into step between the two gendarmes; and with the French officer leading the way, set off along the narrow stone corridor to the iron-grilled door which guarded the head of the steep spiral staircase. A blocky man in soiled waistcoat and breeches unbarred the door and fifteen minutes later Naseby, more than a trifle bemused, was seated stiffly inside a high topped coach, and with an escort of six mounted gendarmes, was on his way along the coast road to Trouville and heaven knew what.

Shortly before nightfall they clattered into a cobble-laid courtyard ringed by trees – burgeoning green branches overlooking suggestively the stone-capped walls as with a promise of instant freedom for a man resolute enough to put paid to half a dozen of the Emperor's gendarmes in the process. At a curt order the coach door was flung open and he found himself being ushered through a low entranceway and into a fair sized coaching house. One of the escort set about issuing instructions to the landlord, while under the watchful gaze of the other patrons Naseby climbed the rickety staircase to the hostelry's upper storey.

Thus far his gaolers had shown themselves remarkably reticent in the matter of vouchsafing him information concerning the purpose of their journey, the courtly Chavalle having merely contented himself by saying that were he, Naseby, to possess any belongings which he should be unhappy to lose, then he should look to their immediate taking up! Naseby hadn't, other than the clothes in which he stood, so there the matter had rested. The one obvious deduction to be drawn from all this was that whatever awaited him at Trouville, and whither bound from there, he should not again be returning to the fort above the town.

The room to which they led him was reminiscent of the lodging house in Cobbs Alley. So much so, in fact, with its sloped attic ceiling and plain appointments, that he felt desirous of pinching himself lest the events of this half year past turn out to be nought more than a dream brought on by an over active imagination and the shock of meeting up with Siras Blount again. But it wasn't a dream, and Siras was dead. Gone to the bottom in the *Resolve* along with Edwards and the others.

Leaving him to his own devices, his guards withdrew. A mumbled '*Vous mangez bientôt*' and a graphically mimed gesture serving to remind him that he hadn't eaten since morning. Downstairs the sounds of revelry far into the night attested to the devotion to the grape of his guards.

The supper provided had turned out to be adequate, and had it not been for the strange sense of foreboding which he had been heir to since entering the hostelry, he might have slept. Instead he lay tossing and turning in the narrow bed while he relived those last shot-torn hours in the *Resolve.* Finally exhaustion must have taken its toll, for it was with a sense of one being awakened out of a particularly troublesome dream that, hearing a noise outside his room, he started up, face beaded with sweat and every reflex keyed for action.

Just what the noise which had roused him had been, he had scant inkling, but as a man long used to trusting his senses, knew straightway his life to be in danger. Reaching for his clothes he dressed silently, ears straining for further tell-tale sounds. It was inky black within the room, the tiny skylight which served the attic being boarded over. The tallow dip by which he had eaten his meal had long since been extinguished. While the folly of alerting those he felt to wait poised beyond his room door (even should, of course, he possess the means for so doing) by showing a light, would suggest itself to no man desirous of going on living.

Cautiously he cast about for a weapon. Nothing presented itself. A click, as of a pistol being readied from half-cock. A further stealthy scuffling. Then chaos: with a crash the door burst inward and his attackers were upon him. Something jarred against his shoulder and a pistol exploded inches from his face, the searing powder flash all but blinding him. Where the ball went there was no time to speculate. Someone shouted something in French and he felt his fist connect with a nearby face. The man let out a howl of pain, but any feeling of triumph proved itself short-lived. Almost at once his legs were swept from under him, resulting in his being sent sprawling – helpless before the flailing boots of hate-filled assailants. Something fetched him a resounding crack behind the right ear, and he felt oblivion, all consuming and inexorable, reaching up to claim him …

The pinpoint of light seemed to be coaxing him tenderly back to wakefulness. Deep in his brain, a throbbing, as of a hundred tiny men with hammers, was doing the opposite. Above him someone was speaking: a gruff and guttural voice such as a man might use in drink. Unwillingly at first, Naseby tried to catch on to it, mentally clutching at each slurred syllable as if it were a lifeline.

It was a surprise at first to realise that it was French that was being spoken. Then not so. His command of the language had never been more than a strictly rudimentary one. But now, hampered by that incessant banging in his head, the thing was proving impossible. Slowly, and at the cost of much concentration on his part, the gruffly uttered syllables began to form themselves into words, the words into phrases. He was being asked a question.

'*Vous nous revenez, Lieutenant! Vous pouvez vous élever?*'

A hand came into focus before his face and the voice, now grown solicitous, asked, '*Combien de doigts?*'

'*Trois,*' Naseby managed to mutter.

Apparently satisfied, the hand withdrew, leaving others to help him sit up. His head swam horridly and he knew what a man must feel when he is seasick.

'*Vous récuperez maintenant, oui? Prenez du vin.*'

Resolutely he fended off the man with the wine. Couldn't these damned Froggies leave a man to recover in his own time!

The room was bathed in lamplight, by which he saw a dozen if not exactly anxious, then certainly curious, faces peering at him. The gendarme with the wine tried again. This time he gave in.

'*Les paysans, monsieur – comment vous dites? –* "mob", *oui?*'

Naseby managed to grunt in the affirmative as the gendarme corporal went on to explain, calling on the odd word of halting English here and there, how, incensed by the idea of a hated '*matelot Anglais*' and an officer to boot, ensconced at the inn, the local peasantry (Naseby supposed that even here, in revolutionary France, the common people of the countryside could not aspire to being termed 'citizens') had contrived to lull his guards from their duty with liberal quantities of wine and attempt to take his life in the night. A calamitous happenstance which all were agreed might, following this night, remain best left untold. After all, had they not roused up in time and saved his life? Just how difficult the contriving on the part of the locals had been was a moot point. However, sufficiently clear of mind now to be fully cognisant of the fact that should he favour any other course his 'saviours' might even now decide that it were as well to be hung for a sheep as a lamb – after all, they could easily claim that he had succumbed later to his wounds – Naseby tendered agreement.

Apart from his guards the room had cleared. The area behind his right ear felt like a cracked walnut, and at some point in the fracas he seemed to have sustained a cut lip. Then he remembered the telling blow which he had managed to deal one of his attackers, and felt considerably better. Of the identity or current whereabouts of his attackers there was no mention. Naseby deemed it best not to ask.

The morning brought a resumption of their journey, which even with the cameraderie which had sprung up between himself and his guards vis-à-vis their shared conspiracy of silence, found Naseby still no further forward in his ruminations concerning its inception. Maybe they were taking him to stand trial for some imagined war crime. Unlikely, certainly, but anything was possible. He had a bad moment then. To die in action with your ire rising and the stuff of life coursing through your veins was one thing; to cold-bloodedly face a firing squad or, heaven forbid! worse – pass from existence on that fiendish contraption of Dr Guillotine's – quite another. Then the thought came to him that were that indeed to be the case, and he was on his way to one of those mock trials so oft in favour with the Emperor, then his way would lie not ahead along the ceaselessly winding coast road to Trouville, but rather inland, to Paris. Even Napoleon couldn't shout that loud!

The coach rocked endlessly, which served little to accommodate his ill-used head. By midday his spirits had sunk to dumb acceptance, while when in the early evening the coach and its clattering escort finally cleared the gorse-fringed roadway and swept careeringly out onto the heath overlooking the little port town, it would have been of scant interest to Naseby were a whole company of marines to come tramping across his person.

Rhythmically the coach swung down upon the township, rejoining the main road after its short cut across the countryside with a patter of sprayed gravel and a sharp invective from the driver. So close at hand that he could almost reach out a hand to it, lay the sea – sparkling blue and silver where the late afternoon sunlight kissed myriad tiny wavelets in a mocking salutation to the dying day.

The Channel – a moat created by Providence, it seemed to dissipate the dreams of conquest of even the most ingenious warlord, bringing to nought a tide of onslaught that, were it once to bridge the narrow gap between the continent of Europe and John Bull's island, would wreak a havoc unknown even in the long past days of Julius Caesar, marauding Norsemen, and even the Norman Conquest. It was a sobering prospect and one which, avowed cynic though he had always felt himself to be, brought a bullish lump to even Naseby's throat. Cautiously, as if perhaps fancying that even now he could see across the glittering expanse of water separating him from freedom, he allowed his mind's eye to fly forward in time to a day when even this present threat should have become merely a part of the nation's memory, a glorious episode which would perhaps pale against a proportionately greater peril imposed by some new world-shaker. Perhaps when men should have found some new way of negating distance and making as nothing the watery divide beyond which stretched his thoughts.

How would the people cope then, he wondered, in those far off days. Well, no matter. He shrugged, fetching himself upright on the hard wooden seat. Such would not take place within his own span of years, nor yet likely those of his children or grandchildren. – Hadn't someone mentioned something about balloons?

But then the coach was racketing through the town, along confining cobbled streets, and he found his attention taken up with more immediate prospects.

He passed that night in a tiny brick gaol scarcely large enough to be worthy of the name. Six by eight with a peephole for a window and a door which gave out onto what could best be described as an alleyway. The place had had to be approached on foot and his nostrils were still tainted by the smell of fish. No bad thing, for his accommodation reeked strongly of baser things.

His supper when it came was foul: odd shaped lumps of gristle floating in a thin, pea-green gravy. Knowing that whatever lay ahead, he would require his strength, he forced it down, mopping up the residue with the morsel of stale dark bread which the town gaoler had reluctantly tossed him. At least there was the comfort of not being privy to just what it was they were feeding him.

Resigned now, he slept soundly, awakening before dawn and easing his cramped muscles while he listened to the sounds wafting in from outside. Breakfast came soon after, and then he was left alone to contemplate his fate for the rest of the morning.

Since his arrival at the gaol the previous evening he had received neither sight nor sound of his guards and judged the six man escort to have by this time departed whence they came. It was strange how that wholly impersonal supposition left him feeling alone.

At midday the bolt was thrown on the door of his tiny, single cell gaol, and silhouetted darkly against the incoming glare stood an officer of the French Marine. A lieutenant of a similar age to himself. The newcomer spoke in English.

'May I have the honour to introduce myself. I am, *monsieur*, Lieutenant Jean Bouvet. I come to escort you to your place of exchange!'

IV

The Girl in the Coach

London stank of horseshit. He had forgotten quite how badly, although truth to tell, Naseby's years in the service had provided little enough opportunity for renewing acquaintanceship with the place.

His uncle had lived in Hyde Street, just a stone's throw from Greenwich. He, too, had been dead these past – how many years? At least four. The false peace of Amiens had just been ratified. Not that he had borne any lasting affection for the man. Yet kinsman he had been, and to one all but alone in the world, that of itself had stood for something. Now his aloneness was total. Odd how he felt it more so today. Or perhaps not so when you thought about it.

The thirty-minute interview he had had with a rather nondescript clerk at the Admiralty had left him more than a trifle bemused – the upshot of which being that he could now recall exceedingly little of what had been said to him. Rather, he had come away with a host of jumbled impressions: a limewood fireplace surround carved with an intricacy of detail which defied description, depicting assorted naval designs; roof-mounted weather vanes, cleverly constructed so that they actuated mechanical dials in the great room, showing at a glance day or night, the direction of wind. Not to mention a majestic-appearing grandfather clock capable of displaying the day's date in addition to recording time, which had, the clerk had reliably informed him, been made by no lesser personage than Langley Bradley, who as everybody knew, had built the clock in St Paul's.

The blessed exchange which, miraculously as it had seemed to him at the time, restored him freedom of action, had taken place a month to the day. A signally half-hearted enquiry, not yet a full court martial, held some three weeks later with the business of looking into the loss of His Majesty's sloop *Resolve* had exonerated him entirely.

It was raining; a delightful summer shower which dampened down the stench from the street and even went some way towards alleviating the perspiration-inducing encumbrance of the heavy dress coat which Messrs William and Charles Prater of Charing Cross had at such short notice, and it must be said, additional cost, graciously made up for him. Nor, as a result of the aforementioned interview, would this be his sole call on the Admiralty cheque for lieutenant's full pay which had been accruing during his short captivity in France.

The sum wasn't large, but with care it would suffice for the articles he needed. First and foremost of which was going to be the plain gold epaulette which in his mind's eye he could already see rested so naturally upon his gently sloping left shoulder. Next would come the task of outfitting himself with sword and sea chest, pistols and breeches, not to mention half a dozen pairs of white silk stockings and all the other many and divers maritime accoutrements with which the sea-going young officer newly taking up command of a ship of war must equip himself. It was, he told himself lightly, hardly an expenditure to be begrudged!

Appointed commander – after scarce more than half a year and one commission spent as a lieutenant. And that not achieved by dint of examination. Unless, he revised, you could call the unflinching facing of cold steel and howling grapeshot a suitable preparation for the rigours of command! A new thought entered his mind. Was it after all possible that those whose onerous burden it was to wear the mantle of lofty authority and thus wield the power of choosing and bestowing rank glimpsed something in him which he had himself not guessed was there? Hardly – and yet – ?

The rain had become heavier. Mentally he made a note to pick up a copy of J.H. Moore's *New Practical Navigator* as a matter of priority to replace the one that he had lost aboard *Resolve*. Unconsciously his steps had taken him back along the Strand into Fleet Street and with Ludgate Hill and the

Cathedral rising before him, he paused for a moment to marshal his intentions. Strong in him was a desire to search out his birthplace in Limehouse, to fill his nostrils with the so well remembered smell of the docks and watch the river where it flowed down the 'Reach' winding towards Greenwich.

The sudden proximity of a speeding coach shocked him out of his reverie, causing him to step back quickly. So quickly in fact that his feet became tangled up together and he sat back, sprawling. The pistol shot crack of the whip, a harsh oath from the driver, and then the wildly lurching vehicle was past. It had all happened so suddenly. His new dress coat was awash with the filth of the roadway and Naseby was left with no more than a fleeting impression of a daintily bonneted face which had looked out at him with wide, frightened eyes. A moment he stared after the swaying conveyance, too dumbstruck even to give voice to the stream of profanity which had sprung to his lips.

Abruptly the coach turned a corner, for the space of a second seemed in danger of turning over as it tottered drunkenly, and then the driver worked the reins and they were gone from sight, the renewed play of the driving whip having to compete for attention from Naseby's hearing with some impudent giggling (no doubt brought on by the unlooked for, though highly amusing spectacle of at the very least a full-blown admiral down on his uppers in the dirt of the roadway) from a couple of female passers-by.

Frowning hotly, Naseby clambered to his feet, setting himself to rights as best he could while his mockers, now less certain of the game, hurried on. More shaken by the episode than he would wish made plain, it was not until he had gained the sanctuary offered by a nearby doorway that he could find time to brush away some mud, or worse, that had adhered to his hat, and speculate on the speeding coach. He had been afforded but a glimpse of its female occupant, yet nevertheless felt certain that he would know her again. Such wide, staring eyes – on account of his plight, no doubt, for the coach in which she was travelling had all but run him down. Indeed, had likely done so, from its occupant's necessarily limited perspective.

And yet – Somehow there had been something more. The single glimpse he had of her had been only that, it was true. In all conscience he found himself loath to decide whether the hair framing her face beneath the bonnet had been light or dark; yet he thought fair. Her eyes had held a haunted look, had sought out his own in plaintive enquiry. He was reading too much into the incident, he knew: the price a man paid for too vivid an imagination. Like enough she had been on her way to an eagerly awaited tryst with some suitor and had told the coachman to hurry. Perhaps she was even married. With no cause for so doing, he at once dismissed the thought. In any event, he would not see her again, so it was useless to speculate.

The coach had been heading north, no, more like north west: Highgate, Finchley, perhaps. She had been a lady, that much was certain, and a fine rare beauty to boot, of that he'd be bound. Far and away above a penniless naval commander whose only call on the word 'gentleman' was owed to the date on his commission.

Awhile he stood there, brushing absently at the black felt of his hat. The rain had ceased and a watery sun appeared. It was nearing midday. He must soon be about the purchase of his wants. Yet he found the previously anticipated excursion, with perhaps the much prized epaulette proving the exception, to have lost much of its lustre.

Nevertheless, he set to with a will, calling first at the establishment of John Salter, sword cutlers of number thirty-five in the Strand: fashioners of fighting swords par excellence. The weapon he chose was short-bladed, heavy enough to cleave the stoutest of shoulders, and whose razor-honed length could be relied upon to hold an edge capable of parting a hair. Sensibly mindful of his purse he had opted for a plain example of the art, devoid entirely of adornment or embellishment of any kind. Satisfied, next on the agenda came calls on Threshers a little way along, and at James Lawson, also in the Strand, where were secured respectively a supply of silk hose and an extra cocked hat to be kept strictly for best. Further calls followed, each of which necessitated deeper delvings into his purse, culminating with a visit to Joseph Dean's premises in nearby Craven Street to obtain the single gold epaulette. As it had turned out, the most sought after item had been left till last.

Now, with his purchases secure in a stout, if secondhand, sea chest and on their way to his lodgings, it only behove him to search out a suitable eating house prior to keeping an appointment across the river with an old acquaintance whom he had bumped into at the Admiralty.

To record that the proceedings had managed to expunge from his mind all thought of the girl in the coach and her reason for haste would be to do less than justice to Naseby's keen sense of curiosity; his knowledge of himself and his foibles assuring him that his fleeting vision of the haunted girl would rise spectre-like before him on many a lonely watch over the forthcoming weeks and months.

However, the exciting prospect of taking over command of the twelve-gun brig *Solent* at present anchored in waters whose name she bore, off Spithead was one which of necessity left little room for ought else in his present comprehension of the scheme of things. Everything which a newly appointed Lieutenant Naseby had once prophesied for his friend the late Siras Blount was, courtesy of the inexplicable fortunes of war, beginning to open up for himself. He, it was, who had now joined the gilded ranks of those fortunate individuals who with the normal passage of time and a satisfactory diligence to duty might reasonably expect to attain 'post' rank. Not to mention the more immediate and highly beneficial adjunctive to his appointment to commander carrying with it the princely sum of seventy pounds per annum!

*

Inextricably bound up are the threads which bind our lives together, one with the other. Weaving inexorably the tentacles of coincidence as converging byways, we come together, cross, then depart, each in his fashion capturing some essential essence of the other so that from that time on the two journey, be it ever unknowingly, as one.

Thus it was with Naseby and with the girl whom he had glimpsed in the coach, reading aright as it transpired, the frightened mien, the cloying clutch of anguish, the stark and awful dread which grips the heart when fickle Providence, finding us ever unprepared, casts its impersonal mantle of death, as a shadow, immediate and final, across those who in trusting innocence we hold to be our most near and dear.

Slowly, and with unfeigned reverence, Sara Throgmorton stooped to plant a kiss on the still warm forehead of her recently departed grandfather. Carslake House, the capacious Carslake Estate, not to mention a goodly cash fortune, were now hers to do with what she would. To her credit, at this moment these and divers other worldly considerations were, however, very far from her mind. Freshly fallen tears shone wetly on cheeks pale from travel.

The kindly Lord Carslake had been far more than grandsire to the sole offspring of his long dead daughter Elizabeth, his only issue, and her husband the deeply mourned Jonathan Throgmorton who had been lost in the West Indies when Sara was but a child. Becoming both father and mother, guardian and tutor, to the girl in the fullness of time he made her his heir; a move unprecendented in the Carslake line, disdaining his own distant blooded clan, whose elder male progeny would now inherit nought but the title. All else passed to Sara – a flaxen-haired and blue-eyed diminutively formed girl, scarce nineteen.

A discreet cough sounded behind her and she rose, half-unconsciously, dabbing a prettily embroidered lace kerchief to her cheeks, eyes which had so recently held fear now devoid of all save sadness as they looked a last fond farewell at the prone figure in the bed. News of Lord Carslake's sudden and totally unexpected relapse had reached her at Putney, where she had been staying with friends these three weeks past. All through that subsequent nightmare drive, as the tall coach had thrashed its way along narrow city streets, meeting carriages and dodging pedestrian traffic to be at her grandfather's bedside, Sara had railed at herself for her untimely absence. If he should die before she could reach him, then she knew that she would never forgive herself. Well, now he was dead. It was hard to accept that fact. And that she had come too late after all. Not that it really mattered, now.

Turning away from the bed she was able to reflect on the

strange duplicity of the mind, that now in her hour of grief she should find her thoughts winging outward, beyond this now defunct sick room, out beyond the terraces and lawns newly alive with their gay borders of sweetly fragrant summer flowers, out to the crowded city streets which would by now be draped in shadow in preparation for the long summer twilight. To a tall young naval officer, who in their haste they had all but run down. Odd, too, that she should be able to recall his face so vividly. For she had only seen him for but a moment, before her scurrying coach had whisked her past. Leaving him there, deposited in the roadway, cocked hat askew and his dignity in tatters! How comical he had appeared. She hoped that he had not hurt himself.

A strong, goodly, face it had been; full of character and holding little of confusion and not one wit of fear at his near injury in the taking of his stroll. More perhaps a look of reproof, as if its wearer had been rudely snatched from some secret inner pondering. Was it, Sara wondered, disrespectful of the moment to be fancying so? Hopefully no, nor assuredly yet so strange. For his had been a face as she imagined her father's to have been. For she retained no likeness and had oft fallen to romantic imaginings in her perception of her lamented and to her, entirely unknown, forebear. Natural, then, to cast up this vision in her mind's eye when all she had known about her had been plucked away. Stolen by unheeding Providence at such times when she had needed them most.

The same polite cough sounded again at her elbow and she quickly took stock of herself, replacing her handkerchief before turning once more to address the doctor. Poor man! He and her grandfather had been first acquaintances, and then later, friends, for many years. He would be taking it badly, she knew. All through Lord Carslake's long illness he had attended him.

'Doctor John,' she comforted, taking hold of his hands and urging him to a chair.

'I only wish he could have lingered – he so wanted to, for you ... ' mumbled the old physician apologetically. 'It was his heart, you see ... '

Sara nodded toward the doorway and a wizened family retainer cat-footed over with a tray bearing a brandy decanter and glasses. She bit her lip; no more would the two old men, master and retainer, secretly partake of a warming glass when once hers and the doctor's backs were turned ...

The morning following the previous evening's liberal partaking of alcoholic beverage was for Naseby a salutary lesson. Not that should the occasion warrant, he couldn't hold his drink with the best of them! The evening's imbibing – coming at a time when even a whole month, three weeks of which had been spent in comparative comfort ashore after his imprisonment at the hands of the French, he was still in the process of recovering his former strength – had taken its toll. Added to which, over these last weeks had been the stress of the enquiry, sympathetic though it had turned out to be, culminating in his being ordered to London and completely out of the blue, handed command of a ship of war! Little wonder, then, that his evening assignation with a service acquaintance and the subsequent round of festivities involving as these things are wont to do, the entire patronage of the public house whereon they had settled to meet, as they drank to and fittingly celebrated the matter of his rare good fortune, had left him with a headache sufficient to sink a fleet!

The evening had also gone a considerable way towards sinking his purse as well. He ruminated, staring sombrely at his reflection in the mirror above the wash stand in his room at the lodging house. Compared to the bleak little attic in Cobbs Alley his present berth in Crown Lane just off Bow Street was luxury indeed. A clean, well appointed house kept by a kindly woman and her two unmarried daughters. Dressing leisurely, the better to fill the intervening time before breakfast, he donned fresh linen, taking elaborate care over making himself presentable before trooping downstairs in company with the other boarders.

The dining room smelt temptingly of freshly baked bread and from a steaming platter in the centre of the table Clara, the landlady's freckle-faced younger daughter, was busy doling out lamb chops onto plates set ready for the purpose. Taking his seat with the rest, Naseby found himself in good appetite – quickly putting away a goodly number of chops while at the same time doing full and equal justice to a half loaf of still warm white bread, served with a crock of butter, with molasses on the side for after. Finished, he washed the whole down with small beer, falling easily into polite conversation with his neighbour.

Fanny, the elder of his hostess's two girls, much to Naseby's delight, appeared at the room doorway dressed for the street, announcing coyly that she was off to market 'an if any o' the fine gennel-men as wanted anythin' special fetchin' ' they should say so now. Naseby didn't, but the chance to follow the girl out and perhaps woo her into warming his bed tonight was one not to be missed. It was a full week yet before he was required to take up command of his new ship and while he was suitably eager to travel to Portsmouth with all dispatch so as to obtain a sight of her, once at sea and in the midst of things it might well be months before another woman so much as hove within hailing distance. Hard living for any man. To Naseby it was an anathema!

Intent then on securing for himself a pleasant week's indulgence of his fancies, he excused himself and pausing only long enough to fish down his topcoat from the hall rack, passed out into the street. In contrast to yesterday the sun was ruling the roost with not a cloud in the sky. So that even this early in the day there was sufficient heat for his topcoat to have been unnecessary. He would need to watch these civilian ways, he mused whimsically. Or before he knew it he'd be chill-boned and soft of belly like any landsman!

Up ahead the girl was already turning the corner with, he was not slow to note, an arch look back first to assure herself that he was following. Pleased now that he had thought to don city clothes, and satisfied with his appearance in them, he lengthened his stride, the silver-topped cane which he had decided to affect tapping rhythmically against the cobbles as he went.

Crossing Bow Street, they headed for the market, Naseby now a scant dozen steps behind her and well content to bide his time. It was a game that they were playing, as both well knew. One which could lead to only one possible outcome. 'No tight-kneed virgin, this!' muttered Naseby to himself, experiencing a premature readying of manhood unlooked for at this time and place.

Of a sudden she turned and faced him – evidently deciding that the chase had run its course and it was now come time to stand and take his measure. Something in which, as Naseby was able to predict comfortably (taking the phrase at its baser level) yon Fanny was not apt to find herself disappointed! Fifteen minutes later, the sortie a success and a promise made, the couple parted company, the girl to go on with her marketing, while Naseby, secure in the prospect of his forthcoming night's entertainment, strolled off to solicit further indulgences.

Mid morning found him negotiating The Mall and pondering on whether or no to take a promenade across the park and watch the dandies prance and prate in Birdcage Walk, before leisurely hunting up a coffee house and settling down for the afternoon. The Admiralty stood bathed in radiant sunshine and it was with an entirely new sense of wonderment mingled with gratitude that he was able to stand here thus and cogitate on his, only since yesterday, now lofty position in the current scheme of things. It was to be hoped above all else that the war went on and on for as long as it should take him to become made post. For if not – if for any reason it should end before that vastly desirable goal should have been attained – then he would be apt to find himself once again back on the beach, eking out a meagre existence at half pay, and with all hopes of promotion vanished as puffs of smoke before the wind. No longer even a commander, but a lowly lieutenant lacking in seniority and one amongst many. A berth as a mate on a merchantman was out of the question, despising as they did the fighting service and requiring anyway of their officers that they be highly skilled in the matters of stowage and the like. Nor, indeed, could John Company be looked to with regard to seeking service in one of their fighting frigates continually on station in the East Indies; the Honourable Company operated a similar advancement by seniority system as did His Majesty's Navy. All that would be left would be a hitch before the mast, and at that he was no great shakes as a seaman.

Putting such gloomy thoughts aside lest they should gain the upper hand and sour what thus far promised to be a most pleasant day, he entered the park, telling himself as he did so –

and not for the first time – that his fears were groundless: England and France would be at one another's throats for as long as Napoleon ruled across the Channel; the current chagrin over the introduction of the Continental System forbidding trade between Britain and the rest of Europe guaranteed that. Long may he reign, thought Naseby treacherously.

*

It was Sunday, and he was attending services in St Martins in the Fields. Not out of any misplaced observance of religion, for if Naseby felt inclined to pay lip service to the possible existence of a god, which same he was not, then that god would be man himself and the great works which it lay within his power to achieve. But rather because in a weak moment he had allowed himself to be talked into accompanying a fellow boarder at his devotions.

He was fast becoming bored with his brief stay in London and growing impatient to get back to sea. Fanny the landlady's daughter had succumbed, as he had known that she would, visiting his room during the night on several occasions, and by now the sport had begun to go out of it. The morrow he had decided should see his departure for Portsmouth. His companion from the lodging house travelling with him.

The man's name was Gray, a lieutenant of Marines and a veteran of the Battle of the Nile where in '98 Nelson, in company with his gallant 'Band of Brothers' and despite a raging toothache, had put paid to a yet to become emperor – Napoleon Bonaparte's – daring plan to strike at India, England's richest colony, by launching an invasion through Egypt. Instead, at Aboukir Bay, the scene of the battle, the French grand fleet had been all but devastated and its admiral, François Paul de Brueys, killed. His flagship, the *Orient*, it had been, that had provided, from salvaged pieces of its mainmast, the coffin in which, some seven years later, the battle's victor – then grown even more illustrious – would be interred.

Gray had until recently been recovering from a leg wound sustained in an abortive cutting-out expedition at Ferrol; moving to London to convalesce before returning to

Portsmouth to await orders for joining up with another ship. Older than Naseby by some dozen years and a devout man to boot, the two would ordinarily have had little enough in common. But pushed together at the lodging house, a friendship of sorts had blossomed.

The pews were filled to capacity, in spite of which the place was deliciously cool. Beside him Gray was bestowing rapt attention on the proceedings, leaving Naseby free to idly scan the congregation while stiff of limb, he waited stoically for the ordeal to be over.

A face glimpsed profile-on and halfway along the leading row across the aisle, arrested his attention, causing his pulse to quicken, so that he craned forward, seeking immediate confirmation that he had seen what he had and that his eyes had not merely played servant to his imagination.

The object of his scrutiny turned out to be a diminuitive figure clothed in black, a modest mourning veil performing scant service in regard to concealing from view the striking flaxen-haired beauty which lay beneath. It was the girl from the coach; Naseby was as sure of that as he was of his own name. Wish otherwise as he might, common good manners, not to mention the formidable press of worshippers betwixt, forbade any bold attempt on his part to solicit her attention; his only recourse being to follow her out and seek then to obtain some clue as to her identity. This he resolved to do.

The sermon, a sanctimonious bleating delivered by a dry elderly cleric to a self-satisfied and largely self-seeking audience, was drawing to a close. Whether more desultory and decidedly discordant hymn singing would follow, Naseby had no firm way of knowing. But if such were the case, then it was to be hoped that it prove shortlived.

In the event it was not until some twenty minutes later that he got a chance to put his loosely formed strategy into operation. Gray, looking mildly displeased, was soon left limping painfully behind as Naseby, his sights firmly fixed on the solicitously shepherded figure in black, shouldered his way unceremoniously through the departing crowd.

Outside, people were milling about in attitudes of polite leave-taking, many of them awaiting an opportunity to step into carriages, handled by soberly liveried coachmen, that circled and gleamed, circled and gleamed, in a never-ending procession in the bright June sunshine. Into one of these – a smart maroon and black affair bearing a crest which Naseby from his present position of optical disadvantage could not quite make out – were handed the flaxen-haired girl and an older woman who attended her closely.

Faced with this unlooked for turn of events, all he could do was to look on helplessly as, head bowed, the girl and her chaperone were driven off – to be swiftly swallowed up in the general throng heading northward.

*

Portsmouth was alive with seamen carrying chests – protected John Company men no doubt – marching marines and people of all trades and walks of life scurrying to and fro in pursuance of their daily round. Breasting the High Street, Naseby and his companion made directly for the Fountain, a hostelry favoured chiefly by lieutenants of the service. The George, haunt of post captains, commodores and admirals and scene of Nelson's final hours in England, opposite the Port Admiral's office, would have to wait upon such time as the glittering gold epaulette should have swapped shoulders.

Despite the heat, or perhaps because of it, the Fountain was packed: a jostling sea of blue coats and sweaty faces.

Searching out a space for Gray and himself, Naseby vouchsafed the lad with his sea chest a shilling and gave instructions for the chest to be transported down to the sally port, where the lad was to stay close by his cart and hence his precious belongings, until such time as Naseby himself should arrive and being satisfied, pass him a companion for the coin which he already held.

This done, he passed a pleasant three quarters of an hour with Gray, seeing off an excellent bottle of madeira in the process, and departed for his ship.

Retracing his steps of the previous day across the drawbridge separating Portsmouth Point from the rest of the town, the thought was strong in his mind that he should miss the stiff-backed marine. Devout Walford Gray may have certainly been, but never dry!

Solent was riding at anchor in the harbour following an extensive refit supervised by her previous commander, a final act before moving on to be made post into another ship. Naseby had had himself rowed out to her the previous day on arriving in the town, being most content with what he saw and in truth desirous of remaining aboard had not his companion in travel, awaited him. Now with Gray ensconced comfortably in lodgings (not, may it be said hastily, those in Cobbs Alley!), mutual toasts drunk and his farewell taken, he was free to turn all his attention to *Solent*'s proper victualling. His orders for sailing could be expected any day now, and until then there was none save he, courtesy of a quite intentional slip on the part of the Admiralty clerk, with the slightest notion of whither the ship was bound. 'The delay caused by refitting will mean that you'll just miss the tail end of the hurricane season,' the clerk had said, winking broadly.

V

Station: West Indies

From Capstan Square and next the coach office; the Blue Posts, well remembered scene of departures of former years; to the sally port, left off the main street. Through the patient victualling, the securing of his meagre cabin stores and all the necessary but vital final preparations inextricably bound up in the making ready for sea of a ship of war. From an offing, watching as the smooth grey undulations of Portsdown Hill slid slowly astern. Farewell to Portsea in whose teeming streets and alleys dwelt the families of many a 'jolly Jack Tar'. The Point alive with a jostling throng of men-of-war men – to a visitor, picturesque this time of year in their striped Guernsey frocks and white canvas trousers. The fleet anchorage at Spithead, with the sun glancing sharply from off naked spars reaching majestically skyward. The wooden-walls-of England: mighty hearts of oak in whom a nation trusted for its salvation and in which men, both commoner and on occasion the vaunted nobility, fought and died so that said salvation might be a reality.

With the incidence of the hurricane season which was wont to ravage the West Indies in June, the bulk of the British fleet in those waters had developed the custom, comfortingly enough emulated by the French, of sailing northward up the east coast of North America, to tread water there until such time as the gradual onset of winter in or about October should signal a general return south. Thus, and for this reason, Naseby had it in mind to swing round up the west coast of Ireland and on northward to pick up the favourable north-westerly wind which he knew to blow from about 55° north latitude, just below Cape Farewell, making for Halifax, home to the small

North American squadron; reliable sources advised him that even should he run into a westerly gale it would blow on his starboard beam and be thus usable.

As it happened, the little brig encountered neither hardship nor gale, making – much to Naseby's secret amazement – a perfect landfall a month to the day after leaving Portsmouth. He was not, however, suffered to remain, Carleton in command there ordering him southward with both urgency and dispatch.

From Halifax it was that the convoy's bearing masts taken from New Brunswick and more latterly the St Lawrence valley, and needed so desperately by the mighty first-rates, began their long and oftentimes hazardous haul to the naval dockyards of England.

In truth Naseby would have tarried there awhile, enjoying the hospitality of his superior's tables, for the outward voyage, largely uneventful though it had been, had placed heavy demands on his hithertofore inferior seamanship and navigational capabilities. Captaining a ship, he had found to his dismay, called for a vastly superior outlay of mental agility and sheer tenacity than that normally required of one of its officers, even an executive one.

Almost as one, *Solent*'s larboard battery of tiny six-pounders went off with a thunderclap roar which heeled her sharply over to starboard and sent a billowing cloud of greasy brown smoke which bit acridly at the back of the throat, swirling about the heads of her officers as they stood easily braced to the uproll on the brig's canting quarterdeck.

'Secure the guns, Mister Perry!' ordered Naseby, fighting to keep the hoarseness out of his voice. 'That will be enough for today.'

Down in the brig's claustrophobic little stern cabin, and alone at last, he could relax; allowing the bone-numbing tiredness which clawed at his consciousness to claim him for its own. What unadulterated bliss it was to collapse loose-jointed onto his cot and to lie prostrate, swinging gently with the motion of the ship. Over-canvassed and never constructed to face a passage fighting the long greenish-tinted rollers of the Atlantic, the little two-masted vessel had fared middling well, and he supposed that he should feel grateful. But he wasn't. There was still so very much to do.

Why, in the matter of gun drill alone *Solent*'s people were scarcely one step above abysmal. As a captain Cuthbert Collingwood had so drilled his gun crews that the best of them could fire their cannon at the lordly rate of three rounds every two minutes! Naseby intended likewise for his gunners.

Clearing the windward passage on course for Jamaica *Solent* beat her way slowly around Morant Point on the south-eastern tip of the island, acknowledged the salute from the cannon on Fort Charles, and glided effortlessly to her anchorage in the bay: a sheltered natural harbour almost land-locked by a narrow weaving sandbar which the Spaniards had dubbed Palisadoes. Perched on this neck of land stood Port Royal and the naval dockyards, seat of British maritime power in the Caribbean.

Kingston across the bay appeared just as he had remembered it – squalid and teeming – yet from here strangely beautiful: Rock Fort commanding the eastern approach, and away in the distance the blue mountains which were really green. With the hurricane season tailing off it felt good to be back again, and turning his gaze inboard, Naseby allowed himself a brief moment of pride for all that had thus far been achieved in this his first command.

Then, as ever, there was much to do. His first call must be on the Rear Admiral in charge of the station, for whom he had dispatches. Naseby knew nothing whatsoever of the man under whose vast and far-reaching authority he now fell, except that like himself Rear Admiral of the Blue Sir Reginald Coxman Purvis was a newcomer on station. A deficit, mused Naseby as he had himself rowed across, which was about to be made up.

The large and palatially appointed day cabin of the *Repulse*, flagship of the squadron, came as a bit of a shock after the confining stuffiness of his own quarters, a pleasant breeze wafting in from the open sternlights playing coolly across his face and ruffling gently his unruly shock of black hair, which he even now could wish he had queued tighter.

The commander-in-chief turned out to be a fussy be-wigged little man with a bulbous nose and over-bright blue eyes. The dispatches which Naseby had brought (one set of which would obviously contain orders for him) both from England and from Carleton on the North American station, had been already handed in, the Admiral no doubt having perused them before deciding to honour his most junior commander with an audience. Seated comfortably in a plum-cushioned wrap-around chair and sipping a glass of quite excellent madeira, Naseby was able to reflect that up until now all had gone reasonably well.

Purvis had a disconcerting habit of looking at one; there he was, doing it now: tiny orbs the texture of diamonds boring coldly into their victim's brain. He stared back unflinchingly. Now had come the time to broach the question which had, both waking and sleeping, been hovering ever more insistently about the periphery of his understanding these past many weeks. Perhaps now with luck he might secure the answer. At any rate, it could be tried. But first befell the obvious necessity of making polite reply to the Admiral's softly-voiced enquiry into how he was enjoying his wine. Perhaps wishing that the young man would do his part towards opening up the conversation, or else drink up so that he might decently be put out, Purvis was drumming stubby fingers upon the top of his long mahogany desk. Naseby took a final sip, nodded appreciatively once more, and then dived in.

'Then it was Lord Collingwood, sir, who was largely responsible for my being considered eligible for exchange?' Purvis had already given him that much in passing.

The Admiral bobbed his head quickly. 'Quite so, m' boy, quite so. None other. As also – ' He held up an admonishing forefinger lest Naseby interrupt (which same he wouldn't have dreamt of doing). 'His lordship it was who nudged the powers-that-be into appointing you commander of the brig *Solent*! A quite extraordinary intervention on your behalf, as you doubtless will not need labouring.' All Naseby could do was reply respectfully in the affirmative. The Admiral had a little more to say on the subject. 'You have a friend there, er, Captain Naseby; look to it that you don't let his lordship down!' The diamond-hued eyes bored still more deeply into Naseby's own.

'Er, no, sir; of course not, sir' – the gulped reply more a product of the disruption to his composure caused by his admiral's no wit patronising and kindly meant use of the honorific 'captain'; a title due him merely by virtue of his appointment as *Solent*'s commander, than the look that accompanied same.

Solent's task in the West Indies was to harry and if possible send to the bottom as many of the 'curse of the Caribbean' fast sailing privateers: pirates for the most part masquerading as patriots under easily obtained letters of marque, as she could. Notable among foreign powers issuing such permits to plunder was France. With the privateers out of commission a constant drain on His Majesty's shipping in the area should have been removed; thus freeing valuable frigates, primarily designed as commerce raiders themselves and currently being utilised as escorts, for more war-shaping service elsewhere.

Naseby's own feelings on the subject were that such miscreant vessels as were unfortunate enough to fall under *Solent*'s guns would fare far better being diposed of by the prize courts than rotting slowly away beneath several thousand tons of sea water. Sensibly, however, he adjudged it politic to keep such mercenary intentions to himself ...

*

Over the forthcoming weeks *Solent* was to come upon and engage four such vessels. The first, a light buccaneer craft, was sent to the bottom. A second, fore and aft-rigged and incautious enough to allow a skull and crossed daggers emblem displayed on a black field to be discovered on board, was sent in under a prize crew; the vessel to be sold by the Crown, her piratical crew to be hanged. A further two, engaged together after they were caught shadowing a friendly trading vessel, were driven off. All this with the loss of only one man killed, an ordinary seaman by the name of Harris, and a hole the size of a fist punched in the foretopsail.

During these first vital weeks spent as a hunter Naseby, ably assisted by Perry, his first and only lieutenant, snatched every possible opportunity to exercise the crew at their guns. The results had been remarkable. In addition, sail-handling, putting on and taking off canvas, tacking, wearing, and all the many and varied evolutions necessarily performed with a high degree of skill by the crew of a Royal Navy ship at sea, had improved one hundred per cent.

In every respect His Majesty's twelve gun brig *Solent* was fast becoming a tautly run and potent weapon of war. One which no privateer captain in the entire Caribbean was likely to be foolish enough to want to trade broadsides with!

The late October sun was casting a watery reflection on the deckbeams above his head. *Solent* was sailing comfortably along under all plain sail and all was well with the world. Perry had the watch. Which left Naseby with a rare moment of idleness, subject to an unlooked for change in the direction of the wind which, as per his standing instructions, would result in his being called on deck immediately. Eight bells would be sounding soon enough. He sighed, and as far as a man can do so from a position with his head permanently bowed, stretched. He would develop a permanent stoop if he remained thus a great deal longer. Pity poor Collingwood, then, for Naseby knew the noble, lofty lord to stand a full six feet two inches.

On the bulkhead chart table spread out before him lay the chart he was currently perusing, and some jotted course calculations. A salt-stained volume of Tampion's treatise on the sextant and a portable hand compass peered mockingly back at him. Moore's book on navigation already into its umpteenth edition, which he had made a mental note to remember to purchase, had in the event been forgotten. Maybe after all he would have better made a soldier, he mused, with a characteristic touch of whimsy.

On their present south-westerly heading they should fetch the isthmus of Panama on the morrow, a fever-ridden sinkhole well remembered from former days. Above his head Perry's monotonous backwards and forwards pacing as he walked the weather side of the quarterdeck set his nerves on edge and conjured up visions of his recent captivity. A restless spirit at the best of times, such morbid associations just now were a distraction which he could well do without.

Resolutely he fell once more to a study of the chart. A brisk turn about the deck he knew would do much to clear his head. But any move in that direction would result in a necessary disruption of his second-in-command's much cherished exercise, sending him scurrying hastily to leeward in time-honoured obedience to an unwritten naval tradition which ruled that as captain of their little floating world he must have the weather side of his quarterdeck to himself. Not to mention causing every one of *Solent*'s forty-one souls who fell under his all-seeing gaze to quake in trepidation lest their lord and master sight something which should incur his wrath.

He shook his head. No, it was too high a price to pay just because he was getting jumpy and in need of a breath of air. Life aboard *Solent*, a pea-sized navy gun brig, could hardly be compared to life aboard a majestic ship-of-the-line. Nor her captain be shrouded in quite the same aloof mystery in which a senior post captain basked. The cold, almost imperious discipline of the one hardly related to the necessarily more liberal familiarity of the other. Nonetheless, as commander of *Solent*, Naseby was every bit as lofty a personage in his own right, and every bit as autocratic, as any captain when aboard his own wooden-walled domain. With, at least in the sight of his minions, only God and King George perched above. A heady responsibility.

Prey to discontent, he straightened up from the chart. Naseby hated to see frightened men about him, and unlike the vast majority of naval officers of the period, did not accept such to be the natural order of things. The thought of mindless, abject terror stalking the lower deck appalled him. Men were born to live, act and think freely, such being their birthright as men. Anything else was unthinkable. And some day the world would wake up to that fact; of that solemn and prophetic truth he was convinced. The thought pleased him. Why, then the arbitrarily autocratic, self-perpetrating and habitually cruel ruling classes would needs look to their powder, by thunder! For on that most blessed of days, when every man and his brother arose … ? He broke off the thought to fish a long-stemmed clay pipe from a rack adjacent the table. The smoking utensil secured, he again picked up the thread of his thoughts. Such a day as he envisaged would not, he knew, come during his lifetime. Not in England. Perhaps not for generations to come. The French had had the way of it;

at first, that was. Until sadly, Jacobin fervour had turned to nationalistic sabre-rattling. With that destiny-besotted bumboy Napoleon ruling the roost, a wholly laudable move towards emancipation had become totalitarianism. How had Pitt phrased it? 'Liberty for the many, used as a stalking horse to secure licence for the few.'

Four double clangs sounded the end of the watch. Pocketing his thoughts with his unsmoked pipe, Naseby left the cabin and mounted to the quarterdeck, the unformed resolution going with him that at least aboard his ship command should not perch on such archaic foundations of self-seeking bestiality such as the rope and the cat. The gun brig's people had not yet had sufficient time in which to come to know him. Not for Captain Philip Masterman Naseby a cowardly sheltering behind the crushing weight of authority imparted by a shiny bauble of an epaulette. Nor did he need an act of Parliament to feel capable of leading men; nor yet the lordly sanction of Admiralty. Leadership was a talent with which he had been born. Any man who didn't wish to obey an order of his need not fear being seized up to a grating and having the flesh flogged from his back – Naseby would simply toss the lubber overboard with his own two hands! That was fair; that, he told himself contentedly, was democracy.

Up top the air was the texture of velvet; scarce a wisp of cloud visible anywhere in the sky. Perry grinned, momentarily oblivious to the element of presumption inherent in the gesture. Aware of this, Naseby returned the like. The wind was full in the sails. Tilting back his head, he could spy the lookout perched aloft and watch as the dizzily spiralling masthead punched holes in the sky. A glance at the compass assured him that all was well, and after a word or two, Perry disappeared below.

Ever beautiful, the Caribbean had always fascinated him: for the greater part of the year unbelievably calm and peaceful; rich blue and shoal green merging together in constantly merging undersea patterns as the ship moved from deep to more shallow waters. At his back, the wind was quartering slightly, but would not yet necessitate any change of trim. Running before the wind the slate showed *Solent* to have been making nine knots at the last casting of the log. Now with the wind backing and beginning to blow more fitfully, that speed would be reduced somewhat. Trust Perry to have had the best of it.

Leaning on the weather rail he was better able to gauge the feel of the ship, finding time as he did so to go over in his mind the letter he was writing to Gray concerning his doings thus far in the Caribbean. Of course, it would be weeks and maybe months until such a letter might be read by its recipient. Particularly so if by the time the post office packet reached England Gray should have been at sea these past many weeks and was even now seeing service on some foreign station. As of course as an experienced and hence valuable lieutenant of Marines, this was very likely to be the case. Nevertheless, writing the letter and betweentimes, such as now, seeing to its composing relaxed him, serving to draw his mind from an endless wrestling with the problems of navigation and the day to day tedium of running the ship. When once it caught up with him, he knew, Gray would be just as happy to receive it, such links with others in their shared world of endless departures assuming an importance impossible adequately to explain to landsmen. Going about their predictable, orderly lives from one day to the next; as like as not for the most of them, being born, rising to adulthood, marrying, birthing children of their own and then one day dying – all not five miles distant from the place of their roots.

Not that Naseby would for one moment deign to trade places with such as they. Nor yet with any other, for the like of it. Loneliness was a companion one grew to live at peace with, as many another had found. Yet, a letter helped; aye, from time to time, a letter helped. Gray wasn't such a bad fellow, for all his devoutness. Besides, who else was there to write to? In all the world he had no one else. While for the straight of it, as far as he knew, no more had Gray.

Forward in the waist, Gideon Moon crouched to his work, replacing a thole-pin on one of the ship's boats damaged during the action with the two privateersmen – the self-same action that had claimed the life of his messmate Harris. Seething inwardly, the man stole a sly look aft, towards the object of his hatred: the pillar of authority on the ship, reposing languidly on his quarter-deck, totally innocent of and oblivious to the dark thoughts that were even now fermenting evilly in his beholder's mind. A Cornishman, Moon had shipped aboard a merchantman as a boy, returning to Falmouth three years later to be swept up in the general 'press' following the brief peace of 1802-3. Since then he had served on three men-of-war, a seventy-four and a frigate and culminating with his present stint aboard the gun brig *Solent.*

Never content with his lot in the Navy, Moon had stubbornly refused to follow the accepted custom of the fighting service; whereby men who had experienced the ill luck of finding themselves captured by a press gang, were once on board, encouraged to 'volunteer' – thereby making themselves eligible for the meagre advantages to be had by appearing as such on the ship's books. Instead, on one occasion becoming a deserter – a foolhardy escapade from which his back still bore the scars – he maintained throughout a bitter and all-abiding contempt for the service, his superiors and whatever one of the King's ships in which he happened to find himself.

Thus it was that even now, with a berth on a gun brig hunting privateers, a berth which, because of the possibility of prize money, many seamen would give a year's grog for, he yet could not keep out of trouble. Bream, *Solent*'s boatswain, had found many an occasion on which to reprimand him of late, including that business this very morning when for nothing at all the bilge-swilling cove had fetched him a whack with his rattan-cane. Just because he had been a little slow getting to divisions. Well, let him once get a chance at the fine and dandy 'Mister' Bream some dark watch when there was no one else around, then he'd know what's what all right! And not with no rattan-cane neither. He'd use a belaying pin!

Straightening from his task, he was in two minds as to which of them he hated most: the puppet-master up on his quarter-deck pulling the strings, or the puppet. In truth there really wasn't very much in it. One bell sounded of the first dog-watch; half an hour left to go before supper. Below in the orlop his confederate, the red-headed Samuel Hinks, would be waiting for him, and it didn't do to keep old Samuel waiting, the devil it didn't!

Hearing the clang of the bell Naseby strode briskly forward, passed a word to the man at the wheel, glanced quickly at the compass card in the binnacle, and pausing only long enough to check that the glass had been turned, ordered another casting of the log. The wind had backed two full points of the compass, hitting them now from somewhere north by east and calling for a change of trim.

Squatting above the beams in the orlop Gideon and his co-conspirator Hinks heard the call for all hands and swore bitterly. 'Gawd spill 'is innards,' muttered Gideon, stirring, ' 'e'll 'ave us 'aulin' an' 'eavin' our 'ands bloody, so 'e will. Damn 'is eyes!' Beside him Hinks made no comment, knowing well the measure of the man to whom he had chosen to attach himself. Samuel Hinks was an old hand and as such had long since learned the craft of using others. Especially such as the fiery Gideon.

Last on deck, the Cornishman was again to feel the rattan-cane of the boatswain Bream, and in his present mood and according to his own lights, pushed beyond all reason, retaliated. Rounding on his persecutor, the nimble Moon planted a wicked back-heel squarely in the bo'sun's groin, snarling wolf-like as he drove in, hitting the man with everything he had. One of the mates tried to grab him and he shrugged him off, sending in a hard right-hander before turning in desperation to seek sanctuary below.

He never made it. Appearing from forward of the main hatchway Burke, the carpenter and one of *Solent*'s three warrant officers, laid a belaying pin smartly alongside the malcontent's head. In the general mêlée Samuel Hinks, who had taken no part in the affair, slunk slowly away.

With the yards braced and her sails trimmed to make the best use of the wind, *Solent* was once again making better than eight knots. Below in his cabin Naseby sat making entries in his personal log and contemplating his evening meal and the precious bottle of wine which he had promised himself. Bream and the problem of what to do about the man Moon could be left until tomorrow. By which time the malefactor should have had a night in irons whereby to contemplate his punishment and 'Mister' Bream a chance to recover.

Under the Articles of War the offence, that of striking a superior, was one of mutiny, for which the prescribed penalty following court martial was death. The prospect of keeping a man perpetually in irons until such time as the gun brig should return to Port Royal where such a court, made up of officers of at least post rank could be assembled, was abhorrent. Why the blazes could the fellow not have contented himself merely with answering back, he asked himself. Then the matter could have been resolved on the spot; the accepted punishment being to have the offender gagged, – clapped in irons in a sitting position, his mouth forced open and an iron bolt put across, well secured behind his head. A sentinel is then placed over him and there he remains until such time as the captain sees fit to order his release. Or until he passes out with exhaustion. – A barbaric enough practice to be sure, but infinitely preferable to what was on offer now.

It was always open to him to order the man flogged. Forty-eight lashes without dint of court martial. Something he knew he had no intention of doing. Nor yet of seeing him hang. True, the offence had been committed, so it followed that Moon would have to be punished. Indeed, as one of *Solent*'s permanent establishment of warrant officers, if Bream wished to press the matter – a rash move indeed if contrary to his captain's wishes – the thing could even now end in a hanging.

Naseby put the matter aside while he sought a fresh quill. His steward would be in with his supper soon and it would fare better with his digestion if his paperwork were cleared.

The middle watch had half an hour still to run. A lump on his head the size of an egg, Gideon Moon sat on the deck with the irons chafing his legs and pondered darkly his prospective fate. As like as not he'd be hanged; taken back for court martialling if he was lucky. If he wasn't and their lord and master was of a mind to handle the entire thing himself, then it would be tomorrow. They'd haul him, gasping and choking out his life, up to the main yard where he'd dangle, legs kicking ludicrously in mid air while the captain and his lick-spittles looked on. Six bells of the forenoon watch it would be; eleven in the morning. Well, at least he'd managed to give that cove of a boatswain something to remember him by. Leastways for a day or two.

With the look-out down from aloft for the night the ship was being 'watched' until morning from the deck. His hands had been tied tightly behind his back, but other than that, and of course save for his leg irons, he wasn't secured. Not that there was anywhere to go. With the watch overseen by a 'snotty', and soon to change anyway, it was odds on that the hands, lolling under a warm Caribbean night, would by now be asleep. So if he wanted to go quietly over the side and cheat his mess mates out of their forthcoming entertainment? – Even wearing leg irons the thing might be managed.

For a moment he considered the possibility, the idea of a watery grave holding little appeal. From scant feet away a voice hissed his name in the darkness. Half on his side facing the forward hatchway, he lay still, listening. On warm sultry nights, provided the watch-keeping officer allowed it, it was no unusual thing for a number of the hands to take a turn at sleeping on deck. Thus the incident neither alarmed nor excited him. Until, that was, he remembered that the custom of those who made a practice of this invariably congregated on the main deck, around the area of the ship's boats where they were largely out of sight, thus leaving the foredeck to those employed on watch.

The voice came again, soft yet insistent. Here in the Caribbean the nights never got really black, and presently he spied a head raised slowly above the hatch coaming. Straining his eyes to the rail, senses alive to every sound, every faint movement, he delayed answering. But there was nothing. Only the motion of the ship and the expected sound of the water overside.

At the third time of asking he answered his name, sure now who it was. Above the coaming a form took shape. It was Samuel Hinks, come, or so Gideon hoped, to rescue his young shipmate and set them both free. Just as they had so often planned down there in the orlop: steal up top during one of the night watches, preferably when there was a 'snotty' aft, take care of the hands nodding contentedly at their stations with belaying pins, break out the dinghy and – Even thinking about it, made his breath come faster. Of course, they had planned to be a deal nearer land when they made their try. Also, to have stowed water and victuals ready. Grog, too, should they have managed to save any. But that couldn't be helped now. They would just have to go as they were, leg irons and all, unless Samuel should have discovered a way to effect a miracle.

Writhing and bunching his muscles, he managed to raise up. So that he half sat, half lay with his back against the foremast. There was a man on watch over there beside the starboard bow-chaser, unless he missed his guess, and those infernal irons had raised enough clatter to rouse the dead! His hand before his face, as if motioning for silence, Samuel Hinks knelt before him. His heart racing, Gideon held his peace. A while they listened thus, the rash young malcontent and the older, wiser hand ...

They found him there, at the changing of the watch. Half sitting, half lying with his back against the mast. It had been one of the departing watch on his way below who had found him, almost stumbling over him in the dark. Thinking him asleep, the man had proceeded to bestow a kick where it would most be guaranteed to elicit response. Then when it didn't, and realising something was amiss, running aft to summon the 'snotty', while calling at the top of his voice for someone to fetch a lantern. Arriving on the scene the midshipman, having secured the necessary lantern, was able to see clearly what had taken place and report to Lieutenant Perry, who, fresh up from below, came hurrying forrad.

Most of his blood, in the flickering light visible as a dark stain on the deck, had already flowed into the scuppers, although the body was still warm. Whoever had done the deed had got right up close, you could see that, the throat having been cut perfectly. Moon even had a comical sort of smile on his face; only the eyes, if one looked closely, betrayed yet a hint of surprise beneath their fish-like glaze of death. One of the hands even commented on the fact that their late, departed shipmate's visage had borne something akin to a look of expectancy. Almost as if he were looking forward to something much to be desired, and was excited about it.

Roused from his cot, Naseby's first question received laconic reply: 'Oh, freshly done, no doubt about it. Should think he even heard the ship's bell ringing out his death knell!' Peering owlishly, Naseby thought Perry's ill-timed levity less than appropriate, but let it pass. It was doubtful if anyone would mourn the murdered seaman anyway.

In which opinion he was somewhat wide of the mark. For at that very moment forrad in his hammock, swinging gently to the slight rise and fall of the ship, Samuel Hinks silently mourned his friend. Mourned the man, if not the deed. For he'd had to do it, there hadn't been any other way. Once before one of those terrifying Admiralty courts, or worse still, seized up to a grating with his flesh laid open by the cat, and it would all have come out. About their long talks in the orlop, their plans to steal a boat and desert; everything! 'Mutinous assembly' they would have called it; them and their fancy 'Articles of War'! And for that, as for many and divers other crimes, a man was hanged.

They'd have been too far from land, that had been the straight up and down of it. Otherwise he'd not have had to silence him. Shame really; they'd have made a great team, the pair of them. Him with his experience and knowledge of the world and young Gideon, fiery and hot-tempered but full of go. Couldn't have been much above an age with the captain, Gideon couldn't. Maybe not that; it was difficult to tell with a man that had shipped to sea, before the mast. A deal more so with a pock-marked cove, like Gideon had been.

Well, now one of them was dead while the other still strode his quarterdeck, or at least would do when he felt the urge. Oceans apart and precious little reason for it either; at least as far as he, Samuel Hinks, could see. Merely an accident of birth; no figuring it, really – Aye, they'd have made a fine pair right enough. He'd have to seek out another now, with whom to share his dreams and hatch his plots. He'd been a good shipmate, had Gideon Moon. As had also been Harris before him. 'Aft the most honour, forrad the better men.' Aye, that was the straight of it, right enough ...

VI

The Spaniard

'Sail ho!' sang out the look-out from the masthead, a paroxysm of suppressed excitement funnelling down with the haunting cry, to make itself felt even on the deck far below. *Solent* was skimming an azure sea in the grip of a soldier's wind, her holystoned deck planks shining white and dazzling in the bright morning sun. It was Wellard at the foretop.

Running forrad, Naseby fashioned a speaking trumpet from his cupped palms. 'Where away!' he bellowed, powerful voice rising easily to the man perched aloft on the foretopmast crosstrees.

'A couple o' points off th' sta'bbad bow!' came the return. 'Rigged like a Span'ard!'

Wellard had a keen eye and Naseby was ready to take him at his word. Springing to the starboard shrouds, perspective glass to his eye, he was already able to discern a bobbing pyramid of white low on the horizon.

A scrambling movement at his elbow marked the arrival next to him in the shrouds of Lieutenant Perry. Grudgingly, Naseby handed over the telescope. *Solent* was making a good seven knots by his reckoning. It would be at least an hour before the two ships bore down on one another. Six bells had just sounded. Had Moon lived, like as not the approaching Spaniard should have signalled a temporary reprieve from the hand of justice. Perhaps even a chance to redeem himself; such things had happened. But then he had not, and Naseby found himself thinking that perhaps this way it had all worked out for the best. At least now he was absolved from the dire responsibility of ordering, at the very least, some awful mutilation to be carried out on the hot-tempered wretch.

It was disconcerting, however, to realise that he had a murderer aboard. Even knowing that in something over an hour's time they would all likely be involved in doing their very utmost to slaughter their fellow man. Such was war, and his was a fighting service. It was highly unlikely that they would ever find out at whose hand the malefactor had died. Which same, he mused, was likely just as well.

'Send the hands to dinner, if you please, Mister Perry, and get something yourself,' he ordered quietly, breaking free of his musings and recapturing the glass from an already retreating Lieutenant Perry. If the gun brig's people were called on to fight an action in the next hour or so they would fare all the better for having a hot meal inside them.

Cleared for action, the galley fire would needs be pitched over the side. Then they should all be on cold commons. As he himself intended to be, aware that he must stay, conning his ship until her approaching hour of danger should be fast fled.

Quickly he glanced inboard: at the scurrying mêlée as the bo'sun's mate piped the hands to dinner. Lord only knew when they'd eat again. Maybe never, if yon Spaniard turned out to be a well armed frigate, or even yet a too heavily gunned schooner. Well, he thought, turning his gaze outboard once more and glass to eye, engaged in studying the everso steadily approaching vessel: at least the next fifteen minutes or so should serve to settle that question, one way or another.

Solent carried an armament of ten six-pounders and a pair of long-fours mounted as bow-chasers forrad. Ample firepower when dealing with the average privateer, but lamentably lacking in weight of metal against a national warship of any size.

Descending to the deck, he strode aft, careful to keep his gait regular and his actions unhurried as he checked their heading, passed his orders to the man at the helm and cast a weather-eye aloft at the dog vane flying rigid at the maintruck. As always at such times, *Solent*'s people would be watching him, he knew. Ever ready to take their lead from him in deciding how great the danger they were sailing into. Should he, be it by word or deed, display but a moment's hesitation or anxiety, then as captain he could have a panic on his hands. Not that the seamen were in any way cowards; far from it. Merely was it that as arbiter of their joint destiny it was his bound-in duty to have 'got it right'.

Finished with his playacting, he went below to his cabin. The seaman who was acting as his steward had laid out cheese, several slices of cold meat and some of the ship's biscuit for him. In truth he was not overly hungry, but in this again was aware that not to eat would be construed as fear. Seating himself, he started to eat, remembering automatically as he did so to first tap the biscuit sharply on the edge of the table in order to dislodge any tunnelling weevils. There was also a jug of beer from which he helped himself liberally, thirstily conscious of its reviving coolness.

Having done justice to the meal, he could now look to the business which had brought him below. Namely that of arming himself against any eventuality. Some ten minutes later he emerged on deck, if anything, looking more like a figure from some pirate opera than an officer engaged in the sober service of King and country: the short-bladed fighting sword swung from a broad leather cross-belt worn rakishly across his right shoulder; a pair of pistols, side by side twin-barrelled flintlocks jutting formidably at his waist. His relatively plain undress lieutenant's coat, sensibly minus his commander's epaulette, was close-buttoned and as was his wont, he had opted for black Hessian boots in preference to shoes and hose.

Cleared for action and scooping noticeably on a sou-westerly heading with the wind abaft the beam, *Solent* hurtled onward, her people standing silent at quarters as with all sail set she raced to keep her appointment with the oncoming Spaniard. Balanced easily to the send of the deck, the gun brig's burly-sinewed commander snatched the perspective glass from his eye.

'I'll have the starboard battery loaded and run out, if you please, Mister Perry!'

'Ball, sir?' enquired Perry, standing ready to bark his instructions to Hawkins, the brig's master gunner.

'Aye, ball, Mister Perry!' Naseby replied at once, appending as the thought occurred, 'And I'll have a charge of grape on top of each!'

The Spaniard – a fore-and-aft rigged schooner with a trimly swept hull and flying her national red and gold at her stern – was bearing round with the wind on her port quarter in an effort to bring her larboard battery to bear.

'A point to larboard, helmsman!' ordered Naseby, his tone even, businesslike.

The vessels were within a cable's distance of one another now, with the schooner's officers plainly visible on her afterdeck.

'Wait for my order, Mister Perry!' This time he was only partially successful in keeping the excitement out of his voice.

The Spaniard was turning, turning – allow a little more – Gauging his enemy's manoeuvre with a practised eye, he had almost left it too late! The time was now but his tongue felt stuck to the roof of his mouth.

'Fire!' he bellowed.

Solent's deck lurched and then dipped under the recoil of her five starboard six-pounders.

'Stop your vents! Sponge out!' rang Perry's stentorian tones from his position forward by the guns.

The freshening wind whipped the smoke clear as the Spaniard's neat row of four-pounders made reply. *Solent*'s broadside had scored at least two hits above the schooner's waterline and her heavier six-pounders were thundering out again even as the other vessel's weight of metal slammed mightily into her own side timbers.

'Fire as your guns bear, Mister Perry!' Naseby heard himself roar, eyes peering intently at the Spaniard's smoke-wreathed sides as he weighed up his enemy's and his own next move. An ominous whirring overhead caused him to look up; just in time to see a rude notch gouged from the mainmast.

'He's turning to the wind!' sang out Perry, looking aft to the quarterdeck and struggling to make himself heard. The pall of smoke forrad was blinding.

He needn't have worried. Naseby was alive to the move. The schooner's captain was attempting to bring his vessel's bows to the wind preparatory to making a stern-raking pass behind *Solent* using his thus far unengaged starboard guns. Naseby was glad now that he had deliberately chosen not to shorten courses, thus robbing the ship of vital manoeuvreability. Filling his lungs to capacity he made his voice carry the length of the ship.

'Hands to the braces there! Wear ship!'

Here was where the weeks upon weeks of endless sail drill paid off as men ran to their stations as if nothing in the world was more natural than that they should be here, fighting for their lives three thousand miles from their homes. Overhead the rattle and squeak of blocks replaced the intermittent rumble of guntrucks forrad.

'Tops'l sheets! Larboard helm!'

Nimbly *Solent* spun on her heel.

'Braces there!'

Presenting her stern to the enemy thus was taking a measured gamble which every man aboard knew was dependent for its success upon their beating the Spaniard to the wind. Glancing aft, Naseby could see that it was going to be a close run thing. With the foreyards hauled right round the wind was on the other quarter; *Solent*'s bows swinging with maddening slowness to put them on a parallel course with the enemy schooner.

His eye on the brig's shivering canvas, Naseby knew that the moment must be judged just right. There was no room for error. Not if they wished to avoid becoming a helpless, wallowing target for the Spaniard to pour broadsides into as he pleased. It called for every scrap of Naseby's seamanship and confidence in his own best judgement to wait it out.

Standing close abaft the waiting helmsman he was more than a little surprised to find his voice so steady.

'Ease your helm! Let go and haul!'

He had judged the thing perfectly. Yards braced hard round, courses and headsails sheeted taut and drawing. *Solent* settled comfortably on the larboard tack.

'Keep her full and by!' he said to the man at the wheel.

'Full and by it is, sir!' echoed the helmsman.

Naseby felt uncommonly good, but there wasn't time to enjoy the feeling. Wearing round to pass to leeward of the other he had allowed the Spaniard, who had now also completed her manoeuvre, a chance to gain the weather gauge.

Fortunately, however, the schooner was some distance astern of them. Which happy circumstance could quickly change given the two vessels' differing sail plan. Fore-and-aft rigged as his ship was, the Spaniard could lie considerably closer to the wind than could *Solent*. A fact which was amply demonstrated as the brig began to fall off to loo'ard.

'They top's'l schooners us just made fer a nifty bit o' privateerin', zur!' offered Bream, quite unsolicited, from adjacent the main mast.

'Quite so,' muttered Naseby, more to himself than the loquacious boatswain.

Already the schooner was gaining on them. Once let her draw level and up to windward like she was, and there'd be precious little *Solent* could do to stay in contact with her. A single broadside, perhaps two, and the Spaniard would be away. Flush-decked and with her trimly swept hull scything through the water like a dolphin, they could soon find themselves dogging the schooner's wake all the way to Havana.

Mentally measuring the fast-dwindling expanse of water that still separated the two ships, as he grappled with the angles which the problem presented, Naseby made his decision. Likely the whole thing would result in a fiasco and the prize elude them. But at least they should have tried.

Summoning Perry aft he outlined his plan, adding a little something for insurance should his calculations be off. 'Now comes your part, Mister Perry. I want the long-fours manned and ready. You understand?' Perry nodded, his mobile expression and alert bearing assuring Naseby that his second in command was fully alive to what was expected of him. 'See to their laying yourself, will you!'

Satisfied, Naseby turned to bark his orders to the expectant-faced seamen on *Solent*'s deck. 'Prepare to put her about! Helmsman! Lee ho!'

All at once ordered confusion reigned as the gun brig's people fought to lay their charge up into the wind, the rattan-cane of boatswain Bream landing smartly on the smoke-blackened shoulders of a laggardly seaman nearby. Then her bows were swinging, coming round head to, in a desperate evolution designed to foil her enemy. Overhead, canvas cracked and shrouds thrummed as *Solent*'s sails were taken aback and she staggered falteringly across the eye of the wind. Naseby gulped. For a single, heart-stopping moment it appeared that, not having sufficient way on her, the gun brig would miss stays and be held in irons. And then they were past, swinging clear and free, a cooling wind singing amidst her rigging. Naseby was himself again.

'Meet her, helmsman! Mainsail haul! Make fast and belay! Starboard battery!'

But already it was too late. Spotting the move, the schooner's captain had hauled her even closer to the wind. Naseby's gamble to put *Solent* on the starboard tack and come up behind the Spaniard had gone awry, leaving the gun brig firmly in the schooner's wake and her guns with nothing at which to fire, save empty sea. From the gun deck forrad a heartfelt growl of dismay attested the hands' disgruntled assessment of their apparent predicament.

However, *Solent*'s commander was not done yet. This was the exurgency for which he had planned. Projecting his voice, harsh along *Solent*'s glistening length of decking and against the wind, he cried: 'Mister Perry! Bow-chasers! Fire as your guns bear!' Then, almost quietly to the straining man at the wheel, 'Keep her full and by, helmsman!'

'Aye, sir, full and by,' mouthed the man, his words lost in the booming report from *Solent*'s forward facing guns.

Leaning far out over the weather side bulwark, Naseby could see, even as a cheer from the deck forrad attested, that Perry's carefully laid long-fours had scored a hit. Even as he watched, Perry's guns fired again. With a lead of less than a cable and minus stern-chasers all the Spaniard could do was mutely to await the fall of shot. The first ball missed, raising a plume in the water off to larboard. The other didn't: smashing straight through the schooner's stern-rail and wreaking; it was only to be imagined what havoc amongst the Spaniard's people and along her deck.

' 'E's 'auled 'is wind, zur!' someone cried from forrad.

It was true. The Spaniard had put his helm hard over, throwing his vessel full bows on to the wind. No wise could he be tacking. Such a move being tantamount to committing suicide, handing *Solent* all the advantages.

But, damn his eyes! – he was doing just that. A stupid, reckless gamble on the part of the schooner's captain that, close-hauled on a similar tack with *Solent*, the more weatherly capability of his vessel would yet prove sufficient to claw her clear. As of course it might; but not before her resolute and more suitably-armed enemy should have had ample time in which to pound her into matchwood with his bow-chasers! Watching, Naseby's heart went out to the man. The graceful schooner was duck bait now.

'Fire!' screamed Perry, *Solent*'s long-fours booming out across the water almost as one.

Naseby could well imagine the pandemonium attendant on the Spaniard's deck as both balls hit home. The distance between the gun brig and her prey had shortened. One of the balls from *Solent*'s long-fours had kicked high, all but dismasting her, and the schooner had gybed. Hardly disposed toward sending such a fine prize to the bottom, Naseby ordered the helmsman to lay her alongside. The schooner might yet be hard won, but he was damned if he was going to forego the attempt.

Unfortunately he had misjudged the wind, and *Solent* could claw her way no closer than half a cable's distance from, and broadside on, to her adversary. 'Damn your eyes!' he gritted at the helmsman. Then, 'Why doesn't she strike?' If, however, as Naseby hoped, the Spaniard did indeed entertain any notion of lowering his colours, he was evidently not yet ready so to do.

To the accompaniment of a crashing crescendo the schooner's broadside belched forth tongues of orange flame. The battle was joined. *Solent* reeled and curtsied to the weight of metal as the schooner's shot took her amidships. A gurgling shriek sounded from the hammock nettings and Samuel Hinks, a gaping red hole the size of a melon in his naked chest, turned slowly inboard, swayed drunkenly, and then melted to the deck. Forrad of the mainmast a blue-coated 'snotty' whimpered in disbelief as he painfully strangled to death on a vagrant musket ball which had taken him in the throat.

By now *Solent*'s own musketeers were popping away, adding their own minute contribution to the overpowering din.

Sparing a look for the fallen midshipman, Naseby found himself wishing devoutly for a like fate to befall the Spaniard. The stench of gunpowder clogged his nostrils. Vagrant tears, doubtless a product of the blinding smoke which everywhere pervaded, stung his cheeks.

Overside the Spaniard's people were cheering raggedly. Lieutenant Perry was yelling instructions to *Solent*'s gun-layers. Hawkins himself could be glimpsed kneeling at one. Sighting carefully on – Naseby knew not what. The fighting sword was slapping against his leg and he felt impatient to clasp his enemy up close.

The gun brig's broadside spoke at last, a pall of powdersmoke obscuring all. Forrad on the gun deck men were gesticulating and shouting, their words lost in a holocaust of sound; mouths which opened and closed with nightmarish unreality – dazing the mind and making it difficult to comprehend just what it was that had taken place. Wrenching his gaze from the cavorting figures, Naseby peered outboard. Then, raising his hand, as if to clear a path for his smoke-tortured vision, he arrested the motion. A helpful gust of wind had cleared a channel for him, through which could be plainly seen the enemy schooner wallowing drunkenly, beam on, to a broaching sea. The wreck of her foremast trailed overside, set out like a sheet anchor, drawing her inexorably round. The sea filled with tangled cordage. The stump of the mast, splintered and jagged, reared some nine feet above the schooner's flush decking. Mute testimony to the efficient gun-laying of Elias Hawkins.

Crippled, the schooner had begun to gather sternway. Frantic figures could be seen labouring furiously to free the wreckage at her bow, the schooner's people obviously expecting the cursed Englishman to seize his opportunity and go in for the kill.

At this stage of the proceedings a cautious commander, and certainly one less concerned with avarice, might bring matters to a satisfactory conclusion by standing away and pounding his stubborn enemy into submission at long range. Naseby, however, was fashioned from stiffer clay. Snatching out his sword, he gave orders to the helmsman to lay *Solent* alongside.

With the Spaniard wallowing beam on to the wind something like a cable's distance down to loo'ard, the required evolution demanded but little of the gun brig's commander: *Solent* turning on her heel and with the wind abaft the beam, and under full press of canvas, bowling easily down upon her helpless opponent. While up forrad the ever dependable Lieutenant Perry was already engaged on getting the brig's long-fours primed with grape.

'Boarders to me!' Naseby bellowed, flourishing his sword and bounding forrad.

Solent was closing fast, bow on to the Spaniard. A wild chorus of cheering broke out around him, all but drowned by the double bang of *Solent*'s two long-fours. Hastily formed up amidships to repel boarders, the lethal charge of grapeshot cut a wide swathe across the schooner's deck. A further chorus of cheering, and then the gun brig was grinding relentlessly alongside her enemy. The grating impact as the vessels came together transmitting a judder which seemed momentarily to live throughout the entire superstructure of the ship.

Yelling at the top of his lungs, Naseby led the wild carousing charge along the deck, swarming heedlessly over *Solent*'s bows and vaulting onto the schooner's populous deck. A pistol, wielded by a red-shirted brigand, hung fire directly before him. His sword cleaved the man's shoulder and then he was past, dragging one of his own pistols left-handed from his belt as he went. The heavy recoil of its twin barrels jarring his arm to the elbow as the weapon, held hitherto at half cock, discharged full into the face of an advancing Spanish officer. All about him was the cruel mindlessness of men locked together in mortal combat.

Lashing out to right and left with his sword, he cut a bloody path to the vessel's mainmast. Muskets were popping from aft, and a one ounce ball tore a jagged sliver from the mast, sending it whistling past his ear. Bream, *Solent*'s boatswain, was over by the lee rail, his Herculean sinews glistening as he wielded an over-sized fighting axe as if it were a toy. Seeing him thus, it was hard to imagine Gideon Moon besting him now.

'*Solent*! Solents to me!' sang out Naseby, in time-honoured fashion, using the ship's name as a rallying cry for her people.

A sharp pain burned his forearm, and he turned to face a gaudily bedecked Spaniard flourishing a rapier. The schooner's captain! Once more the gleaming blade flicked towards him, but this time he was ready and instinctively parried the lunge. Something hefty struck his back and he stumbled forward onto the Spaniard. The man danced away along the deck, the rapier's long-bladed menace doing service to cover his retreat. No mean swordsman himself, Naseby nonetheless knew that there just wasn't time for this. Hurling his discharged pistol at the man's head, he let out a wild banshee screech, launching himself bodily into the attack. No match for the fighting sword's heavier blade, the Spaniard's slender rapier was easily broken in twain, as by sheer main force Naseby, snarling, bore his adversary writhing to the deck.

Yet his enemy wasn't done. Frantically fumbling fingers sought the brass-capped butt of Naseby's remaining pistol, seeking even now to turn the affair. Pinning his lighter opponent with scant effort, Naseby pried loose the man's grasping fingers, himself drew the pistol, thumbed back both hammers and, pressing it hard up against the underside of the Spanish captain's jaw, rasped, '*Bastante, amigo?*' It was over; the prize was his!

San Juan del Norte bay lay shimmering opaquely in the early afternoon heat, the cooling breath of the trade wind conspicuous by its absence. Allowing the rich blue waters of the bay to assume a glass-like sheen that to Commander Philip Naseby as he gazed out upon it from *Solent*'s open stern light, seemed almost as if this whole south western corner of the Caribbean Sea was covered by a kind of huge, invisible skin; so utterly devoid of motion did it appear. A biscuit toss away the captured Spanish schooner, *Salamander*, was having a spare spar fished to the stump of her foremast.

Perry had laboured heroically to bring the crippled vessel in. It was a meritorious mark to Lieutenant William Perry which Naseby was fully determined should ring out loud and clear from the carefully worded pages of the report which he was currently engaged in writing. Judging other men according to his own lights, Naseby, disdaining the man's haughtily proffered *parola de honor*, had ordered the schooner's captain clapped in irons and stowed in *Solent*'s cramped manger forrad. The animals wouldn't mind, and besides, there was scant place else.

To *Salamander*'s crew he had offered a straight choice: over the side and swim for it – they were still half a day's sailing from land at the time – or volunteer for the King's service. Reasonable enough under the circumstances, he had thought, since anyway he didn't have the men to guard them. Perhaps not surprisingly, to a man the rag-tag mixture of half castes and Indians had chosen to volunteer. With the exception of her captain, none of the schooner's other officers – all Spanish, of course – had survived the action. Which was, mused Naseby with absolute indifference, all to the good.

This stretch of coastline, as *Solent*'s commander well remembered, was an unremitting expanse of fever rife jungle and stinking mangrove swamps. 'A veritable paradise of menace,' one never to be forgotten gun room wit had aptly dubbed it. A tropical hell-hole would have been Naseby's somewhat more direct summation of the place; its lush and many-hued vegetation hiding all manner of poisonous things and ill humours waiting to pounce on the unwary and, as yet, still largely unacclimatised English seamen. Not a place a man would wish to revisit.

Which was, of course, why he was here. Neglected by all, even the acquisitive Spanish after a period of time, the place made a perfect base. There was a fine, sheltered anchorage and, providing a man knew what to look for, an ample abundance of tropical fruits. Northward the coast climbed, reaching ever outward as it did so, far farther than a ship could sail in a good day and a half.

Laying aside the quill with a firm resolution to put the finishing touches to the report later in the day, and minus his coat, he went up on deck. His shirt hung open to the waist, exposing the heavy muscularity of a by now nut brown torso, much of which was covered by a thick mat of coal-black hair. He had taken to wearing white canvas duck trousers over these past days spent anchored safely in the bay. Most of the men went barefoot, as was the seaman's wont, weather permitting.

Naseby, however, had resisted going that far.

Another day would see both vessels' water casks replenished, and a goodly store of fresh fruit taken on board. *Salamander*'s three parts Indian crew had proved their worth here, gathering many times as much in half the time than could have any white men. Bream – *Solent*'s boatswain and, with Mister Perry away, unofficial acting lieutenant – was presently ashore with a party foraging for anything else that could be had. Gazing outboard he could see that Perry had succeeded in giving the schooner an improvised foremast now. *Solent* had been extremely fortunate in possessing an extremely able carpenter in the shape of the American Nathan Burke. A blessing for which her captain felt duly grateful. He could well conjure up a vision in his mind's eye of the gangling Nathan going about his work and grumbling the while.

Solent had got off relatively lightly in her action with the Spaniard, being holed in only two places, both above the waterline and both now patched.

Eight bells sounded and the starboard watch padded on deck, their ranks somewhat decimated by virtue of the fact that Perry had needed every available pair of hands and brawny back aboard the captured schooner. Despite the unlikelihood of an enemy frigate, or even a roving privateersman, looking into the bay, and the sheer improbability of there being Spanish soldiers in the vicinity, he had chosen to man all watches as if they were at sea, not trusting to the usual anchor watch only. The hands would be better off squatting forrad under the rail than milling aimlessly about below.

'Boat putting off from *Salamander*, sir!' piped up a look-out from the bow.

That would be Burke with *Solent*'s extra seamen returning to the ship. Perry had done exceedingly well. An odd bird, as thin as a rake and burdened with a lugubrious-looking horse face and buck teeth. Yet for all his unprepossessing appearance, a first rate lieutenant and an able subordinate. If Naseby's memory served him aright, Perry was a year his junior and the son of a baronet. Still, he amended, you couldn't really hold that against him. Any more than you could his unfortunate appearance. Fops aplenty in the service there most certainly were, all blue blood and minus a backbone. But Lieutenant William Perry wasn't one of them.

On the following day Naseby had the Spanish captain brought to his cabin. Three bells of the forenoon watch had just sounded; nine-thirty in the morning. The Spaniard, one Don Juan Castaño, in the company of the bo'sun's mate and a half caste negro topman known as 'Rings' (a reference to his piratical affectation of sporting enormous ear decoration) who had been pressed into service as interpreter, standing stiffly, heads bowed to the height of the deck beams. The trio presented a comic appearance.

'*Estoy muy enfadado. Usted me guarda con los puercos* – !'

Naseby cut him off with a sign.

'*Por dios*!' exploded the prisoner, grunting as the burly bo'sun's mate jabbed a formidable elbow at his cadaverous ribcage.

'*Bastante*!' ordered Naseby, largely exhausting his knowledge of the language. To the topman, 'Rings', he addressed his carefully thought out questions. The interview was a laborious one. At long last, however, and thanks to the able and grinning assistance of 'Rings', not to mention the ready elbow of his gaoler, the Spaniard was ready to offer up his story.

And a riveting enough one Naseby found it. En route for Havana, carrying dispatches for the resident Spanish governor (dispatches which in accordance with naval custom and the standing orders of each nation's fighting service had gone over the side in a lead-weighted metal box at the first moment when their capture seemed imminent) the schooner, a national warship for all she was fitted out as, and behaving like a privateer (no doubt her main function) had run onto *Solent.* Taking her at first for a trading brig the Spaniard had borne down, only to find too late just what it was that he was sailing into. There followed the action.

The part of the Spaniard's story which held Naseby riveted, however, was when, seeking to secure his freedom by same, the man offered to acquaint his captor with the contents of said dispatches, to which unaccountably he had been privy. Dispatches of sufficient import, the Spaniard had volubly assured him, to make 'the most honourably English *capitano*'

'*Más rico que Usted puede imaginar!*' Which liberally translated meant rich beyond his wildest dreams!

Here was a turnabout which Naseby, inveterate cynic though he was, had not envisaged. So much for Spanish gentlemen! Choosing his words carefully so as not to appear to bite too quickly, he acceded grudgingly to the Spaniard's terms. Keeping it firmly in the forefront of his mind that should, as seemed eminently possible, the man indeed impart such wondrously valuable information, he should do far better to cut the fellow's throat and have his body sent to feed the sharks. That way the information should remain valuable.

A heavily laden treasure ship was making ready at San José, about a hundred and twenty miles down the coast, to the south. She was an armed galleon named the *Santa Rosario*, with a cargo of silver ingots bound first for Havana, and thence to Spain. According to his prisoner, she was due to sail on the fifteenth, wind permitting. Today was the first. His Excellency the Governor of Havana had been exhorted in the dispatches to send warships to act as escort for the treasure ship.

Upon hearing which, Naseby was more than a little surprised, if not to say scornful, that charged with the bearing of such important tidings, the Spaniard had seen fit to jeopardise his mission by seeking to engage what he thought at the time to be a likely prize! It was a salutary lesson in greed. Yet uncommon good fortune for him. 'Question not the hand of fate, for it be turned in thy favour,' would have been Naseby's present motto, should, that was, he have felt inclined to pen one.

Ridding himself of the Spaniard with a lightly given promise to look to the matter of his being released that very day, he fell immediately to laying his plans. The schooner's captain could scarce be allowed his freedom; so much was obvious. Be so ever it may, that was a detail which need not remain a problem overlong!

VII

Treasure Galleon

Twelve days had passed since the Spaniard had gone to his reward. *Solent*, a cable and a half to leeward of the captured schooner *Salamander*, was riding hove-to over a glassy sea. With luck tomorrow would see an end to the rigours of poverty for all time. Or at least for as long as his mortal body would sustain life. Which amounted to the same thing.

Naseby inhaled deeply of the fragrant tobacco in his pipe, closing his eyes as its pleasant aroma bathed his senses. The only fly in the ointment might arise should the errant schooner be expected back at San José before the treasure ship sailed. Many times over the last days Naseby had cursed his own stupidity in not having ascertained this fact before disposing of her captain.

Mister Bream, the brig's unofficial acting lieutenant who had the watch, joined him at the rail. It would be sunset in an hour. As if to echo his thoughts a double clang chimed out from forrad to signal that half the first dog watch had run its course. There was an air of quiet expectancy about the men lounging up forrad this evening; each man no doubt savouring some private dream, perhaps long cherished, which the morrow's prize money would serve to make a reality. Even the bluff Bream at his side seemed caught up in silent musings.

Naseby sighed. However good it was to dream, such things were elusive and had to be fashioned into substance by one's own hand. The *Santa Rosario* had still to be taken. On which thought Naseby tapped out his pipe and went below. Doubtless Perry in the *Salamander* was prey to likewise restless doings ...

The lantern swinging from the deckhead beams was smoking

evilly, giving off an acrid stench which pervaded the entire cabin. Naseby held on to the edge of his cot as he shaved. The wind had freshened considerably overnight and was blowing from almost due east. Dead foul for the Spanish treasure galleon, which would have to claw its way wearily out to sea in an exhausting and time-consuming series of short tacks. That was, if her captain decided to come out at all, but chose instead to lay to and await a more favourable wind. The Spanish were a lubberly lot of seamen at the best of times! Not to mention the fact that the national warships which the Spaniard would be expecting as escort should, with a strong wind abeam, be hourly drawing nearer to their precious charge. Which fact alone, Naseby mused sourly, would doubtless encourage the man to put off sailing for as long a time as possible.

Solent gave a particularly violent roll, causing Naseby to nick himself. Swearing softly he splashed water over his face from the bulkhead attached canvas wash bowl and towelled himself dry. Spenby his steward ghosted in with his coffee.

'Mister Bream's compliments, sir, and can he clear for action, sir?'

God, the man was keen. It still lacked a good hour and a quarter till dawn. Bream must be feeling his new found responsibilities weighing heavily. Well, that was all to the good.

'Very well. My compliments to Mister Bream, and you may inform him that I'll be on deck directly!'

Spenby tugged at his wispy forelock and padded silently from the cabin. Naseby took a cautious sip of the scalding coffee and reached for his coat.

Solent was bucking bow on to the still freshening wind and providing but poor footing for men grown used to a calm sea. Bream touched his hat respectfully and moved away from the binnacle. Outside its muted yellow halo the world was still a canopy of near blackness. Two bells struck musically up forrad. Naseby coughed.

'Very well, Mister Bream, you may stand the hands to quarters and have the guns loaded, but don't clear for action just yet!'

'Guns run out, sir?'

Naseby smiled in the darkness. 'No, not yet, Mister Bream.

I'll give you the necessary order in good time, never fear!'

Bream's stammered 'Aye, aye, sir!' sounded a trifle stilted, and then he was barking his orders and the brig became a bustle of barely seen confusion. Clucking to himself, Naseby returned below. Time enough to clear for action in half an hour; after the galley had had time to rustle up some breakfast.

Dawn came up as suddenly as it always did in the tropics and revealed their consort *Salamander* faithfully hove to a cable's length to larboard. From aft Perry waved his hat in salutation. Naseby returned the courtesy and then resumed his pacing. There would be no sight of the treasure ship before mid morning in any event. Momentarily he allowed his thoughts to dwell on the prospect of his share of the prize, before abruptly shaking himself and casting a wary eye aloft. *Solent*'s masthead pennant was pointing aft, as stiff as a board. 'Damn this wind!' At least he would hold the weather gauge from which to run down on his opponent should the chance come. Which of course, would avail him nothing if the Spaniard were land-bound.

The next couple of hours passed exceedingly slowly, and then another. At the guns the crews lolled disconsolately while Naseby sweated. Sweated and paced, up and down, up and down, the wayward motion of the decking beneath his feet forgotten as he willed the look-out aloft to conjure up their prey.

The forenoon watch came and went and still he paced. Still the hands lounged at the guns. Bream had wisely kept to his own side of the quarterdeck, for which fact Naseby was grateful. The wind had dropped this long hour past and was now blowing little more than a sharp breeze from north of east. What the devil was the Spaniard up to! Naseby was about to order the men by watches to a cold dinner when the long awaited cry from the mainmast crosstrees snapped his mouth shut.

'Sail ho! Standin' out from lan'ard!'

Barely able to contain his excitement Naseby sprang to the taffrail. It could only be the treasure ship. It *must* be the treasure ship ...

*

The wind had died still further to light airs from the north-east. *Solent* and her consort drifted steadily over the sun-sparkling waters of the Caribbean within half a mile of the high-pooped galleon, looking for all the world like a throwback to some fifty years ago, with her limply curling flags at the mastheads and heraldic shields from mainmast to stern.

'A four-master, by the powers!' muttered Bream conversationally.

The *Santa Rosario* sported a bonnie-venture mizzen within a spit of her taffrail, a relic of earlier times.

'She'll most likely be armed with long culverins and a half a dozen brass cannon on the broadside,' offered up Hawkins from the gun deck. At any other time such unsolicited comments might have drawn swift rebuke, but not today.

Leaving aside the walking wounded aboard both the ships under his command, Naseby had something under seventy men with whom to take the treasure ship; barely enough. There was also the danger, real but necessarily acceptable, that some among the recently 'volunteered' crew of the schooner might, in the heat of battle, decide to revert to their old allegiance. A discomfiting possibility: to lessen which Naseby had seen to it that the erstwhile Spaniards had been evenly distributed aboard both ships. Also that each among their number had had it patiently explained to him that, once the treasure galleon were taken, he stood personally to benefit to the tune of some nine hundred pounds.

A King's ransom to the denizens of the lower deck. The best of whom, the topmen, received (when they were lucky enough to be paid at all) the sum of thirty-three shillings per month. Out of which were deducted various sums for their clothing, etc. Indeed, how much more this vast sum would appear to the largely Indian and half caste dregs of the Main that made up the ranks of *Salamander*'s people could scarce be imagined.

Naseby's own two-eighths share of the two hunded and fifty thousand pounds sterling (the estimate given him by *Salamander*'s late captain concerning the value of the silver ingots in the galleon's hold) would amount to some sixty-two thousand five hundred pounds, with a further one eighth – thirty-one thousand two hundred and fifty pounds – going to the Admiral commanding the West Indian station. A dazzling prospect for them both!

The Spaniard had crowded on all sail in an effort to pass to windward of her adversaries. But in the present light airs it was a forlorn hope.

'We'll have the colours run up, if you please, Mister Bream!' Naseby ordered, and then to the crouching Hawkins, rapped, 'A shot across her bows, Master gunner!'

Solent's foremost starboard six-pounder banged off and an answering plume of water rose half a cable ahead and to larboard of the galleon.

In the interval since the sighting of the *Santa Rosario* Lieutenant Perry had managed to work *Salamander* up to windward of the brig, and now lay beam-on to the rippling cats paws, presenting her broadside to the Spaniard, a cable's length astern, and to starboard of *Solent*. Under which threat the captain of the treasure ship would be forced to strike despite his own token armament. Accustomed as they were to sailing in close convoy with a heavy frigate escort, her crew would be unused to fighting and as such, no match for determined British seamen, not to mention superior British gunnery.

Levelling his glass on the Spaniard's poop, Naseby wondered if her captain would offer even a token resistance. The time-honoured single broadside aimed into the sea for the sake of honour. While at the self-same moment when the last gun would fire, the colours should be furiously hauled down and the ship surrendered …

The little triangle of white-sailed ships barely moved over the surface of cobalt blue water now, but even so as the gap between them gradually narrowed, the Spaniard suddenly threw her tops'ls aback, killing what way she had, and lowered her colours, flapping gently, to the deck.

Naseby smiled inwardly. So the game was won! Now all that remained was to lower away a boat and have himself hauled across to the fortune which awaited him.

'Sail! Fine on the larboard bow.'

Naseby's heart sank. Snatching up the telescope he sprang onto the rail, oblivious of the shark-infested waters rippling bluely scant yards below. Living in his brain was the thought that this unexpected late arrival might be a belated escort dispatched by a suspicious captain-general of San José. Perhaps the schooner *Salamander* was due to have returned, following her hop to Havana …

She would be nothing as large as a frigate, that much was certain. Else she would have been detailed as escort for the treasure ship already. Scant comfort, for even the arrival on the scene of something as small as a 'guardacoaster' could dangerously swing the balance of power the wrong way at this delicate stage in the proceedings. Technically the treasure galleon had already stuck to him. But with no British seamen yet aboard her, her captain might well gain fresh heart from the prospect of help so near at hand and decide to make a fight of it. These thoughts and others chasing one another across his brain, he levelled the glass.

The newcomer was too far distant to make identification easy, but from the scrap of sail which hovered in the object lens the vessel had the look of a tops'l schooner, of a type with *Salamander*. If, as seemed likely, she proved to be Spanish – ? Leaping down onto the brig's quarterdeck, Naseby rapped out his orders.

It was odds on that in the kerfuffle of making ready to surrender his ship, and under the menace of English guns, the Spaniard had not as yet sighted the still distant vessel. Bream had managed to get a boat away now, and under the vituperative lash of his tongue, her crew were pulling lustily for the galleon.

In the circumstances Naseby had deemed it politic to remain aboard the gun brig. With the present lack of wind it would take the approaching schooner the better part of two to three hours to bring her presence to bear, by which time, all being well, the galleon should be securely in British hands.

Of course, there was the slight possibility that the newcomer might herself turn out to be British. In which case her commander might conceivably expect to share in the prize, having questionably been in sight at the moment of her taking. Taking? Yes, but not of capture, for the Spaniard had already struck! It was a moot point, and one which, Naseby decided irritably, was hardly worthy of consideration at this present precarious point in time.

At any moment the captain of the treasure ship might spot the interloper and snap off a broadside. Colours or no colours. In the self-same position, Naseby was in no doubt at all as to what his own course of action should be. But then, he would not have struck in the first place.

With a devout sigh of relief he saw that *Solent*'s boat had lashed on to the galleon's mainchains and Bream was already scurrying up her steeply canted side.

With her officers and crew securely battened below hatches and with all sail set to make what use she could of the prevailing light airs, *Santa Rosario* was being warped agonisingly across an almost level expanse of sea by her ship's boats. *Solent* and *Salamander* ranged a cable's distance on her either beam.

On the quarterdeck of the gun brig Commander Philip Naseby paced backwards and forwards, hands clasped beneath coat tails, a resolute cast to his ivory tanned features.

The newcomer – she was close enough now to be definitely recognisable as a tops'l schooner, and Spanish – was having hardly a better time of it. Not that Naseby's little flotilla had anything directly to fear from her solitary presence at the moment. Rather the danger would come later, when having passed 15° north latitude and somewhat over half way to Jamaica, they might expect to run foul of a hunting enemy frigate, likely French, engaged in keeping a weather eye open for enterprising English privateers sailing south-westward from Kingston in the hope of snapping up a prize or two off the Main. No doubt with that very thought in mind the Spaniard was doing his utmost to keep the flotilla in sight. Ready, if and when required, to lend such an ally any assistance he might.

Sunset found them lying to and with the morrow's dawn a usable wind had them beating northward preparatory to making an easting for Jamaica, and safety. All that day Naseby held his little command, hampered by the cumbersome *Santa Rosario*, as close to the wind as could be contrived. The eagle-eyed Wellard at the masthead scanning the horizon for suspect craft.

On two occasions the time-honoured cry of 'Sail ho!' sent icy shivers of alarm arcing down Naseby's back, but on each occasion the sighting turned out to be nothing more than bona fide trading vessels only too anxious to steer well clear of ships of war, no matter how small.

Downwind the Spaniard kept her station like a faithful puppy, neither lagging too far astern, nor beating up too close. Several times during that long, hot day, Naseby was tempted to run down on the shadowing schooner and give her a taste of roundshot, but resisted the urge. An unnecessary battle now, when he was within an ace of achieving the notable distinction of leading his prestigious prize triumphantly into Kingston Harbour, would be the most crass folly.

Kingston Harbour was a sun-drenched panoply of translucent blue with the gaily fluttering flags and hastily strewn bunting adorning Port Royal setting up a dazzling field of colour. As, with the *Santa Rosario*, the union flag streaming from her masthead, in the van, and with the gun brig *Solent* a cable's length astern, herding her in like a wayward sheep, the two sailed regally into the bay.

Cognisant of the dignity of the occasion, and determined to receive his due, Naseby had sent Perry in the *Salamander* on ahead with his reports to the Admiral, and in all justice the astute Purvis had done him proud. On the quay a band was striking up with 'Heart of Oak' while a marine honour guard, their red coats and pipe-clayed crossbelts adding to the festive blaze of colour, stood drawn up at attention.

Naseby, attired for the occasion in his best lieutenant's coat, snow white breeches and silken hose, drank it all in. Success. The stuff of dreams. From Fort Charles astern a welcoming salute banged; instantly echoed by her cousin across the bay. From each, only one gun it was true, but then as a lowly commander, no matter how successful, he could hardly be given more. While the majestic ships of war in the harbour dipped their flags and the tars lined bulwarks and rigging, hats waving and huzzahs rising, Naseby's single epaulette grew another layer of gold on that sunny November day.

That evening he dined with the Governor of Jamaica, Sir Wesley Graves.

The official residence stood screened from the roadway by a neat row of acacia trees. Their pinnate-shaped leaves twisting gently in the cooling breeze that filtered down off the hills to eastward. Still the designated capital of the island, despite Port Royal's new-found pomp, or Kingston's urban sprawl, Spanish Town had changed but little in the slightly over one hundred and fifty years of British rule. Lying some five miles inland from the original harbour, an inlet of Rocky Point and the headland west of Fort Charles, the town retained a certain elegance and charm as yet unmatched by anything which its rivals could offer in its place.

The residence itself, seen by Naseby on but one occasion previous (and that but a glimpse from the driveway, midshipmen hardly being bidden to enter) was of typical colonial pattern: gleaming white with an imposing bay-shaped portico, comprising five columns.

Alighting from the carriage – the Governor had sent his own – Naseby was met by a coloured servant in pale blue livery and ushered within.

Despite the splendour of its exterior, that which awaited the visitor's gaze inside, could only have been described as 'austere'. Sir Wesley had neither kith nor kin, which perhaps went some way to account for it. Or maybe it was just that the powers-that-be back in England had determined that never again should the excesses of Henry Morgan be repeated, and had levied accordingly.

The entrance hall itself was dark and shaded. While the main staircase that wound upward on his right rose cheerless and was noticeably bereft of portraits. Naseby found himself speculating as to where the likenesses of former Governors were situated.

His escort's place was taken by another of even darker hue, whose livery bore slight difference to the first – a sign of rank, perhaps? – and he was shown into a reception room. This at least showed some sign of comfort. The door closed, and he was left alone. Choosing a seat by the high, jalousied window, his best cocked hat perched carefully on his knee, Naseby settled himself down to wait, and, as always when there was nothing better to do, to think.

The preceding days: capturing the treasure ship, running with his flotilla before the late-arriving schooner, not to mention the but hours old triumphant entry into Kingston Harbour, had taken much out of him, both emotionally and physically, and he felt drained. Once turned eastward the shadowing Spanish schooner had lost interest, or perhaps grown more cautious, and Naseby and his two prizes had been allowed, entirely unmolested, to beat for home.

He should be sent back to England now, he knew; to be posted captain. Admiral Purvis had hinted so much aboard his flagship that afternoon. He would be sorry to leave *Solent*, but a gun brig was a lieutenant's command. And Purvis having no vessel suitable – that is, one requiring of a full post captain, in his squadron wherein there was a vacancy – the return home spoke for itself. The disposing of his prizes would take place over the forthcoming weeks, Naseby himself free to stroll about Port Royal, and any place else on the island that happened to take his fancy, to his heart's content. His duty to the ship was done. His report made, Rear Admiral of the Blue, Reginald C. Purvis, KB, as commander-in-chief on station had officially relieved him. In effect, he was again beached. Although, hardly in the manner of on former occasions.

Perry would remain in *Solent*, until such time as a new commander be appointed. Here Naseby had cautiously proffered his own recommendation, which same had unfortunately fallen on deaf ears. Doubtless the Admiral had a favourite of his own whom he wished to promote.

The clock in the hall was chiming musically. He took out his own watch. It was five forty-five. Dinner was set for eight with the guests to arrive any time after seven-thirty, Sir Wesley purportedly having requested the pleasure of Naseby's company somewhat earlier 'so that he might enjoy first hand hearing how he had captured the *Santa Rosario*.'

As the Crown agent in Jamaica, he too would be sharing in the prize money. Which perhaps meant, thought Naseby facetiously, that the old boy would be able to afford to do the place up a bit!

The 'old boy' turned out to be a merry, round-faced individual, whose open mien and infectious jollity appeared vastly out of keeping with his present sombre surroundings. Not only did he address Naseby as 'Captain', but until checked seemed determined on the appellation 'Sir' as a forerunner. Thus bestowing on his tall young guest a distinction which, to his certain knowledge, he had neither earned nor owned.

In such company the intervening period before dinner sped quickly enough, with at table Naseby finding himself adjacent a colonel's wife and opposite a general. Exalted company indeed for a modestly born son of Limehouse who had snatched his present position by his martial skill with weapons and a willingness to fight. Not to mention the murder of the Spaniard Don Juan Castaño ...

'Vice-Admiral Nelson commanded here in '79,' the fresh-faced midshipman assured him knowledgeably. 'Of course he wasn't a vice-admiral then, sir!'

Naseby himself had paid a fleeting visit a decade later, but doubted anyone would remember. The 'here' to which the midshipman was referring was Fort Charles, where Nelson (in the same year in which he had been posted captain) had indeed passed several fretful weeks as commandant; while he paced its elevated wooden walkway and awaited a French invasion which never came.

The fort itself was on two levels – conspicuous for its squat turreted wall – and boasted a hundred cannon (several of which were mounted picturesquely in arched openings) which covered both land and sea approaches. Quarters for the officers and post commander were provided by plain two-storey houses situated in the fort's centre, while a stout low-roofed structure inside the east wall did service as a munitions store.

'Shall I tell the Commandant you're here, sir?' enquired the midshipman solicitously.

Naseby shook his head shortly. Captain Styles, a one-armed giant of a man whose name was steadily making its way up the bottom half of the Admiralty's seniority list, was not a man too easily digested so soon after breakfast. Naseby knew; he had taken dinner with the man the previous week.

He had been in Port Royal some ten days now and had run out of people to visit. Perry, as his duty required, spent most of his time aboard *Solent*, and truth to tell, Jamaica's latest and much fêted hero felt lonely.

Politely ridding himself of the midshipman he mounted to the platform lining the seaward wall and, oblivious to the pacing sentry, stared out to sea and smoked his pipe. Of late he had taken to remembering the girl from the coach. Conjuring up mental pictures of her and fantasising about a time, as yet far off, when they should meet. By then he would be a senior post captain; with the three years spent in the rank necessary to see his own name commence its climb up the captain's list.

It was a sour note to realise that had it not been for his sloth that day in the church he might yet know her name and where she came from.

The sea, which came right up to the wall, was a translucent turquoise-green, the colour of jade, changing dramatically to blue and thence deepening in hue the farther out one looked. In the quadrangle a party of marines were drilling, their NCO's strident commands borne inland on a cooling sea breeze. His pipe had gone cold and he stood awhile, sucking pensively on the stem as he leant against the parapet wall.

Of course, she would have had to have remained unmarried. As of a certainty in all his best dreams she had. At first the mourning black which she had been wearing, and to which at the time he had paid such little mind, had returned to trouble him. For could they not in truth have been widow's weeds? He thought not. Rather was it likely some relative had died. Someone for whom she had borne a deep regard. He recalled the solicitous way in which the older woman had shepherded her from the church, and how the two had huddled together in the carriage as it was being driven away. Only the girl had worn black, from which it followed that they could scarce be kin. For if that were so, then what caused one to grieve must surely be acknowledged in dress by the other. Besides, in truth, as he now remembered, it had been the girl who had sat head bowed, seeking comfort, the woman merely bestowing it.

If only he had managed a look at that coat-of-arms on the carriage door! Yet somehow he felt he should see her again. Felt it just as surely as he felt the wall against which he leant, the breeze on his cheek.

Styles would be out for his morning inspection of the fort in a while. If he would duck their meeting, then it were best done now. So thinking, he descended to the quadrangle, and with a last admiring glance at the marines, quit the fort.

Once outside the main gate a tree-fringed road led away along the Palisadoes. Past the naval dockyard, a product of the 'new' Port Royal and, by-passing the town, wound away eastward to where the sand-spit (for all the world like a monstrous boom protecting the harbour) joined up with the headland below Rock fort. In times gone by there had been wooden palisades all along here, laid down by the Spanish as defensive works and from which the sand-bar had derived its name. However, like the Old Port Royal and the Spaniards who had founded it; and the more notorious buccaneers who had greatly added to it, they were now long gone.

Turning his footsteps towards the town, Naseby passed a group of fishermen sitting cross-legged as they worked at repairing their nets. Off the road the sand was pearl-white and ankle deep. Stretching away on his right to where sea-pounded beaches lined the shore. Beyond the town the road was flanked by cactus, while on the left as one journeyed toward the island, rose salt water mangrove swamps, dense and luxuriant. The sun was already high and, uncomfortably conscious of the heat even in his light nankeen jacket, he yearned to be at sea.

Since his arrival on the island he had chosen to stay in a small house he had rented for himself in Port Royal. Graciously and with genuine sincerity, Sir Wesley had extended an invitation for him to remain as his guest in the official residence. A deep honour, and one of which Naseby had been sensibly conscious. However, feeling perhaps that this might in some way jeopardise his freedom of movement, he had politely declined.

A decision which he now regretted. The bluff and cheery companionship of Jamaica's Governor would be infinitely preferable to the bland solitude attendant on his own homecoming. That day he dined alone. As, at least in prospect, probably one of the richest men on the island, there was little enough in all conscience with which, for his amusement, he could not furnish himself. And that included female company. Yet strangely, even in regard to the latter, normally his first port of call, he found himself reticent.

Letting himself in and stripping off the sweat-stained jacket, he supposed that once he had returned to England things would be different. Here in Port Royal, belonging to, and yet not a part of, the naval establishment, he was like the town itself. Existing in a kind of limbo. Whereas once back in England he should again be a part of things. Once more in the swim, as it were. And what was more, on a far grander plane even than when he had left! Already he felt better.

The old woman who kept house for him had left some cheese on the table and what to Naseby, as a sailor not yet that long in from the sea, was even more appetising, a loaf of really fresh bread. 'Soft-tack', the seamen called it. As opposed to 'hard', which was what that infernal ships biscuit was!

Viewed from the circular solidity of the Martello tower, (which as Naseby had mentally remarked on upon his arrival in Kingston, had not been there on his previous visit) Port Royal appeared pink-tinted and oddly romantic, caught in the last rays of the setting sun. Across his shoulder to eastward, or windward as the islanders would have it, and similarly illuminated, the Blue Mountains did indeed appear blue.

Tomorrow would see an offing. Home to England, a fortune and – And what, a post captaincy? Probably. Only time would tell. Further adventures, certainly. There was yet a war on and he must needs be in the thick of it. Not for prizes, nor promotion. Nor even for glory. For what was that once savoured, but a wilting bloom.

No, to fight; that was his real vocation. An end in itself. He would fight, be it for a palace or a lonely retirement in a one-roomed garret somewhere. He knew that about himself now. And the knowing brought comfort.

Solent's new commander having been appointed, William Perry would be going with him on the morrow. A fine prospect! A fine farewell, at least for the present, to the West Indies; for doubtless but that he'd be returning some day. And a right fine beginning for them both back home in England …

VIII

Impasse!

It was Christmas Eve, a cold miserable day aboard the homeward bound packet *Chrysanthemum*, and Commander Philip Naseby, a surly passenger at the best of times, hugged his pea-jacket close about him and resolutely kept his cabin. On deck the morning watch had just expired and the vessel was being laid on the larboard tack before a blustery headwind amid a timber-groaning crescendo of discordant sound and the stamp of endless booted feet.

In the next cabin Perry would doubtless still be abed. Finally promised a step to commander for his part in the capture of the *Santa Rosario*, the lugubrious-looking lieutenant was being shipped home for duty in the Channel.

Lacking his senior's hardy constitution, the abrupt change from a tropical to a northern clime had had the effect of laying him low with a racking chill which, as the bucketing post office packet climbed ever higher amid the wintry latitudes of the Atlantic, was growing steadily worse.

The last link in Naseby's Caribbean trio, the redoubtable boatswain and erstwhile acting lieutenant, Nathanial Bream, the man who had actually conned the majestic treasure galleon into Kingston Harbour, had remained in Jamaica, using a small portion of his tidy share in the prize money to secure his release from the Navy and purchase an imposing hostelry in Port Royal. Naseby wished him well.

As for himself – well, with some sixty thousand pounds invested in the Funds as well as a sizeable sum in cash, the world, even a world torn by the mindless ravages of war, was his oyster. Added to this was a personal letter of recommendation from Rear Admiral Purvis to William

Marsden, First Secretary to the Admiralty, urging in the strongest terms that Commander Philip Naseby, hero of the West Indian station and captor of the treasure galleon *Santa Rosario*, be immediately posted captain. A gracious gesture, to be sure, but, reflected Naseby realistically, certainly no more than was his due in consideration of the princely addition which his short tour of duty in the Caribbean had made to his Admiral's personal fortune!

Seating himself on the erratically swinging cot as one of the packet's boys brought in a steaming mug of coffee, Naseby allowed his mind to race back over the events of the last year to the previous Christmas Eve spent in the cheerless lodging house in Cobbs Alley, and the drab attic room which it had been his to occupy. Siras Blount had been alive then. Bluff and red-faced Blount suffused with the excitement of his first command and willing to extend a helping hand towards a friend whom he had not seen for several years. Naseby sighed and gulped at the scalding liquid. Whatever the burgeoning suspicions which he had begun to harbour regarding his late benefactor's qualities of leadership, the genuineness of the man's friendship had been fulsome enough.

Collingwood. Now there was an odd happenstance. Why, by the powers, should a lofty vice-admiral, intimate of the late lamented Lord Nelson, and a hero of the nation in his own right, stoop to concern himself with the fortunes of a lowly lieutenant? There could be no personal motive; of that much he was at all wise aware. The noble lord being no kin to him – more was the pity! For the good of the service then? Well, obviously. Although to admit as much, even to himself, smacked of the unwontedly pretentious. Ah, well, it could not be doubted but that the fullness of time should vouchsafe him an answer!

Once again in the space of less than a year, Philip Naseby was to find himself alone and inwardly grieving over the loss of a friend. For poor, thin, lugubrious-looking, aspiring Lieutenant Perry had died aboard the *Chrysanthemum*. Almost within sight of the Lizard and what would without doubt have turned out to be a promising career.

February 1807 came in like a raging torrent with gusting snowdrifts that rose thigh high and reduced the narrow London

Naseby was just another Collingwood oak

streets to a clogged quagmire of slush and ice. Having discharged his duty to his late subordinate and friend, Naseby was at last free to present himself at the Admiralty, being duly ushered into the steely-eyed presence of Mr William Marsden, the First Secretary.

Directed to a seat, he sat rigidly and ill at ease; conscious of a fine trickle of melted snow that had worked its way down inside his left boot-top.

'Ah, hum, Lieutenant, ah, or rather Commander Naseby, is it not?' The steely eyes plumbed Naseby's own – until he supplied the required response. Evidently his fame had not yet spread as far as the hallowed halls of Admiralty.

The First Secretary lowered his eyes and began a careful perusal of Rear Admiral Purvis's missive, leaving Naseby to reflect ruefully on how different things had been in the West Indies.

His thoughts were dragged back to the present. Finished with his reading, Mr Marsden was speaking. An odd look bent on the tall and (unusual for the Navy) straight-backed young officer seated uncomfortably before him.

'You no doubt realise, er, Commander – ' The First Secretary appeared to be echoing Naseby's own thoughts – 'that, er, Jamaica and the Caribbean sea is somewhat distant from our thoughts at the present time. Distant, although let me say at once, not forgotten.' An afterthought, that. 'As indeed are the exploits, meritorious though they certainly may be, of the, ah, junior officers attached to that station.' So much for old fuzzy-wig's letter, mused Naseby. 'You will therefore appreciate, Commander, that while this office extends yourself and your officers all due felicitation and credit on your capture of the, er –' Marsden referred briefly to the letter – 'Ah, yes, *Santa Rosita* – The pinch-faced bastard had even got the name wrong – 'when viewed against a wider backdrop of events worldwide – ' The measured, even tone, now fully into its stride, droned on, leaving a no longer listening Philip Naseby studiously inspecting the ceiling, and recalling a waiting room full of dejected half pay officers which lay just across the buff walled hallway.

It was shortly after three in the afternoon when he finally regained the street. The Secretary's parting words echoed sourly in his head: 'Look to yourself, Commander; doubtless twill not be overlong before England has need of you again!'

The upshot of it all then was that, far from being immediately gazetted captain, Philip Masterman Naseby, for his pains, did not now even have a ship! At least they couldn't take his prize money away; that was something for which he was thankful. This time half pay wouldn't seem quite so bad. So thinking, he set off for the suite of rooms which he had taken at the Lord Lincoln and some much needed feminine company.

The large four-poster felt incredibly warm and strangely solid after his months at sea. What's more, it was blissful to think that he could lie here and luxuriate in the tasteful opulence of these exquisitely expensive surroundings for howsoever long as he felt inclined. That, and hark back in his mind to the delightfully abandoned young female with whom he had pleasured himself last evening.

Promptly at eight-thirty a maid entered with his breakfast: tender slices of cold roast beef cut wafer thin, a trio of eggs lightly boiled, soft bread, a crock of fresh butter, and a pewter tankard containing small beer. A feast fit for a king, let alone a passed over, and no doubt already forgotten, naval commander.

Minus a ship to command he had to all intents and purposes reverted to being one of a steadily growing list of half pay lieutenants. If Nelson and Trafalgar had finally and irrefutably established the Royal Navy's dominion over the seas, it had also largely written finis to the Emperor Napoleon's offshore operations and put countless officers ashore. Naseby was almost tempted to wish that the French had won! Determined to enjoy his breakfast, he put all such thoughts resolutely aside and stumbled, yawning, to the table.

An idle and largely unmemorable three weeks were to pass in this fashion until, inevitably tiring of such a meaningless existence, Naseby had decided to take up Sir Walter Perry's gracious offer, (made on the occasion of his one and only visit to the household bearing a letter from the baronet's deceased son) namely to introduce him around in the 'right circles' and so generally show him off.

Renting an enclosed carriage for the trip, he had himself driven through the still slushy city streets to the gracious townhouse which Sir Walter, a widower of sixty with a daughter of marriageable age, kept in Sharrington Square, a stone's throw from St James. The short drive, even through congested thoroughfares, was soon over, and Naseby found himself in the same elegantly appointed morning room as on the occasion of his previous visit.

The baronet, he was informed, was not at home, but the Lady Anne would be pleased to receive him and would grace him with her company presently. Naseby uttered his thanks and sat back on a comfortable settee to while away what he construed to be a lengthy wait. The entry a scant five minutes later of a dark-haired girl whom he judged to be in her very early twenties and who, unfortunately, bore a striking resemblance to her late departed brother, proved him wrong. He was further dumbfounded to find after a very few moments spent conversing with her that, despite her undeniably unprepossessing appearance, Anne Perry was an extremely accomplished and intelligent young woman.

For the best part of an hour they chatted away busily, discussing everything from the course of the war to the cost of a decent madeira. By the end of which time Naseby, well aware of the attraction which his complete maleness held for certain women, was acutely conscious of having made a conquest. Not that he cherished any base notion of mounting an assault on the lady's virtue; indeed, perish the thought. Her quite obvious equestrian ancestry ruled that out! Rather that, ever the opportunist, he was quite willing to garner to him any and all means of furthering his own currently blocked progress along a road which, as a gangling midshipman of tender years, he had been started, and which ever since he had been tenaciously engaged in following.

He had required money. Well, in the shape of the treasure galleon *Santa Rosario*, fortune had so favoured him. Favoured him beyond his own wildest imaginings, as it had turned out. As to promotion, while it was true that in this most vital aspect his career had of late experienced something of an impasse; at least until such time as his gradually reawakening native wit having attained its customary sharpness should arrange to secure for him a ship (any vessel below twenty guns and therefore suitable for a commander); this in itself was some way short of being the nub of the problem. It ran deeper than that; its basis lying in the indisputable fact that what he really craved was action. Craved it as strongly as he had recently craved a woman. So strongly, in fact, that if needs be he would accept a berth as junior lieutenant on a ship of the line!

But even for that he would need influence at court, since a like commodity in the Admiralty he obviously didn't have. To this end a seeming alliance with the daughter of Colonel Sir Walter Perry, Bart. – ? Yes, the campaign had merit …

The following weeks, avidly supervised and carefully organised by Anne and her father, were for Naseby a revelation. A gradual setting aside of the gossamer-woven yet steel-sprung veils of acceptance through which one passed before gaining admittance to the rigid circle of exclusivity which made up polite London society – the 'drawing room set'. A seemingly endless and slightly bewildering round of balls, soirées and presentations. A month of which, as an aside, found him some five hundred pounds the poorer!

His dressing room at the Lord Lincoln was literally festooned with new clothes: suitings and accessories of every possible style and pattern. The number of hats and canes he had purchased, rich silk cravats, not to mention a prodigious supply of linen, could hardly be guessed at. He had even managed to coerce a protesting tailor into making him up a pair of the new pattern trouser of the type affected by that Brummel fellow. Of a certainty, the new garment was eminently better suited to the exigencies of normal daily living than were breeches and hose. Needless to say, seamen, notably the lower deck, had been wearing the like for years. Naseby himself oft-times preferred them, as did many another officer. Especially at times when his customary and much beloved Hessian boots seemed inappropriate.

Which was not to suppose that they would soon find favour with the Admiralty. In any event, the new full length breeches had caused a goodly commotion on the occasion of their first outing before the Prince of Wales; or so the story went. Had he to choose, Naseby would probably have plumped for the 'seaman's version', offering more freedom in the leg and being fashioned of coarser and therefore stouter material.

His necessarily subtle wooing of Anne Perry had been put well in hand. Almost a constant visitor at the house in Sharrington Square now, his suit was being given every chance. Of a certainty the girl was enamoured of him. So much was plain. He was seated now in the Perrys' drawing room, watching attentively as Anne and her friend Charlotte Maybury played two-handed whist. In fact, he felt desirous of a pipeful of the fragrant mixture made up for him by the tobacco sellers patronised by Sir Walter but was loath to broach the subject.

The noon post had brought him a letter from his friend Gray. A letter which he had as yet but partially read, having barely had sufficient time before being due at the Perrys'. From his brief reading it was apparent that as he had foreseen, the lieutenant had received orders, firstly to report to the marine barracks in Portsmouth and thence aboard the thirty-six gun frigate *Nimrod*, before his own letter had arrived. As was customary in the service, be it the corps of marines or the navy proper, Gray had been unable to do more than speculate on whither bound his floating home, for perhaps the next couple of years, might be. Said speculation being the Indian Ocean in joint operation with John Company's ships to wave the flag at the Moors. He must remember to pen a few lines covering his windfall in the shape of the *Santa Rosario*. Gray would be happy at his friend's good fortune, he knew.

About his niggardly treatment at the hands of the Admiralty he would say nothing. Ill tidings were best hid safe at home. Besides, he thought, visibly brightening, by the time his errant missives should have caught up with the marine his new found friends in high places should likely have succeeded in securing for him a ship!

'What are you smiling at, Philip?' Anne wanted to know, patently pleased at finding him in such good humour. Oft-times of late she had peered beyond the patient mask behind which he had endeavoured to hide himself, he knew, and glimpsed the inner restlessness of spirit which as ever when on land, he was heir to.

'I was merely recalling a jest made by one of your father's friends at dinner the other evening,' he lied.

'Oh, do please share it with us, Captain, won't you? Please do,' wailed Charlotte, curdling his blood with the thought that were he to marry Anne Perry it could well be his lot to have to listen to that ridiculous female for the rest of his life.

Skilfully he managed to dissemble, compounding the lie with a veiled reference to the possible indelicacy of the mythical quip. It worked, at least in Anne's case. Leaving Charlotte, he felt, even more eager to learn what it was that had been said, and more importantly, about whom.

He was growing fonder of Anne. She might never stir his loins, but she was a good companion, and when the occasion warranted (which he had contrived should be rare) a sympathetic listener. 'Anne is good for the soul, my boy, as you'll doubtless find out!' Sir Walter had said to him in conversation one day. Naseby could already vouchsafe that this was so.

It was to be at one of the more intimate gatherings of the capital's élite, Lady Dalrimple's convivial week-ends at Kew, that Naseby was to run into an unexpected, although to be sure not unlooked for, vision from the past.

'Her name is Sara Throgmorton, Commander,' confided Lady Dalrimple with the merest inclination of her head, screened discreetly behind an elaborate lace fan, in the direction in which he was unashamedly staring. Closing his mouth, which he realised had been hanging foolishly open, he hastily averted his gaze. Without doubt, the lissom flaxen-haired beauty who so captivated his attention was the girl from the coach. Also the very purest vision of loveliness Naseby had ever seen. At his side the predatory Lady Dalrimple was asking if he'd like to be introduced and Naseby was vaguely conscious of being propelled gently but unerringly through the ranks of gossiping acolytes to find himself moments later face to face with a ramrod of a man, fully his equal in height if not in breadth, wearing the short black military wig and scarlet coat of an officer in the King's Grenadiers.

'Lord Carslake, may I present Commander Philip Naseby of the Royal Navy. Commander Naseby, Captain Carslake.'

The officer bowed curtly, subjecting Naseby to a cool appraisal. Naseby returned the compliment as stiffly as he could, and then turned his attention to the frankly smiling girl at his side.

'And this – ' (Now was there not a hint of mischief in his hostess's honeyed tones?) 'Commander – is Lord Carslake's second cousin, Miss Sara Throgmorton. Delightful, is she not, Commander?'

Naseby managed to mumble something clumsily in the affirmative and bowed awkwardly over the girl's proffered hand.

'The naval officer from the street. I knew you the moment you entered the room, Commander. But perhaps you do not remember?'

So it seemed that, like himself, Sara Throgmorton had found occasion over this past year to call their 'almost meeting' to mind. The thought went far to restore Naseby's customary aplomb so that when he answered it was with suitable restraint.

Lady Dalrimple, much to the obvious annoyance of the gentleman concerned, had skilfully manoeuvred Lord Carslake out of earshot and was currently engaged in bending His Lordship's ear with some mildly malicious nonsense or other. Leaving Naseby feeling patently more at ease, and the lovely Sara to acquaint him with the background to her careering drive through city streets, ending with the sad death of her grandfather. Naseby now had the answer concerning what had lain behind the girl's fear-haunted visage that day.

'So you see, when grandfather died, the title passed to cousin Nigel. Of course, I didn't know him at the time. While everything else, the prodigious estate, a considerable fortune, even dear old Carslake House, passed to me.'

'And, er, the captain, I mean his lordship,' ventured Naseby, already sure of the answer.

'Oh, Nigel.' She flashed cool green eyes at him. 'He intends, I think, to marry me.' Naseby swallowed. He had not been expecting such directness. 'Well,' she continued matter of factly, 'how else might he and his family contrive to restore the Carslake fortune and estates to what they consider is their proper line? Perhaps after all they are right. However – ' She held up her hand before Naseby could make utterance. 'I have no intention now, or at any time in the future, of becoming Lady Carslake!'

Perhaps understandably Naseby was, by this time, feeling just a trifle bemused. Added to which, he had not thought to find such candour beyond the streets of his own humble origins.

'You find me refreshing, Commander?'

Naseby laughed; there was nothing else to do. 'I apologise for making my thoughts so obvious,' he said, 'although I must admit to a certain feeling of relief at your, um, lack of entanglement with the captain.'

Her smile was radiant. 'Why, Commander, if I hadn't heard already about the legendary Captain Naseby and his daring capture of the Spanish treasure galleon, I might assume that you're fortune hunting!'

Naseby cast a quickly searching look at the freely smiling face before him, but finding nothing there of female mockery, answered honestly enough.

'Hardly legendary, Miss Throgmorton, at least not with their lordships of the Admiralty. Also, I'm afraid, very little of daring.'

She laughed unaffectedly and Naseby found himself liking her all the more. 'I'm sure you're being unduly modest, Commander.'

'My name is Philip, Sara,' he said.

'Philip. Yes, it's a strong name and worthy of you.'

For a moment they sobered, their eyes meeting and holding. It was a moment of mutual understanding and – dared he hope – of promise?

Then it was past as the circle of general conversation once more entwined them and Naseby found himself gathered up in a twittering gaggle of well meaning but rather inane adulation. Kept busy until the dinner hour answering endless questions about shipboard life, from a chorus of people who would never venture to sea in their entire lifetimes, much less be capable of having any understanding of what it meant to walk the quarterdeck of a king's ship.

Naseby found little excuse to seek the exclusive company of Sara Throgmorton over the remainder of that wonderful week-end. For always it seemed, where the delightful Sara trod, there also went the gallant Lord Carslake. As stiff as a Prussian and twice as dour. He had, however, on one occasion managed to slip a hastily composed missive to her through the good and ever willing offices of Lady Dalrimple, enjoining her to meet him outside His Lordship's box at the opera a fortnight hence; being the best that could be managed under the circumstances. While she hadn't actually been able to openly avow her acceptance of their secret assignation, Naseby had correctly, he hoped, interpreted a compliant glance which she had cast in his direction during a lull in the conversation at dinner on the Sunday. The next fourteen days for Naseby were to prove an agony of expectation.

Two days before the secret assignation, 1st April, a Wednesday, brought an unexpected snippet of information which augured well for his chances of getting back to sea. Quite naturally, it seemed, he had moved into the Perry household; finding himself regarded in a quiet and as yet unspoken way, as a substitute for the ageing baronet's fallen son. A state of affairs highly agreeable to the largely friendless Naseby. A little to his surprise, he had grown genuinely fond of the kindly Sir Walter and his homely daughter.

He was ensconced in the comfortable upstairs first floor study when the news came, happily engaged in cleaning his brace of twin-barrelled pistols. A tap on the arched oak door admitted Anne, bright-eyed and obviously bursting with news.

'Grand tidings, Philip. Lord Collingwood is in London. He's invited to the palace on Sunday. Father is to be there as colonel of his old regiment, and will doubtless be able to speak to the Admiral on your behalf!'

So overjoyed was she on his account that before Naseby realised what he was doing, she was in his arms and he was gently stroking her long dark hair. On his part the gesture had been nothing more than instinctive. A surge of emotion brought about by their shared purpose; namely, that of furthering his career in the Navy. However innocent its intent, it was, he realised, an unpardonable blunder – for confirmation of which he need only steal a look at Anne's upturned face resting happily on his shoulder.

Cursing himself for a clumsy fool, he extricated himself awkwardly from her embrace. While at the same time vowing inwardly to exercise a deal more restraint in his handling of the delicate balance of their relationship in the future. By now Naseby was sufficiently endeared to the gentle Anne as to find the prospect of callously wounding her wholly abhorrent.

Forcing a smile, he sought sanctuary in his labours with his weapons, leaving Anne to depart gaily. For a long moment he sat staring after her. 'A rum go all round,' he muttered aloud. Collingwood in London! It was the answer to a prayer. He could almost taste the tang of salt on his lips and hear the steady thrum of the wind in the rigging. Funny how once you were at sea you soon learned to become blithely unmindful of those things.

Fladongs was jammed to capacity at seven o'clock that evening as Naseby jostled his way across its packed threshold. Never a believer in 'wait and see', he had decided to seek out the quarry for himself. And what better place to start than London's premier coffee house and favoured haunt of senior naval personnel.

As a lowly commander he was aware of hardly qualifying for admittance to this unofficial retreat for post captains and above. Nevertheless, his resolve undaunted and the single bullion epaulette polished to perfection, he adopted a jaunty air and looking neither to right nor left, shouldered his way authoritatively into the smoke-wreathed mêlée, heading unerringly for the high-stepped long table at the oblong room's farther end whereat resided the time-honoured benches of the coffee house's more illustrious patrons. From Hawke to Nelson, commoner to viscount, post captain to full admiral, Fladongs had known them all. Well, thought Naseby whimsically, now they can serve the needs of an out of favour commander!

In the corner sat Sir Edward Pellow, engaged in rapt conversation with another Sir Edward – Berry, one of Nelson's famed band of brothers at the Nile. On his left was 'Bounty' Bligh, a veteran of Copenhagen, while nearer to hand were the redoubtable Fremantle and sure enough, Vice-Admiral Cuthbert Collingwood. Doll-like of visage, somewhat of an anacronism in these days of martinets afloat, and an authority on the planting of oak trees. For a moment, conscious of the unpardonable temerity which he contemplated, Naseby hesitated. Perhaps he would have turned and run. But already it was too late, for Collingwood had spied him.

'Why, Naseby, by the saints. Come over, m'boy, here by me.'

The admiral was clearing a place for him. Bligh didn't look too approving. Still, with Collingwood as his mentor he had little to fear from that quarter, and Fremantle and another officer whom he didn't recognise seemed friendly enough.

'What! But not a post captain yet. I heard that you were to be gazetted?'

'It's a long story, m'lord,' spoke up Naseby brightly, deeming it better to show a brave face on the matter.

His lordship sobered; round, almost sensual eyes touching Naseby with a look of careful appraisal. 'Well come, then, sit here and confide us your tale. Have no thoughts for reserve. For here we are all friends, are we not?'

Eyes that were but a moment since almost womanlike glittered briefly along the table and received, as was their due, dutiful nods. Even Bligh managing a look of bland resignation.

Thus Naseby recounted his tale. When he had finished the admiral slapped the table in unfettered consternation.

'A pox on that scribbler Marsden! How by all the powers are we to win this war when influence and nepotism be the criterion by which its prosecutors are chosen?'

Silent, Naseby thought it unwise to remind his lordship that influence was the quarry which he himself sought. Fremantle was muttering something in the admiral's ear. Naseby's spirits lifted, only to falter a moment later as the admiral looked doubtful. 'Yes, but it's hardly command – ' Collingwood mumbled. Then with a sidelong glance at himself, seemed abruptly to come to a decision.

Twisting fully around, the better to face his protégé squarely, his lordship began, 'Well, see here, Naseby. I'd like to help advance your career in the service in any way that I can. England needs fighters, in addition, that is, to good seamen and navigators.' A humorous twinkle lit his eyes a moment. 'I said as much to Purvis when you were assigned to him.' He paused, then continued in quieter tone. 'Unfortunately, even an admiral's opinion doesn't always cut the ice it should. Were we on a foreign station I should merely draft you a frigate, or at least a twenty gun sloop, and inform the Admiralty after the event. Let Marsden fail to confirm your appointment then, by thunder!'

With an effort his lordship brought himself back under control. While Naseby watched silently, and hanging grimly on the admiral's every word, wondered at the unexpected vehemence exuded on his behalf. However, now wasn't the time for wondering, for Collingwood was speaking again.

'As it is, well, Fremantle tells me the frigate *Nemesis* is short a lieutenant. As a substantive commander I could get you in there as first. Hardly a command of your own, I know, but at least it would get you to sea again!'

Commander Philip Naseby, veteran of the boudoir, the drawing room and on occasions the bedchamber, these past many weeks, was off to sea once more.

IX

Dual Appointment

It was Friday, 3rd April. The day of his eagerly awaited assignation with Sara Throgmorton, and three weeks to the day before, as his orders were phrased, he was 'required and directed' to report aboard the frigate *Nemesis* 36, commissioning at Plymouth.

As the ship's prospective first lieutenant, he was well aware that to him would fall responsibility for the lion's share of the work which must be completed before the vessel were ready for sea. Another nail in the coffin of the Emperor Napoleon soon to be off to beard the lion in his den!

The night was starlit and carrying a gibbous moon as he alighted from the carriage and trod the silvery cobbles to the wide steps of the opera house. For the occasion he had chosen to attire himself in olive green tailcoat, brown velveteen breeches and shoes that had buckles of solid gold. The turnbacks of the coat were edged in gold lace and on his head, set at a jaunty angle, was a black tricorne hat. His hair was arranged in a neat queue bound up in a black satin bow. Disdaining a court sword (whose carrying was by now largely unfashionable) and not wishing to bulk his clothing with a pistol, he had chosen for his protection – still a very necessary precaution on the streets of London in 1807 – a silver-topped swordstick with lion's head engraving. His sole reference to things naval – the lion's head being similar in style to that adorning the pommel of the uniform sword, that since an Admiralty minute dated 4th August 1805 had become regulation for commanders and above.

The performance, or show, as Naseby was gauchely wont to refer to it, was a dreadful bore with absurdly garbed fops bawling Italian into a seemingly inexhaustible supply of lace handkerchiefs, and a series of cavorting, lank-breasted matrons whose banshee wailings put him strongly in mind of a chorus of bo'suns' calls in the midst of a howling gale.

Not that he overmuch minded, not tonight, and to be fair, most of the house's other patrons appeared to find the whole thing far less painful. From his seat near the aisle, he could just manage sufficient room for his handsome length of leg; while at the same time arranging to keep an attentive eye on the larboard-situated box of Lord Carslake.

The reward was well worth the effort; if such a thing were possible, Sara Throgmorton appeared even lovelier tonight than she had at Kew. Naseby's heart went out to her. She was the very epitome of feminine beauty. All that he could wish for in a mate for life. That he was hopelessly and irrevocably in love with her was not a case in point; nor yet had it been since their companionably frank conversation at Lady Dalrimple's. That battle – if indeed there had ever really been one – was irretrievably lost. 'Aye, and right happily so,' he found himself muttering to no one in particular.

Lady Dalrimple, he now knew, had been Sara's middle-aged companion in the carriage on the Sunday he had attempted to learn her identity. A good friend and a staunch ally, Sara had called her, having provided both comfort and steadfastness to the grieving girl since her guardian, and paternal grandfather's, death. Naseby was conscious of owing Lady Dalrimple a deep debt of gratitude. Particularly so with the 'gallant grenadier' sniffing around!

He didn't know Carslake, but on a single, brief, meeting, had instinctively disliked the man. Nor was this dislike – perhaps mistrust would be a better word – based solely on jealousy. For while it was not to be doubted that he found the cove's ease of access to the society of the girl whom he loved, obnoxious, there was yet something more; something fundamental, he –

On the stage all had become a huddle of desperately gesticulating figures. The finale before the first curtain? By the powers, he hoped so! Endless minutes more he had to endure with stoicism: the dread cacophony; and then it was over.

Springing to his feet almost as the last, long note sounded and before the curtain began its unfurling descent, he was straightway at the gilted stairway and racing, heart pounding, for his light of love.

The task of locating the velvet-curtained doorway to Lord Carslake's box from all the other velvet-curtained portals was accomplished with a seamanlike sense of direction and in moments Naseby had positioned himself at, and a little to one side of, the curtain's overlap, affecting nonchalantly to twirl his cane. He was glad that Lady Dalrimple was in the box with them, otherwise he should have stormed the thing ere now. A picture of himself, honour wounded, prancing hot-foot above the audience, flourishing the sword-stick, struck him awry and he was hard put to it to suppress the belly laugh which resulted.

At his elbow a door clicked and she was there. God, but she was beautiful. Naseby could only smile, unaccountably shamed by the stirring of his loins. She spoke breathlessly.

'Oh, Philip, I can't stay long. It was all I could do to slip away, and – ' Come to think of it, she did look flushed. If Carslake had been forcing his attentions; but no, there was Lady Dalrimple, and – There just wasn't any time for this! He clasped her arm abruptly. Anne Perry could never stir him thus. Not for all the captaincies and all the battle fleets in England.

He spoke harshly, unable yet to honey his tone. 'You must forgive me, sweet Sara – ' The almost coarse urgency in his voice caused her flesh to tingle and she knew that she was blushing unashamedly. But if she was on the verge of expecting something crude, she was proved in error when in hushed, concise tones, he informed her swiftly of his appointment to *Nemesis* and of the date of his departure.

'So you see, Sara, my dearest love, there will be little enough time for me to court you. But only to declare, here and now, my sincerest affection, honest respect for your unfettered character, and pledge my deep and undying love. To beseech you most humbly – to consent to become my wife!'

There, it was done. His own shallow breathing sounded unnaturally loud in the hushed atmosphere of the upper gallery. He had been clumsy, he knew. Had declared himself too soon. Such arrant foolishness. What right had he to expect that – ? Yet, there, she was smiling. Her cool emerald eyes appraising him in – In what? Surrender? Certainly not. Resignation, then. No, that he knew was too strong a word for what his own anxious gaze beheld. Understanding! Yes, that would bear up. She was looking at him with a measured, one might almost say strangely dispassionate female light of understanding in her eyes; of the mutual bond which had, unbidden and wholly naturally just seemed to have blossomed between them. She loved him too. Yet if so, she seemed unable still to resist a heaven-sent opportunity to tease him. If not in word, then in tone.

'A pretty speech, Commander,' she began, but couldn't keep it up, at once relenting; her voice soft, gently serious, as she told him all that he wished to hear. And more; that which he did not but which was, in truth, his due.

'Yours is the second proposal I have received tonight. The first from Lord Carslake – an insincere man whom I neither hold honourable nor yet own any regard for – and your own sweet avowal. From a gentleman I not only love but honour greatly. Of course my answer is yes, my own dearest Philip!'

Then she was moving, close in his arms, her lips soft, yielding, as his heart rejoicing, he crushed her firmly to him.

In truth their courtship, if either could deign describe it thus, had been something brief. Although perhaps not yet so, as Naseby himself was happily conscious as the male ardency of his kisses was met and readily matched by the fire of the girl's own. For if he were to own to it, had he not wondered on her, fantasised about her, loved her these many months past? He could only assume that matters had fared likewise with her. That evening neither one returned to sit distractedly through any more of the opera.

Anne Perry had applauded his tidings with a careful dignity which left Naseby feeling base. Not for all the world would he have so wounded her could he but reclaim these weeks. Sir Walter, fortuitously innocent of his favoured guest's erstwhile motives, positively exulted for him. Which in a way only left him feeling worse. Whether the old nobleman had in fact harboured a hope that they might one day be joined in blood by his taking of his daughter Anne in marriage, Naseby couldn't now be sure. Although he had judged so at the time. Nevertheless, the thing was done, and that was an end of it.

Besides which, there was much to occupy the attention of Commander Philip Masterman Naseby over the following seven days, what with the necessarily hasty preparations for the wedding, which was to be held in St Martins in the Fields. Initially he had feared that the unaccountably weighty matters of banns having to be read, or some such nonsense, would be allowed to stand in their way. But following a patient and very solemn recounting of the situation: the imminence of his sailing, exigencies of the Service, and with the good offices of Sir Walter Perry, Bart., the way had been cleared. Lady Dalrimple laboured like a Trojan. There was to be a reception at the Admiral Hawke in the Strand, and everybody, but everybody had to receive an invitation. How in the world she expected to achieve this in the time, Naseby couldn't imagine. But only found himself wishing heartily that he could have the woman with him when it should come time to provision *Nemesis*! Those notoriously stingy dockyard officials wouldn't stand a chance.

Exercising her feminine prerogative, Sara had already decided that they were to reside officially at her much venerated Carslake House. A choice which Naseby was quite happy to go along with, thinking privately that with the vast Carslake estate providing a county seat, all that was required now was for himself to win a knighthood!

Tomorrow was Saturday, *the* day, and after laboriously readying his raiment for the occasion, Naseby set off for the Jolly Admiral in Thames Street, and as his new found friend Captain Thomas Fremantle had promised, 'As right royal a setting sail on the stormy seas of matrimony as any a jolly tar could wish!' Well, concerning marriage, Fremantle should know, reflected Naseby, smiling, having five children! Privately he also thought the tag 'jolly tar' hardly appropriate, but looked forward to passing as joyous an evening as its celebration demanded.

It was just gone eight when he stepped out of the carriage before the Jolly Admiral. Almost half an hour before the time fixed by Thomas Fremantle. Taking a glass of madeira in the tap room he sauntered across to the fire. Early spring already, the days were moderate to warm, yet this evening held a chill. One of the tavern's three upstairs banqueting rooms had been booked especially for tonight's 'wetting': an intimate enough gathering, to be sure, with scarce half a dozen revellers to be catered for. Time enough to go up in twenty minutes or so, he fancied, sipping contentedly at the madeira.

He had already ascertained from the landlord that Fremantle and the others had not yet arrived. Well, it was after all only fitting that, as captain of the forthcoming sortie, he be piped up the side first. Pleased with the play on words he resolved to save it, or something like it, for the evening's later toasts, wherein no doubt it should go down exceeding well.

At his back and to the right of the fireplace were situated a row of discreetly curtained off private booths, several of which as Naseby had unmindfully noticed on his entry to the room, were already occupied. It was nothing of any great import. As like as not one or two would house secretly courting couples from the lower orders, or perhaps a gang of London cutpurses busy divvying up the day's spoils. At least one, he knew, would be sure to hold some vinegary old whore industriously engaged in working her gums over an early evening customer.

His glass drained, he was starting for a refill when from one of these booths a voice, seemingly deep in drink and pitched carelessly loud, arrested his attention.

'Man's a deuced nobody. A cutlass-in-teeth pirate bent on turning the ill-gotten booty from some plundered treasure galleon or other to the base cause of purchasing for himself a place in polite society.'

There followed a pregnant pause, during which Naseby stood stock still. The blood in his veins turned to ice.

'What's more, he's managed to insinuate himself into the affections of a woman of quality and ingratiate himself with people who are his betters. Why, sir, do you know where it was they say the fellow was spawned? Limehouse, by the powers!'

No drink-loosened tongue conjured these words. A low mumbling ensued, then that same intemperate voice.

'A gentleman, you say, a gentleman? Dammee, sir; dammee I say again! Why, that broad-faced jackanapes isn't fit to wear the King's coat. Dammee if he is!'

The wide ground floor room had begun to fill up by now, Allowing a goodly cross section of London citizenry, ranging in breeding and social standing from bluff Thames lightermen over in the corner, through a smattering of prosperous-looking merchants, to a trio of red-coated marine officers leaning nonchalantly against the bar. All had heard the deliberately insulting words. As, of course, it had been intended that they should. Nor, as is the way of such things, were many of them having overmuch difficulty in deciding who the intended target was. Indeed, the room had fallen ominously silent. And all – or so it seemed to Naseby, conspicuous in full dress naval uniform, – were now intent on subjecting him to a curious, if cautious, scrutiny. Put up job or no, it was more than any man with blood rather than bilgewater in his veins, could stand. And Naseby would have none of it.

Deliberately he set down his glass, straightened, and turning on his heel paced slowly toward the nearer of the close-curtained booths. The room was now totally devoid of all sound, save for his own gold-buckled shoes clumping steadily across the polished wooden floor. As he reached it the booth's vivid crimson curtain was whisked aside, revealing to sight a quartet of scarlet-coated officers, already on their feet. Foremost of which was a triumphantly beaming Lord Carslake.

Just for a moment Naseby, now in complete possession of himself, treated the nobleman to a contemptuous stare. Had he but possessed the acumen to do so, the stiff-backed Captain of Grenadiers might just have read in the assured manner of the man facing him the steady resolve and cool deliberation of the true born fighting man; the seasoned combatant. But he did not. Seeing instead only uncertainty in the silent stance, and mistaking same for a lack of physical courage, he compounded an already long list of errors with an incautious laugh.

He wasn't to finish it; his head snapping back under the perfectly timed impetus of the naval man's brine-toughened right fist. A startled exclamation broke forth from several of the house's more genteel patrons. Much as it had become the vogue of late for the strutting peacocks of aristocratic birth to take sport in a carefully orchestrated bout with the mufflers against some pugilist of professional renown, for a 'gentleman' to strike another with his bare fist was the most unpardonable insult.

Viewing the fallen grenadier with studied detachment, Naseby coolly placed his card on the table, and in a voice pitched so that all might hear, said, 'Since, Lord Carslake, we are both not of the same service, I doubt our difference in rank applies. Lest, however, this not be the case, I herewith absolve you of all responsibility in the matter by rendering both insult and challenge at one and the same time. I await, therefore, your lordship's pleasure. Goodnight, gentlemen!'

It was a splendid gesture! For not only did the duelling etiquette of the day explicitly state that no officer of junior rank might issue challenge to a superior (for obvious reasons), it was also expressly forbidden for said superior to strike a subordinate. As a commander in His Majesty's Navy, Naseby's substantive rank was equivalent to that of lieutenant-colonel.

Judging the matter at an end, at least for the present, he was thus in the act of turning away when the trap was sprung.

'Not so easily done, my fine fellow!' snarled the nobleman, lurching unsteadily to his feet and brushing peremptorily aside the solicitous attentions of his brother officers. With a sinking heart, the naval man realised what was coming. Carslake was like an enraged animal, a copious amount of blood masking his lower lip, and an insane cast to his eye. In his voice the ring of triumph.

'Tomorrow at dawn behind the Horseguards! The Grenadiers will provide the physician!'

Had he but had his wits about him, Naseby should have glimpsed at once the fuller ramifications attendant on his, as he now realised, ill thought out and precipitate course of action; have perceived the vile duplicity of the man. That the entire episode had been carefully stage-managed with the express objective of drawing him into combat had been readily apparent. That being however, as far as his currently addled thinking had carried him; assuming only, if indeed he had bothered to assume at all, that following the issuing of the challenge a period of truce would ensue. Wherein, by dint of card and officiating second, an acceptance be received and a time and venue laid down. So much for observance of etiquette! Yet enough, it was done. He had walked – nay, leapt – straight into it. Honour – no, that was not a word for which he vouchsafed any use. His 'manhood' demanded that a brave face be put upon it. What use now to cry previous engagement; even would his pride so allow. Which it would not – by the powers! – it would not.

In a rock steady voice he enquired, 'Your lordship has yet to mention the choice of weapons?'

'Pistols!' snapped the nobleman. 'I trust that the "commander" can count among his friends for his attendance?'

'*I* shall deem it both a privilege and an honour to attend Commander Naseby,' spoke up Thomas Fremantle, resplendant in captain's full dress uniform; stepping regally forward.

Until this moment Naseby had been in total ignorance of the arrival of his fellow celebrants. They stood now, implacably ranged about him. A comforting wall of blue; gold lace and gleaming epaulettes. It made his spirits soar to see them. There was, however, to be scant celebrating that night.

Rising sharply at four the next morning, any regret concerning his imminent appointment on the 'field of honour' had given way to a stoic fatalism. If the thing had to be done, then better it were done at once. Sir Walter had been beside himself with rage, threatening to place the entire matter in the hands of Lord Carslake's commanding officer. A course of action which thankfully Naseby had been able to talk him out of. He had not, however, been able to dissuade the gallant old baronet from accompanying him to the Horseguards. He could hear him now, bustling furiously around his apartments, readying himself for the off. Naseby smiled at his own lamplit reflection illuminated softly in the full length wall mirror. Awhile it flickered and danced. It seemed that at long last young Philip Naseby, 'spawn of Limehouse' as Lord Carslake had vividly termed him, orphan and until recently, friendless, had procured for himself a 'family'. It was to be hoped, he appended whimsically, that he survive to enjoy it.

With which thought he caught up his linen; noticing the fast fading scar on his right forearm where the Spaniard's rapier thrust had burned him, and briskly dressed. His last act before quitting the apartments set aside for his use in the comfortable house in Sharrington Square, was to place a briefly worded letter beside the clock on his sitting room mantel. The plain buff wafer bore the forbidding superscription: 'For Miss Sara Throgmorton. To be delivered in the event of my death.' He knew that he could rely on Anne to see to its delivery.

The Horseguards was shrouded in a light morning mist common to this time of year; the park strangely silent and somehow ominous. Captain Fremantle and a lieutenant named Wills had proved the final choice of seconds for the morning's affair – a double engagement for Thomas Fremantle, who had also graciously consented to stand up as 'best man' at the forthcoming wedding. An office that Naseby, alighting from the coach and turning to render unnecessary assistance to the sprightly Sir Walter, was duly conscious that he should perform.

Fleetingly he recalled another day, another time. Sauntering aimlessly through the park with the sun glinting on the Admiralty building and with nothing better to do than watch the dandies at their sport. Before *Solent* and the West Indies. He had been looking forward to bedding the landlady's daughter Fanny at the time.

The time lacked ten minutes of six when the covered carriage bearing Lord Carslake, his seconds and a Major Duxbury, a military physician, wheeled up. As courtesy demanded, a brace of steel-breasted guards, swords drawn and held at the 'present', and a regimental officer, awaited the combatants and their entourage beyond the arched walkway leading to the green. Carslake's cronies were to be congratulated, mused Naseby grimly; the thing had been well arranged. Doubtless too but that friend Nigel was an expert shot!

'Harbour no fears regarding foul practice, Philip, there'll be no greased priming pans this day!' voiced Fremantle, trudging briskly off to supervise the loading and readying of the pistols.

The long oblong of the stables loomed greyly in the gradually dispersing gloom; the rectangular bulk of the barracks as yet indistinct in the near distance. At their back the lofty arches breaking onto the Parade arose forbidding and ghostly in outline.

Shivering slightly in his crisp white linen, Lord Carslake nonetheless contrived to present a bold enough figure as they stepped up to select pistols. Inured to all weathers by his long years at sea, Naseby was himself completely untroubled by the chill in the air. The demand to fire in shirtsleeves had come from Thomas Fremantle and had nothing to do with the cold. Skilled with weapons though officers of the senior service undeniably were, the vast majority of naval engagements called for little more than laying one's enemy so close as to scent his rancid breath, taste his briny sweat, and carve or blow out his innards as you tussled cheek to jowl. All the time swept on from behind by a wildly yelling boarding party. Blistering stuff and no argument.

Yet hardly up to the standard of markmanship required of a line officer in His Majesty's much vaunted regiment of Grenadiers. Hence Fremantle's astute reasoning that a side on presentation in the customary dark clothing might prove a far from satisfactory target for his charge.

They were to shoot from twelve paces. Each man to turn and present on the count of six. Then, at a prearranged signal from the guards officer presiding, each combatant would fire at will. As a point in passing, the ebony-butted brace of duelling pistols which they would use were also courtesy of the Horseguards.

It had by now grown full light and the aristocratic Carslake's aquiline features held a thin, predatory leer. Reinforcing Naseby's opinion of the man, and doubling his resolve that his adversary should 'die hard'!

'One – Two – Three – ' The guards officer's parade-ground bellow rang out sharply on the thin morning air.

The pistol felt over light and foreign to Naseby's hand.

'Five – Six! Turn and present!'

Naseby pivoted. Before him his field of vision appeared to have contracted to a tunnel-shaped killing ground. At the end of which, stiff and correct, stood Lord Carslake. All else, Fremantle and the other seconds, Sir Walter, standing on the farther side with the physician – the better to 'keep an eagle eye' on the proceedings. All had dissolved into what for the duel's protagonists had become a haze-shrouded background, no longer holding any substance in their adrenalin-heightened perception of time and space.

The officer's sword sliced the air.

'Fire!'

Something burned a path across his chest, the sharp detonation assaulting his hearing on the instant. From the nobleman's now impotently levelled pistol a thin plume of smoke spiralled lazily upward. A moment he held fire, sighting carefully, intent on making certain of his aim. To his credit, Lord Carslake remained stiff and unflinching.

At this juncture, in a fictionalised account from a romantic novel of the period, the hero would magnanimously discharge his pistol towards the sky. So much ran through Naseby's mind as tightlipped he shot for the groin. It was a difficult shot, requiring extreme care lest his outstretched arm be perceived to 'dip' too far from the horizontal: a foul and as such, liable to call forth a shot from the adjudicating guards officer.

The soft lead ball took the nobleman on an acute angle with his hip, was not deflected, and ploughed remorselessly on to bury itself, misshapen and finally spent, in his lordship's crotch.

The peer went down in a fountain of blood, a thin, highly-pitched screech of mortal agony wrenched from his lips. Satisfied, Naseby turned away. Lord Nigel Carslake would indeed die hard.

Day had fully dawned. The Admiralty etched in bold relief. Across the 'ride' the park showed green and verdant. Sir Walter was bidding him hasten. As the coach sped them swiftly from the Horseguards, the nobleman's shrieks ringing piercingly in their ears, it was the consensus, first expressed by Captain Fremantle, that the shot responsible had been an unfortunate accident. Even if a richly deserved one. Having nothing to say, Naseby sat silent and inwardly smiling.

Even as a spindle-shanked midshipman, young Philip Naseby had proved expert with a pistol. As indeed he had since, with everything from a belaying pin to a thirty-two pounder. Now for the wedding!

X

To Sea Again

The wedding of Commander Philip Naseby of His Britannic Majesty's Navy to Miss Sara Throgmorton in the church of St Martins in the Fields, had gone off according to plan. The happy couple, accompanied by a few intimate friends, retired immediately to the banqueting rooms of the Admiral Hawke in the Strand for a sumptuous wedding breakfast organised by Lady Dalrimple and courtesy of the kindly Sir Walter Perry. A characteristically generous gesture from a nobleman of the first degree.

It had been a time too short in every respect, this idyllic period between his bachelorhood of youth and the enforced bachelorhood of the sea. Days spent in a necessarily imperfect compromise between readying himself for sea and the precious moments which he passed with Sara. While the nights – these the couple passed in unfettered passion; in the tremulous delight of amorous exploration that is the province of the young and newly in love. Never had Philip Naseby been so happy. Wildly, exultantly happy. While the knowledge that his lovely Sara shared, and indeed luxuriated in the consummation of that joy, wantonly heedful of her own unselfconsciously sought fulfilment, served only to add to his happiness. Perhaps it was a period whose very shortness perforce abetted such feelings of tender abandon.

In any event, it was a period all too soon over, for the days were lengthening even as they passed. Spring was growing stronger, and their so very brief interlude was suddenly at an end.

Thus it was that on the morning of the 24th Naseby, once again in his plain, undress lieutenant's coat and minus the heavy bullion epaulette, sat in the wherry boat being rowed up the long length of the Hamouze and staring pensively at the water. The wherry was pair-oared and danced on the suntipped wavelets like a herring gull.

Uncharacteristically he hardly noticed the divers assortment of shipping through which they pulled. Nor yet spared a glance as the victualling and dockyards swam past, raising his eyes only slowly to take a first long look as *Nemesis* swept up, riding gracefully to her moorings off Bull Point. If until now he had been engaged in reliving in mind moments only lately spent, adjudged himself lost in melancholy musings: again the impatient bridegroom; how they had stood together that day side by side and then later, much later on the terrace at Carslake House and how the setting sun had looked in her hair – he was now fully himself, reclaimed to the service by a skilfully put together mass of wood, sailcloth and tar.

Truly she was a sight to behold: one of a class of recently built 36 gun frigates, and a very monarch of the waves – from her towering masts and neatly furled sails to the gleaming black and ochre of her hull. A perfection of man's genius and inventiveness, of his ability to harness the hostile forces of nature, to command them, to use them, to so bend them to his will as to lift his own comparatively fragile creation and send her soaring upon the wave tops, a lithe oak and canvas bird bearing man's own footsteps safe therein upon the oceans of his world.

All this and more rose to Naseby's own private consciousness as awed by the spectacle and his own poetic conception of it, he gazed upon *Nemesis*.

Her maindeck armament, he already knew, consisted of twenty-six eighteen pound carriage guns, thirteen a side; supplemented by eight quarterdeck nine pounders and a couple of forecastle twelves. In addition to which she also mounted four stubby eighteen pound quarterdeck carronades – these latter, as accorded with the custom of the day, not included in her official armament count, although nonetheless for that, wholly welcome. The slide-mounted carronade, ranging all the way up to the mighty sixty-eight pounders; it had been whose awesome firepower at close range had been largely responsible for visiting such terrifying destruction on the combined French and Spanish fleets off Cape Trafalgar. A worthy enough recommendation. Low, fast and long in relation to her beam, able to sail half a point closer to the wind than the mighty ships-of-the-line, *Nemesis* represented the complete commerce raider. The ideal fifth rate! And if she was not his to command, then at least as her first lieutenant he would bear a very real share in the proud task of fighting her should the fortunes of war so decree it.

The following three days were a hectic race to get *Nemesis* properly provisioned and ready for sea by the 27th. A mammoth task to which Philip Masterman Naseby settled like a duck to water. Cask upon cask of salt beef and pork in brine, flour to be baked into ship's biscuit (in addition to that already taken aboard from the nearby biscuit bakery, whose tall chimneys could be seen smoking day and night) and kegs of rum for the daily ration of grog – all had to be manhandled carefully aboard and stowed securely against the roll and pitch of the ship. Spare spars and cordage, canvas for the sailmaker and his mates, powder and shot – each and yet a deal more besides had all fallen to his weighty concern. Then finally, and perhaps ironically, the seaman's greatest and always hardest-to-provide need: fresh water, tens of thousands of gallons of it. The livestock and fresh food would be coming aboard at the last moment, along with the captain's cabin stores and those for the wardroom.

Naseby had yet to meet Thomas Tewksbury, but knew him to be a post captain of more than three years' seniority with a formidable reputation for discipline. 'A stickler for detail, but fair,' had been Fremantle's dispassionate assessment of his brother captain. Well, thought Naseby philosophically, be he the archangel Gabriel or a fiend incarnate, once aboard the *Nemesis* Tewksbury was his lord and master, and would remain so until an Act of Parliament, the King, or the Lords of Admiralty decreed otherwise. Or until such time as a French roundshot knocked his head from off his shoulders, he amended with relish.

In the event Captain Thomas Tewksbury turned out to be a tall, cadaverous man with a pronounced limp, whose hawk-like nose and yellowed teeth put Naseby in mind of a bird of prey in search of a meal. Reading himself in to the assembled ship's company, Tewksbury's hunting eyes seemed to devour every detail upon which they fell, leaving Naseby feeling more than a little apprehensive as the high, reedy voice droned inexorably on and a light top's'l breeze sighed wistfully through the rigging.

By the 30th with the Narrows and Devils Point, Staddon Heights and to starboard Mount Edgcumbe left far astern, Drakes Island and the creaming waters of the Sound but a memory, *Nemesis* heeled to the wide Atlantic rollers while a brisk nor'easterly drove her 'flying' across the Bay of Biscay.

Naseby was on deck supervising young David Knowles, their nineteen-year-old third lieutenant who had the morning watch. The captain was below in his cabin and as the senior officer topside, Naseby had the weather side of the quarterdeck to himself. It was a privilege to be jealously guarded and a moment which to savour.

Pausing for a moment in his steady pacing, he cast a weatherly eye aloft. It was all here: the fresh tang of salt on his lips, the pungent smell of newly tarred cordage, the heave of a deck beneath his feet. For a time he stood, balancing easily to the ship's at present predictable rise and fall, drinking it all in and letting the bittersweet memories of a thousand such days wash blithely over him.

Captain Thomas Tewksbury (or 'old T.T.' as the wardroom had irreverently tagged him) had amply lived up to Fremantle's assessment of him. Hardly a one of the *Nemesis*'s two hundred and seventy-three souls: officers, seamen, marines, ship's boys, and even Flawson the surgeon, had not felt the caustic rasp of his tongue. And already but three days to sea, mused Naseby wonderingly. Still, for all that he was forced to reflect, the old man certainly knew his onions. Nothing, it seemed, escaped his ever probing gaze. The trim of the sails, a vagrant splinter sticking up from the deck planking. Their captain espied them all, and was not slow in setting to and ferreting out the hapless culprit. Thus far they had not had a flogging; but it would come, as surely as dark followed dusk, it would come.

Simmonds the sailing master was casting a leery eye at the set of the maincourse and giving the benefit of his rather considerable experience to Lieutenant Knowles. Naseby resumed his pacing. Life at sea for an officer was all too lacking in physical exercise, hence the many portly captains and admirals. Naseby had decided to make it a definite rule to manage at least one hour's such each day. As a matter of fact, he was on his third thirty-minute stint now.

A contrived-sounding cough alerted him to the imminent presence on deck of the captain. With a discreet nod of gratitude to Simmonds for the tip, Naseby began to make himself scarce, only to be arrested by a high nasal tone.

'Ah, er, Mister Naseby, a word with you, if you please!'

Dutifully Naseby halted in his tracks, touching a finger to his hat as Tewksbury emerged fully onto the quarterdeck. The sailing master had moved discreetly out of earshot while the two quartermasters were maintaining their customary stoic indifference to the affairs of their betters.

The captain signed for him to fall into step and they began a steady side by side promenade, hands clasped beneath coat tails, turning inwards at either end of their precisely demarcated stroll in time-honoured navy fashion, lest their conversation be needlessly interrupted.

'I've been watching you, Mister Naseby,' Tewksbury was saying. 'Watching, I might say, for any hint on your part that could point to your harbouring notions above your station!'

Naseby remained tactfully silent, knowing that as a commander who had tasted the responsibilities of command, such notions or more precisely resentment at having to subordinate himself to another – albeit a post captain – might well be expected.

'Well, Mister Naseby, I am pleased to find that not to be the case.'

In truth Naseby himself was less than sure about this, but decided it politic not to disillusion his superior.

'In fact, I will go further, and say that I find myself well pleased with your conduct. Both towards myself as your superior, and as first lieutenant of this ship.'

Naseby found himself somewhat relieved at this and not a little pleased at the compliment which he was sensibly conscious was being bestowed upon him.

Tewksbury was still talking. 'Of course, I should not really have expected otherwise. Vice-Admiral Lord Collingwood does not hand out recommendations over lightly!'

So there it was: Tewksbury had seen Collingwood. No wonder he was being so honoured! Always Cuthbert Collingwood. Naseby was almost tempted to believe the man to have become a kind of fairy godfather! So diligently did his august lordship appear to labour on his behalf.

The captain's voice took on a more serious note. 'It is therefore because I hold you in, er, some esteem as an officer, that I intend to take you into my complete confidence with regard to my orders from the Admiralty.'

Naseby felt privileged. Although as *Nemesis*'s first lieutenant it was his place, if not perhaps his prescribed right, to be acquainted with the ship's ultimate destination, he was equally well aware that a good many captains saw it not only as their bound in duty to keep their executive officers in total ignorance as to the precise missions on which their ships were engaged, but sought also to confound them concerning whither bound – Supposing, perhaps, that such added to their lofty mystique. It was a bad practice which was unfortunately not confined only to post captains; many an admiral had been responsible for sailing an entire fleet into an engagement with an enemy about whose conduct and tactics his poor bemused captains languished in sorrowful ignorance.

It was to be supposed, perhaps, that constrained by the rigid line-ahead inflexibility of the 'Admiralty Fighting Instructions' which lamentably still remained in force, such a policy of cavalier indifference to one's subordinates did not greatly matter. Although from his own experiences as a midshipman, Naseby knew this decidedly not to be the case. But since Nelson and that Scotsman Clark had each in their own way – the former at sea and the latter courtesy of a Leith tabletop – amply demonstrated what could be accomplished when each captain of each ship were free to exercise his own judgement, both before and during said engagement – ! 'Delegation of responsibility,' Nelson had so aptly termed it. A measure of the little man's genius which Naseby was privately convinced had gone a very long way towards contributing to the Admiral's most assuredly deserved successes. The model, perhaps, for a navy of the future!

The mission on which *Nemesis* was bound was, to say the least, one of some delicacy, and fraught with considerable danger for the lucky officer on whose broad shoulders (his own) rested the onerous responsibility for its ultimate success – or failure.

A certain Mademoiselle Delacourt, it seemed, had of late managed to inveigle her somewhat dubious way into the good graces of, and more importantly from the viewpoint of Admiralty, incautious confidences of the renowned French Admiral of the Rear, Pierre Magendie. The latter now well into his sixties and commander of the Mediterranean port of Toulon.

Just what information this amateur courtesan and sometime spy had managed to ferret out of the old boy, Naseby hadn't been given to know. Largely, he suspected, because Captain Thomas Tewksbury himself hadn't been told. But it was obviously something of sufficient import as to require the immediate dispatch of a frigate for its securing! To Naseby had fallen command of the landing party whose task it would be to snatch Mademoiselle Delacourt from the lion's mouth as it were.

It was a task for which the first lieutenant knew himself to be well fitted. A chance to show himself in a good light to his masters at Admiralty, and one which he accordingly viewed with some relish.

As day followed day the *Nemesis* pursued her plunging south-westerly course, meeting the wide Atlantic rollers as to the manner born; soon leaving the choppy Bay of Biscay on her larboard quarter and steering more southerly so as to sight Cape St Vincent and make a run for the strait; dropping off dispatches at Gibraltar, they were off again sailing east before bearing steadily nor-east by east on a heading for the Gulf of Lyons.

Coming into the wardroom on their third day out from Gibraltar, the seventeenth of the voyage, Naseby found Edward Manners, *Nemesis*'s second, in rapt conversation with the surgeon Flawson and Snelling the lieutenant of Marines.

'Why, you only have to look at the man,' the surgeon was saying, 'he's the colour of seaweed and bent double with pain!'

Manners was looking uncomfortable.

'I tell you, the captain's not long for this world,' continued Flawson relentlessly.

'Ho, and what's all this?' broke in Naseby with mock horror. 'Taking our gallant captain's name in vain? I'll have none of it, I tell you. Why, if old T.T., ah, er, pardon me – '

'Tch, pipe down, man!' chided the surgeon, smiling despite himself. 'This is serious, I tell ye. Captain Tewksbury's bin vomiting blood for an hour or more.' He paused to bite a chunk from his quid before repeating himself: 'Thomas Tewksbury's not long for this world, or I'm a Dutchman!'

Naseby took a vacant chair, somewhat sobered by what this unlooked for piece of news implied. 'Ah, hum, and how long has he been like this, Mister Flawson?' he managed at last.

Manners, he noticed, was viewing him speculatively, as well he might. Were it not for Naseby's presence on board Manners, as a middle-aged lieutenant of vast seniority, would doubtless have been first. And hence now would be sitting privately anticipating becoming *Nemesis*'s captain in what seemed the imminently likely event of Tewksbury's death. As, of course, was he.

According to Flawson, the first he had known of the captain's malady was when he had been summoned by a white-faced ship's boy to attend the captain in his day cabin during the morning watch. Tewksbury had appeared a little green about the gills and been complaining of severe stomach cramps. Flawson had duly administered a physic and advised him to keep his cabin. Whence he had duly returned at seven bells of the forenoon watch to find his patient's condition worsened, beyond belief.

'And the blood, Mister Flawson,' prompted Snelling, the officer of Marines, ghoulishly making his first breathless contribution to the recounting.

'Well, as I wuz saying,' the surgeon supplied obligingly, 'the blood had started to issue forth on the occasion o' my last visit. Shortly before the end o' the forenoon watch. God only knows what state the poor devil's in now.'

'Then you'd best get along there directly, Mister Flawson!' Naseby made no bones about this being a direct order. The surgeon hurried off to obey. 'And Mister Flawson, you will keep me informed!'

'Poor bugger hasn't a clue what ails old T.T.,' Snelling muttered resignedly.

Naseby remained silent. For the most part physicians were only appointed to ships-of-the-line, and not always then, frigates and the like having to make do with a ship's surgeon. Little more than a literate butcher, whose chief curative measures were confined largely to a dose of rum, a good clear out, or amputation. Although perhaps in all truth, hardly more nor less than could be managed by a physician of the time.

'Humph, Captain Tewksbury can thank his lucky stars he's got a frigate under 'im. Were he commanding a sixth-rate, he'd have to make do with a surgeon's mate!' growled Manners uncharitably.

That evening as he paced the quarterdeck Naseby could not help but hear the ghastly cries emanating from the stern cabin beneath his feet as the 'poor devil' as Flawson had termed him, fought his last desperate engagement against a foe which they must needs all some day lay alongside.

It was not until the end of the second dog watch, 8 p.m., that he was summoned to the musty sleeping cabin to receive his final orders from a dying Thomas Tewksbury. The man presented an appalling picture, lying knees doubled up to his chin in a pool of bloody vomit, a leather 'bite' forced between pain-clenched teeth and a stained cloth around his forehead. Naseby drew up short on the threshold, doing his best not to gag. Then summoning up his will power, stepped forthrightly in. Crouching beside the cot in an attitude of helpless bewilderment, the surgeon Flawson shook his head slowly. So this was it. Bending over the stricken man, Naseby softly announced his presence.

The hunting eyes opened briefly, allowing a glimpse of the man within, a flicker of recognition glowing weakly from their depths. It soon became apparent that the poor wretch was beyond speech; a long talon-like forefinger stabbed feebly in the direction of a rectangular metal box reposing significantly on the foot of the cot. This would, Naseby knew, contain Tewksbury's orders from the Admiralty along with *Nemesis*'s papers and copy of current recognition signals. Swiftly he nodded his understanding. For a brief moment the eyes seemed to wish him godspeed, before glazing slowly over and becoming dull.

Naseby drew a ragged deep breath. He was now the captain of *Nemesis*!

Topside, one bell sounded. With the look-out down from aloft, the ship was being watched from the deck. Lights out having been piped some time since, the hands were swinging restively below decks in their hammocks. Mounting to the quarterdeck it felt good to clear his lungs of the tainted smell of sickness. Tomorrow, after a brief service, Tewksbury would be feeding the fishes. The thought was strangely incongruous with the balmy Mediterranean night working its magic on his soul.

The sky was a blanket of stars, the sea overside dappled and silvery in the moonlight. Walking to the taffrail he began to whistle softly beneath his teeth. The air chosen was 'Spanish Ladies', mildly evocative and rife with all the heave and surge of the sea. Beneath him the ship creaked and sighed as no merely dead mass of timbers – frames, beams and planking – ever could.

He had now taken to keeping a private journal and from this would come material for the three letters which he was now regularly obliged to write. Gray, of course; and in addition there was his beloved Sara, not to mention his new-found family, Sir Walter and Anne (whom he now looked on as a sister) to be kept informed. He would have much of which to write this night, he mused, with perhaps just a trace of genuine sadness.

That night he slept soundly, untroubled as yet by the awesome responsibility which the sudden turn of events had thrust upon him.

Awake with the morning watch it was a revelation to find himself still the same man that he had been the day before.

Unusually, his strange sense of things impending had not seen fit to visit him on this occasion, and he found himself mourning the omission. Gulping down coffee, he shaved quickly, nicking himself in the process.

Today he would be moving into the captain's cabin, a vast improvement on his present cramped cubby hole. The deck-head lantern was rocking gently with the motion of the ship, the rudder pintles groaning in their gudgeons. The wind was freshening. On deck the hands were at work rigging up the washdeck pump. Soon the task of holystoning could begin.

Naseby kept out of the way, leaving the officer of the watch to his duty. As *Nemesis*'s first, let alone captain, as he now was, his mere presence topside demanded the immediate vacating of the weather side by all save those he chose to summon to him. A privilege which on this occasion he deliberately chose to forego. Taking instead a position by the lee rail and the opportunity of a quiet pipe. Soon enough he would be bearing the brunt of things, but for now this was enough.

'I tell ye, the body should be set in spirits for carrying home,' asserted Manners belligerently. 'As captain, it's his right!'

Naseby treated him to a hard stare. The other officers: Simmonds, who as sailing master (the highest obtainable by warrant) and who, under the captain was responsible for navigating the ship, held rank even above that of a lieutenant, young Knowles, Snelling and even Flawson the surgeon, were waiting.

His voice when he spoke was edged with flint. 'You say 'Sir' when you address me, Mister Manners; is that clear?'

The silence which ensued was deafening.

Just in time Manners relented. 'Aye, aye, sir!' he managed. Still, at least to Naseby's heightened perception of things, a mite grudgingly. He chose to overlook it.

'*Nemesis*, gentlemen,' he said, addressing himself to all assembled, and he hoped laying stress on the co-operative entity of the ship, the officers and her people as a whole, 'has her orders from My Lords Commissioners of the Admiralty. Orders which must, and shall, be acted upon!'

His glance fell again on the veteran Manners, who remained now sensibly silent. He continued in milder tone. 'To which end, as her captain, I deem it imperative to expedite the matter before us; namely that of the late Thomas Tewksbury R.N. as befits the time and place – a sailor's funeral. That will be all, gentlemen!'

Ordering 'on hats' as the roundshot-weighted bundle disappeared beneath the deep blue waters of the Mediterranean, *Nemesis*'s new captain could truthfully reflect that he would not have wished for command, even of such as the beautiful frigate that heeled beneath his feet, at the cost of such terrible suffering. 'Conveyed home in spirits', indeed. Who did they think it was the man had been – Nelson!?

XI
Ambush

Since Trafalgar the French naval base at Toulon – or 'Too long' as the jocular British tars had renamed it – had been under only a somewhat intermittent blockade, the virtual destruction of the combined French and Spanish fleets under Villeneuve having largely removed the need. At present the Mediterranean port was blithely unmolested. A circumstance with which Naseby, once again sporting his single bullion epaulette – albeit on the commander's left shoulder as was clearly proper – was not sure that he entirely agreed. In accordance with the pink ribboned orders which he had found in the metal documents box which her late captain had vouchsafed him, he had brought *Nemesis* to the tiny Provence fishing port of Fréjus, about fifty miles along the coast from Toulon, where she now lay, hove-to, just out of sight from the shore.

It was now mid May and *Nemesis*'s seamen frolicked barefoot on her sunswept upper deck as they went about their duties. In his shirt sleeves and minus his hat, Naseby sat perched contentedly on the mainmast crosstrees, swaying gently, as he focussed his telescope on the distant blue smudge of enemy coastline. A welcoming breeze fluted softly from off the Alps flicking playfully at vagrant strands of his coal black hair, fastened as always in a neat queue.

They were two days ahead of the first date tentatively suggested for the rendezvous, with little to do now but wait. That and to go over again and again in his mind the deliberately loose laid plans which he had formulated for the accomplishment of their mission.

Mademoiselle Delacourt was purportedly summering at a modest château, one time home of some minor nobleman who had long since paid the price for his aristocratic blood on Dr Guillotine's fiendish device, about three miles beyond the town.

Each night from and including the 19th, a Tuesday, Mademoiselle and her escort – this latter unspecified – were to make their way to a bluff stretch of headland a mile further along the coast, and there to burn a single blue flare at half-hourly intervals until midnight.

Common sense dictated that now that he was captain of the *Nemesis*, Naseby should pass command of the landing party to one of his lieutenants. However, the thought that the success of such an important mission should depend on the qualities of imaginative leadership, or lack thereof, of either the elderly and singularly unimaginative Manners, or the stripling Knowles, filled him with abject horror. While Soames, *Nemesis*'s senior midshipman who courtesy of the frigate's commissioned officers, having each received a step up, was now acting third lieutenant, being hardly in the running. No, he would command the landing party himself. After all, he reflected, using the thought to square away any last lingering doubts which he may have harboured on the subject, since responsibility for the thing had been laid originally at his door by Tewksbury his predecessor – perhaps even before him, by Collingwood himself – it would seem churlish to attempt to duck it. In truth, of course, it was a peculiarly lame argument. He was justified in going himself simply because he was the best man for the job. Hence all such half-hearted prevarication was not only superfluous but positively time-wasting. Which was, of course, precisely its intent.

It was pleasant enough here at the masthead, out of the way of the skylarking going on below. Above it all, as it were. Being Sunday he had earlier had to conduct 'Divine Service' on the quarterdeck; not a chore he had relished. Far rather would he have read out the 'Articles of War', something which took place on every King's ship one Sunday in three, deeming this a more useful and appropriate beginning to his tenure of command. Unfortunately this had been done but the week previous and woe betide any captain foolhardy enough to overlong deprive his lower decks of their rightful Scripture.

Naseby spat disgustedly, confident of its dispersal before the unpardonable should occur and *Nemesis*'s snowy white deck be stained. Some of the men, he knew, would have saved up their grog ration to be gambled with, bartered, or simply enjoyed later. Which was well enough and of little mind to him provided that it didn't lend itself to disorder. Sunday or no, there was always work to be done aboard a ship of war.

Aft on the quarterdeck acting Lieutenant Soames was pacing ostentatiously back and forth as if the ship were fighting an action and he was attempting to avoid being sighted upon by marksmen in the enemy's tops. He would learn, mused Naseby humourlessly. Experience was a thing which couldn't be taught and something which he, Naseby, at the present time felt woefully short of. True, he had commanded a gun brig in the Caribbean, and very successfully as it had turned out, but captaining one of His Majesty's frigates on a mission of considerable importance to the Admiralty was something else again. Tewksbury had been a tartar, but a fine seaman and an able commander. Was he, Naseby asked himself, really up to filling the man's shoes – as easily as he had thus far filled his cabin? Time would tell, he found himself muttering philosophically, time would tell.

Both the 19th and the 20th of the month were to pass without sight of a signal flare, and it was not until the evening of Thursday the 21st that Naseby was able to give orders telling off the frigate's thirty-man landing party.

With him in the launch would be going Snelling, the lieutenant of Marines, and fifteen-year-old midshipman Horricks, a likely lad with all the makings of a good officer. Command of the jolly boat he had given to Lieutenant Knowles; his task, it was, to stand off from the shore and, in the unhappy event of the whole thing becoming a debacle, carry the news back to *Nemesis* that Manners was now free to clap on all sail and head back to Gibraltar.

Three bells had just sounded in the middle watch as Naseby, complete with fighting sword, clambered over the side and, timing his leap expertly, landed in the stern-sheets of the launch. There had seemed little need for muffling the rowlocks against the possibility of a rather unlikely seeming shore patrol, something which he had nonetheless ordered done. However, he had very wisely given strict orders that none of the muskets issued to the launch's combined complement of seamen and marines were to be loaded until he gave the word. Some fool loosing off a careless shot at the heavens was not a prospect likely to greatly lend itself to secrecy.

It was one of those clear starlit nights common to the Mediterranean at this time of year, with the moon a muted silver wafer suspended low over the water. At the tiller of the launch Naseby found himself humming a melancholy air, and abruptly pulled up short, lest Horricks at his side get the idea that command had gone to his captain's head.

They were within a cable and a half of the shore already, with the sounds of the softly rippling waves lapping against the base of the cliff wafting plainly back to them on the still night air. The section of shoreline which lay ahead was somewhat of an unknown quantity to the landing party's commander at present, although he would have been loath to admit to such. The chart indicated a tiny cove fronted by a shallow stretch of beach situated to the left of the headland. It was to be hoped that this was correct. The sad fact was that such charts as were available to the Admiralty concerning the coastline of Southern France were, to say the least, sketchy with regard to the more minor details. Details such as suitability for landing, location of smaller inlets, depth of water at low tide ... He had been able to make out a little from his regular stints at the masthead with his telescope; but hardly enough to be sure, not without allowing the *Nemesis* to stand closer inshore and thus risk alerting the port.

'Beach ahead!' came a low cry from the bow.

Naseby swallowed his relief. If he had been wrong he would have appeared a fool, and worse.

'Ship oars!' he hissed, the urgency in his voice incongruous on such a balmy night.

Leaping into the shallows he gave the order for the loading of muskets as the seamen dragged the launch up onto the beach. His own twin-barrelled monsters were safely at half-cock and tucked into his belt. Now, if his information were correct, there should be a convenient rope ladder dangling at the foot of the cliff. Swiftly he made his way across. Yes, here it was, swaying less than a fathom above the shingle.

Horricks was at his side, a hanger clutched fiercely in his right hand, long face showing gaunt in the moonlight.

'All right, lad, up yer go!' he hissed, wishing instead that he could go himself. But it just wasn't on; he would be needed here if anything went wrong.

Snelling had his men lined up in front of the launch as a skirmishing party, just in case. For a moment Naseby glanced at the marines. Their scarlet coats loomed blackly and the vivid criss-cross of pipe-clayed belts aided by tall shakoes imparted a certain formidable aspect which was wholly reassuring. The subdued gleam reflected from ten levelled bayonets helped, too. It would be a gallant Frenchman who charged that lot!

Anxiously he peered up at the dark bulk of the cliff, rocking back on his heels and craning his neck in an effort to follow Horricks' dizzy ascent to the top. There he was now, framed for a moment in the moonlight.

Suddenly a dull pop sounded from the head of the cliff and Horricks' tiny figure was toppling backwards – a single sharp cry breaking from his lips as he plunged over seventy feet to the beach at Naseby's feet.

At once all was pandemonium. A second only he stared at Horricks' broken form, then with a dull rasp his fighting sword was out and he was calling his men to order amid a ragged hail of musketry from above. Near at hand a running seaman went down, spinning like a top. Yet another uttered a high-pitched oath before sinking to his knees; several of his comrades moved hurriedly to drag the man to cover.

'To the launch! To the launch!' barked Naseby, flourishing his sword impotently as he ran.

Snelling's marines were kneeling in a patient line, muskets raised to the 'present' as they awaited a target. It would be worse than useless, Naseby knew, to order them to fire almost straight up at the scarcely seen figures hunched on the top of the cliff, and it was all credit to the portly Lieutenant Snelling that in the heat of the moment he had not done so. As these and other thoughts raced unbidden through his mind, a marine at the farther end of the line toppled abruptly over onto his side: a kneeling toy soldier knocked aside by the heedless hand of a delighted infant.

The launch was backing water now, hurtling men clambering frantically across her bulwarks.

'Take order, there, belay!' roared Naseby, but to little avail. The men were fear-crazed, and who could blame them. Fighting an enemy at sea, an enemy whom you could see to aim a gun at, that was one thing; but to remain here to be shot at like fish in a barrel, that was another. Only the marines showed steady. The result of diligent training and iron discipline? Perhaps. Even now Naseby found himself wondering if maybe after all the more individualistic seamen hadn't the right of it!

In any event they would be clear soon. The French were showing no inclination to descend to the beach. Either they were content to pop away into the near blackness below, or were expecting help from a roving guard boat. Which wasn't likely, else young Knowles would have set off one of the red port-fires which Naseby had ordered placed in the jolly boat for the purpose.

Two more of his men had fallen. Bowled down like ninepins. It was taking longer than he'd thought. If they didn't get off this beach soon he would be rowing back to the ship alone.

It was then that he felt the nerve-wrenching pain of a musket ball as it buried itself in his shoulder. His sword had left his hand and he was reeling toward the launch. The burn of the ball in his flesh was indescribable. Another ploughed into the water in front of him, sending up a thin plume of water a good foot high. Above the din, he could hear Snelling's strident orders to his men. Another seaman tumbled choking from the launch and began a blind crawl up the beach. Grimly he fought to steady himself.

A firm hand clasped his arm. Then he was being hefted bodily over the launch's bulwarks, rolling clear, and narrowly avoiding being trodden on as Snelling's marines tumbled tumultuously in after him.

Dimly he was conscious of barking harsh orders to the seamen and of the fact that the pain in his right shoulder and arm had settled to a dull bone-numbing throb. How long it took for them to come up with Knowles in the jolly boat, or how long after that until they had rowed the considerable distance to the ship, he had not the least idea. Nor, incidentally, was he able later to recall conning the launch and managing the heavy tiller totally unaided.

Altogether ten men, including one marine, a corporal whom Naseby had seen fall, were missing when the landing party was finally mustered at the break of *Nemesis*'s quarterdeck. With nothing to say Naseby had himself helped below to the unknown horrors of the cockpit, being mildly surprised to find on the way that some unseen hand had returned his fighting sword to its scabbard.

Situated below the waterline on the orlop deck, *Nemesis*'s candlelit after-cockpit appeared as if straight out of a nightmare. One which, as he stood swaying weakly in the entrance way supported only by an anxious Lieutenant Knowles, he knew he had awoken sweating from on occasions too numerous to mention. Aboard *Defiance* at Trafalgar; he had occasion then to witness the unmanning spectacle, the hellish torment as the ship's surgeon, bathed in blood up to his armpits, a physician in like case, two loblolly boys and the Chaplain, laboured like fiends to hack limbs from twitching torsos and gauge out projectiles from living flesh. The aftermath of a fleet action, that had been. At the time he had felt his bowels start to loosen; a weird fluttering along his nerve endings travelling all the way down to his hamstrings. Like a man falling.

It was all here now, that same feeling: the midshipmen's mess table whereon the grisly work would be done, the instruments (assorted knives and saws) warming above a redly glowing brazier so as to lessen the sudden shock of cold steel. While next to it stood the wooden tub wherein freshly severed arms and legs were thrown.

Naseby felt himself sag. A bandaged marine reached out and caught him; making him heartsick and ashamed of his weakness. Knowles was guiding him, shoving him really, towards the table, helped by the marine and one other whom he couldn't see. Flawson was poking amongst his instruments, the high-powered rum used to lull the patient's pain tight-fast in his other hand. With all his strength Naseby willed to bear upright, to shear off his helpers and march four-square to his coming ordeal. But somehow, try as he might, it couldn't be done.

'Lorst a fearsome lotta blood, 'e 'as,' grunted the marine shortly.

'Heave 'im up on the table if ye please, then, an' I'll have a look at 'im!' returned the surgeon, still fiddling with the warming instruments.

God, how they gleamed in the candlelight. Didn't the fools know, couldn't they understand, they were going to hurt him, badly. Would bear witness to his weakness, his awful weakness. It mustn't happen, it couldn't; he was captain of the ship, he would fight his way out of here – what if they should cut off his arm!

Perhaps he opened his mouth to scream, or else merely to shout; either way a foul leather bite was forced between his teeth and he felt the surgeon's first tentative touch on his skin …

That which followed transcended belief. Suffice it to say that he mercifully lost consciousness soon after, coming to incredibly enough just as Flawson ceased his sadistic probings and announced gleefully that the last bloodied fragment of cloth was now safely extracted from the wound and that he, Naseby, was fortunate that the ball that had struck him had been largely spent. Naseby remembered trying to mutter some inane comment about the fact that if that was what a ball felt like when it were spent, he would hate to think what – But then they were applying the brush containing boiling tar to his flesh, and he remembered no more.

When he awoke it was to find it full daylight and himself in his cot. The self-same cot in which Captain Tewksbury had died, with his right arm – which felt as if it were on fire – securely bound to his chest. For several minutes he lay still, letting the gentle tranquillity of the little sleeping cabin, with the reflections from the water dancing brightly on the deckbeams above his head, wash over him.

Suddenly he experienced a moment of panic. Filling his lungs to capacity despite the pain it caused, he bellowed for the marine sentry standing guard outside his cabin door. Some minutes later, under much protest, surgeon Flawson was removing the binding from the arm. Danger of the wound opening or not, Philip Naseby knew enough about wounds sustained in action and their treatment thereof, to be aware of the fact that if he ever wished to use that arm again it were best left unbound and free to move. Or else carry about with him a useless 'fin' for the rest of his life. Fortunately the wound didn't open, save for a minute aperture which Flawson explained was necessary – 'so as to allow for natural drainage against mortification.' Naseby was satisfied. Nor did he object to the ever present pain, which at least served to reassure him that the damaged limb was still there!

He was up on deck again the following day. His shoulder hurt like the devil, but the invigorating salt tang did wonders for his flagging spirits. *Nemesis* was running along the coast with Cape St Sebastian on the starboard beam, a sighing tops'l breeze lifting at her canvas. He was going home to ignominy, he knew. Of course, nothing that had occurred either on the beach where he had commanded the landing party, or for that matter on the cliff beforehand to the woman and her escort, could properly be laid at his door. Why, for all he knew, Mademoiselle Delacourt had been arrested and made to talk long before the frigate's arrival. Although in truth this seemed unlikely; else why had not the French had a squadron at sea and ready for him. There were ships of war in the harbour at Toulon, as he was well aware. Which pointed to the ambush being a hastily arranged affair, the enemy not even managing a guard-boat! Whatever had happened had happened that night.

No one would blame him. Nothing would be said. It was even possible – no, belay that, probable – that there would be those who would sympathise with him. After all, had not command of the *Nemesis* and consequently the task of carrying out his dead captain's orders fallen as it were out of the blue onto Naseby's perchance over-young shoulders? The Lords of Admiralty would nod their heads in patient understanding. Only Collingwood would perhaps feel disappointment when he returned to Gibraltar empty-handed. Then later, much later, when the prospect of his promotion should perhaps be raised again, if indeed after this it ever were ... Those same Lords of Admiralty would shake their heads in unspoken agreement. 'Unfit for command' would be his silent epitaph.

Naseby felt sick. But what could he do? Going back to Gibraltar to be relieved and sent back to England on the first available transport was a prospect that made his gorge to rise. On the other hand, maybe he wouldn't find himself relieved. Maybe the Commander-in-Chief in the Mediterranean would simply post a captain, some favourite, no doubt, into *Nemesis* over his head. Leaving him to fret away his days as a lieutenant. His brightly polished epaulette put away for ever, slowly to tarnish in his sea chest.

By the powers! It was unthinkable that such a fate should befall him – not now that he had been so close to realising all his most cherished ambitions. Had been so close that he could still taste it. Had held it all in the open palm of his hand, only to watch helplessly as, like a startled butterfly, it fanned out its wings and fluttered mockingly from his grasp.

Gibraltar was out, in any terms. That much was clear. Rather would he sail *Nemesis* into the harbour of Toulon, guns blazing, and so make an honourable end of it. A commander who, finding himself balked at the first hurdle, promptly described an about turn, going back for fresh instructions, was no commander at all. He took order with himself at once. Reflecting on the fact that in the not so distant past the prospect of returning home to a beautiful and adoring wife and living the life of a very wealthy man would have figured as being more than sufficient unto itself, post captaincy or no. Thence was it with some measure of surprise that he realised, in the event, this should prove not to be the case? In truth not. He would end his days as a post captain at least; or he would die trying! He found himself grinning.

With Divisions about to be sounded, Naseby decided to make himself scarce. Up and around before the redoubtable Flawson had deemed wise in any case, he was well aware that Manners would be expecting to be left to his own devices this morning. And was just as happy that this be so. As *Nemesis*'s first, the veteran Manners ran a taut ship and it was much to be doubted that a couple of missed inspections on his part would greatly alter things.

Below in his cabin once more, he fell to studying the chart. If the plan that was currently hatching in his fertile brain were to have any real chance of success he would need to familiarise himself thoroughly with the shoreline as well as the terrain beyond. Steady, measured footsteps sounded above his head as the ever diligent Manners inspected himself.

Life aboard a King's ship was easy on no one, but least of all on the common seamen. They slept, ate, and if they were gunners, spent virtually every waking moment beside their charges. At night those not standing watch unrolled their hammocks, slung them from hooks attached to the overhead deck beams, and in conditions as crowded as any London slum and often as evil-smelling, passed a fitful night swinging above the guns.

The ship's day proper began at midnight with the first four hour watch. The morning watch being roused from their hammocks at four a.m. with the shriek of the boatswain's pipe and the cry 'All hands!' The mates going through the ship with knotted rope ends 'starting' the lazy and the sluggish. Once on deck the pump would have to be rigged up for sea water, the deck washed and sprinkled with sand. Next would come the holystoning, scouring the sand into the planking until it was smooth of splinters, using sandstone scrapers the size of prayer books. The scrubbers would follow, with the swabbers following after them to dry the deck.

The ship's brass and metalwork would be cleaned with brick dust and polishing cloths. These men would work to windward of the holystoning crew so as not to mar their efforts. Hammocks would be lashed with the straw mattress inside, together with a blanket, and bound together by seven regulation turns of a lanyard.

On deck again the men would disperse to their respective divisions and the hammocks stowed in the netting which surrounded the upper deck of the ship with long strips of canvas placed over them for protection against the weather. Stowed in this way they served also as protection against small arms and grape shot when in action.

At eight a.m. the hands were piped to breakfast and the forenoon watch commenced; the meal being collected from the galley by each mess cook and eaten at tables slung between the guns. Further cleaning and polishing followed at eight-thirty a.m., and at nine thirty a.m. (ten a.m. on Sundays) 'Divisions' were sounded.

As was presently taking place. The captain – or in this unusual circumstance Manners the first lieutenant – inspecting the seamen and neatly drawn up ranks of marines, and going round the whole ship from stem to stern looking for errant spots of dirt, dust or grease. Were many such to be found, as executive officer the first lieutenant was due a roasting, with from there, as in all services, the censure passing swiftly downwards.

Once eight bells sounded at twelve noon the midday meal was served and the watch not at work allowed to rest. The grog issue at noon was one gill of pure rum mixed with three gills of water, and as often as not given an extra little zip by the men themselves by adding the lemon juice which they were issued as a preventative against scurvy. As was the custom, any resultant drunkenness was regarded as dereliction of duty and punishable by flogging.

The afternoon would be followed by the first of the two (two hour) or dog watches; these beginning at four and six o'clock respectively. Their purpose being to break up the normal four hourly stints, whereby first the larboard and then the starboard watches took turn and turn about, thus ensuring daily rotation of duties and that each man got, alternately at least, part of a night's sleep.

At an hour before dusk, approximately five p.m., the hands would be piped to supper, receiving their third and last meal of the day; consisting of cheese and biscuits and a second ration of rum and beer. The Royal Marine drummers would then beat to quarters at five thirty p.m. with the men rushing to man the guns. The officers would then inspect the men at gun drill; loading and reloading the guns as quickly as possible. With sometimes prizes of money being awarded the fastest crews. The aim of every gun crew being 'three in five', or three times in every five minutes.

'Down hammocks' would be piped at eight p.m., giving the men just ten minutes in which to retrieve their bedding, get down below and sling the hammocks before lights out was piped mournfully through the ship at eight ten p.m.

With the end of the middle watch at midnight the whole repetitive nightmare would begin again. The only relief from the awful monotony coming on Sunday with Divine Service and on Thursday afternoons which were set aside for 'make-and-mend'.

Naseby leaned almost upright from the chart. Even here in the captain's cabin the headroom was far from adequate. He had foregone breakfast and was beginning to get hungry. Doubtless a sign that he was on the mend. The thought cheered him and he began to whistle softly; contemplating the while what he would have for dinner. Tewksbury had been more than generous in the matter of laying in for himself cabin stores, with the consequence that as captain, Naseby could set a rare and fine table. He would have the duck, followed by a pork and veal pie. There were vegetables aplenty, too, and fruit and cheese for dessert. Not that foul-smelling 'pursers cheese', mind! There was yet some soft bread – hardly fresh but a thousand times preferable to that weevil-infested hard tack. While in regard to wine, there was liberal choice.

Today being Saturday the lower deck would be having salt beef; said meat having been salted a long time, perhaps years. Stoney hard, glistening with salt, dark, gristly and shrunken, the men would carve boxes, mahogany-coloured trinkets and various other fancy items from it. But then, he mused, such was life.

XII

Into Action

Four bells were sounding the end of the second dog watch. Some forty-eight hours since the debacle on the beach. And Naseby was going back. Not to Gibraltar, but to Fréjus. Manners had thought him mad, viewing his afore stated intent as the ravings of a sick man. Although, of course, the ageing first lieutenant had refrained from voicing his misgivings in quite that way. Knowles, to give the youngster his due, had been all for the plan. If plan it could with justice be called. 'Naseby's gamble,' Snelling, the portly officer of Marines, had incautiously dubbed the scheme when it was outlined to him.

Naseby's reasoning was simple, and based entirely on his contention that their expected passenger, or more accurately passengers, had been captured on Thursday night while in the act of signalling to the frigate. Hence, it was reasonable to assume that Mademoiselle Delacourt and her escort, if this latter were still among the living, were currently ensconced in the town gaol, Fréjus having no garrison, awaiting escort to Toulon and perhaps thence to Paris for trial and execution. From the French viewpoint such would seem warranted if one were to judge the lady's importance by the amount of fuss the Admiralty were willing to countenance to bring her safely off.

It was consequently Naseby's intention to take *Nemesis* into the port, land in sufficient force, and under cover of sacking the town, storm the gaol and free their lordship's spy. Put like that, a straightforward enough task. What he hadn't, however, sought to bring to his officers' attention, and a consequence which none among their number had managed to envisage for himself, was the probability that now the French were aware of *Nemesis*'s presence along their Mediterranean coastline, a force would be immediately ordered to sea against her. Especially so, if as her acting captain feared, it were realised in Toulon that the British frigate sailed alone!

Just short of twenty hours later Naseby was ready to go in. Standing at the quarterdeck rail he issued his final orders to Lieutenant Knowles' seventy-strong force of seamen and marines.

'Remember, men, your part in the coming landing is purely diversionary. Make as much noise as you like, and fire some of the empty warehouses.' His voice took on a note of contrived harshness. 'I repeat, it is no part of our duty to murder innocent fisherfolk. Any man among you who forgets this will be seized up and flogged. Is that clearly understood?'

His words were answered by a solemn chorus of nodding heads.

According to the chart the depth of water in the outer harbour was five fathoms, thirty feet. *Nemesis* drew fifteen. He would be able to take the ship within a thousand yards of the quiet waterfront town, thus bringing much of the populace under the grim menace of the frigate's broadside of eighteen pounders. For this reason, and to make the most of the tide, it had been decided to take *Nemesis* into the harbour shortly before dusk.

Fréjus was a gaily contrived hotch-potch such as might be viewed at any one of a hundred such venues along the southern coast, its multi-coloured rooftops reflecting brightly in the dying rays of the Mediterranean sun. Lowering his glass, he descended to the quarterdeck. Manners was by the rail.

'We'll have the guns run out, if you please, Mister Manners!' Naseby ordered curtly.

Nemesis's people had been at quarters and her guns loaded ready for the last fifteen minutes. As the frigate vibrated to the rumble of gun tracks and the rattle of handspikes, her young captain ran an eye of proud appraisal over his charge.

The sanded decks and picturesque marine sentries at the hatchways. Slings rigged from her yards. Eager-faced powder monkeys. And the gun crews standing silent and steady. It was a good feeling to take such a splendid machine of war into action; even if it was only against an undefended seaport town.

As the launch carrying Knowles and his party drew up to the mole, Naseby and a hand-picked party of seamen set off from *Nemesis*'s seaward side, the cutter's course set for a sheltered stretch of beach showing whitely beyond a ragged cluster of fishermen's huts.

By the time they were halfway to the shore a dull crackle of firing had broken out in the town. Naseby set his features grimly. War was war, but the prospect of butchering civilians whose only crime lay in having been born Frenchmen was totally abhorrent. And this from a man who had ruthlessly ordered a Spanish schooner captain's throat cut!

The beach was deserted. Drawing a pistol left-handedly from his belt, Naseby broke into a ground-covering run. The half dozen fierce-eyed seamen at his back each armed with both pistol and cutlass. At the end of a hundred yards the shingle of the beach gave on to a grass-grown bank above which ran the main coast road. Clambering up the bank the little party set a brisker pace along the road; the sounds of firing growing ever stronger as they ran.

Off to their left, bordering the waterfront, a glowing red band had risen into the fast darkening sky, evidence of the incendiary activities of Knowles and his landing party. After a five minute run the party reached the outskirts of the town. Quickly Naseby cast about; the town square, he knew, was straight ahead, perhaps a quarter of a mile. Making a random choice he led the way along a narrow alleyway hemmed in by high stone walls. Emerging at its farther end between a huddle of squalid wooden houses that backed onto the street beside a parade of open-fronted stalls. This would be the fish market – lifeblood of the town's economy.

All about them was fear and confusion. Women, some of them with children tailing desperately onto their billowing skirts, scuttled in every direction. Off to their right a tiny knot of men were busy trying to herd some goats into a rickety-looking barn. Grabbing a passerby, he roared '*Où est le prison?*' He had to repeat the interrogative several times before the terrified man responded. '*Par là! Par là!*' the poor fellow managed to bleat at last, gesturing weakly in the direction of a nearby cross-street. Letting loose the man, who scurried quickly away, Naseby made a dash for the cobbled intersection.

Dusk had fallen rapidly, silhouetting richly the fiery crimson halo that overstretched the southern aspect of the town. The firing had settled into a few sporadic bursts now, something for which he was thankful. The gaol was halfway along the street. A single storey, stone edifice fronting a more imposing building – probably the courthouse. At their approach a blue and red-coated gendarme appeared, half-heartedly raised his musket, evidently lost his nerve, and ducked quickly back inside. Not quickly enough, however, to bar the stout timbered door against the rampaging onslaught of half a dozen brawny English seamen.

The gaol boasted only two iron-barred cells, the first of which was empty. Snatching the large keyring from the belt of the senseless gendarme, Naseby quickly unlocked the second, barking at the cell's quivering female occupant, 'Follow! *Vite, vite!*'

It was full dark by the time the landing party, herding the frightened woman in their midst, made it back to the starlit stretch of beach and the welcoming shape of *Nemesis*'s cutter.

Ahead of them a musket flashed, its report drowned in the thudding boom of a cannon. One of the seamen let out a howl and started hopping. The woman began to scream until another of the seamen nipped it in the bud with a slap. Naseby was more interested in the cannon. Someone was evidently firing on the ship from the headland. With the port minus a full time garrison the thought had not occurred that the French might have a battery located on the point. Likely enough a gendarme post would be situated nearby. No wonder the woman had been taken up so easily.

Up ahead the lone musketeer had found some company, a ragged volley of shots tracing a pattern through the water as they ran for the cutter. One of the seamen used his pistol to fire back, and then they were hoisting the woman aboard. Whether rendered unconscious by the seaman's blow or merely fainted, Naseby didn't know, but as he made his way to the sternsheets he had to clamber over the top of her prone body. He hoped that she wasn't dead.

On the headland the cannon boomed out again, but with what result there was no time to see. Curse Manners – why didn't the man fire back! What with the fire from the town, which by now must be burning wholesale, and a rising moon, *Nemesis* would be lit up like the second coming!

'Jenks is bad, zur,' a voice hissed in his ear. The man sent hopping by the ball from that first musket. ' 'is leg, zur, it's proper bad!'

It was true; even from here he could see that the man would likely lose it.

They were away from the beach now and well out of range of the muskets, which even now were popping off hopefully at them. They would be at the ship soon. She was indeed a sitting target, illuminated vividly against a panoply of darkness.

It was to be wondered how Knowles and the main body were faring. Then a source of comfort to call to mind the steady Snelling and his tall-shakoed Marines.

Forward in the cutter the woman was stirring. It was then that *Nemesis* opened fire. Her side gouting flame and the shot roaring overhead while the cutter, in close proximity, danced on the wavetops to the sudden concussion. Craning around from his position at the helm he could see plainly where the frigate's eighteen pound balls smashed into the bulge of the headland; their combined effect dislodging a great wedge of clifftop and sending it cascading down into the sea below.

Whether or not the enemy battery had been put out of commission remained yet to be seen. But *Nemesis*'s gunlayers had performed well. Lieutenant Manners was to be congratulated. With a bump they were against the side of the ship; a moment more and they had hooked onto the frigate's mainchains and were clambering up her gentle tumblehome, himself in the van in accordance with tradition, and stepping gratefully onto the deck. Manners was on the gangway gazing fixedly towards the headland. Passing the word for his servant to escort Mademoiselle Delacourt aft to his cabin, Naseby joined him at the netting.

'Frenchie's firing high and wide, sir!' reported the first lieutenant, touching a finger to his hat.

As if to prove the veracity of his words, the battery on the headland banged off again. The balls sailing high overhead to raise unseen plumes far out to sea.

Young Soames had a party of waisters at work getting the cutter hauled inboard; *Nemesis*'s gun captains crouching impatiently on the gun deck as they awaited the chance to lay another broadside on the point.

Naseby's arm was paining him. Immediately his thoughts flew to the seaman wounded on the beach. What had his companion called him? Jenks, yes, that was it. The man would be below now, down on the orlop in the after-cockpit having his leg sawn off. For a moment Naseby's hands gripped the hammock netting, holding him upright, steady, whilst a paroxysm of pure horror passed over him.

Then of a sudden he was himself again. At his side Manners appeared not to have noticed. Keeping his eyes fixed firmly on the foreland. Whether or not this studied disinterest on the part of his first lieutenant were affected, Naseby had no way of telling. With a final heave the cutter was swung inboard.

'Fire!' bellowed Manners.

Instantly the decking recoiled beneath their feet, *Nemesis* heeling hard over to the crash of her broadside eighteen-pounders. From nowhere a telescope was pushed into his hand and he half turned to see the Master, Simmonds, balancing easily on the gangway behind him. With a curt nod he raised the glass to his eye. *Nemesis*'s broadside had demolished another section of the cliff.

'How many guns do you make it on the point, Mister Manners?' he asked, swinging the telescope to take in the port.

'Two, thus far; but they're firing separately for the most part,' returned Manners promptly. 'Takes 'em five minutes to reload, sir!' The entire port was on fire. Knowles' diversion had got completely out of hand.

'Just be grateful they Frenchies 'avn't gotten round ta trainin' red'ot shot down on us, Zur!' put in the sailing master bluffly.

Floating wooden walls against fixed emplacement; often heavily fortified, land batteries. Able, given sufficient time, to heat a furnace to hurl sizzling-hot spheres of iron which kindled hidden fires to life the instant they became embedded in a ship's timbers. To his knowledge a seaborne force had never yet fought a successful action against adequately prepared onshore fortifications. Not that those two abysmally laid guns up on the point could be rightly described either as 'onshore fortifications' or as being 'adequately prepared'. Nonetheless, he frowned – worried despite himself; they could always get lucky!

The intermittent battle with the cliff top battery was to continue a full forty-five minutes, neither side managing in that time to do anything more than bombard the seabed with a score of roundshot and great wedges of cliff, while throughout Fréjus burned.

Knowles and the main landing force were aboard unscathed. Not a man lost and but a smattering of minor wounds to show for the raging inferno which they had made of the town.

'You will understand, *Capitaine*, that I can convey nothing to you of the information which I have for your Admiralty. But may I offer you my heartfelt gratitude, *mon brave*!'

Naseby bowed courteously. They were in the frigate's sunlit stern-cabin with Mademoiselle Delacourt seated demurely on the green leather-cushioned locker which extended the full width of the velvet curtained stern-lights. Naseby's servant entered with a silver tray bearing decanter and glasses.

'Madeira, Mademoiselle?' Naseby enquired solicitously.

Mademoiselle Delacourt smiled her acceptance, taking the brimming glass which the elderly Walker held out to her.

Nemesis had cleared the outer harbour of Fréjus without mishap and was now some fifteen hours after the twilight raid on the thriving little seaport, sailing briskly along under all plain sail in a bid to fetch the Strait of Gibraltar before the French could act.

Which hope was soon to prove a vain one.

Mademoiselle Delacourt was a petite, dark-haired woman with a pleasant, if not exactly beautiful, face, and what could only be described as a voluptuous figure, which on many another occasion prior to his marriage to the lovely Sara, Naseby would have found irresistible. Today, however, his fatigue-reddened eyes saw only a passenger whom duty demanded he entertain. He would also, he decided ruefully, have to give up his sleeping cabin to the wanton baggage!

*

Naseby had made the enquiry tentatively, knowing already what it was he would hear.

'Had to take the leg off above the knee, sir!' replied the surgeon matter-of-factly. Naseby bit back an oath. After all, there was nothing of real callousness or lack of genuine concern for his patient in Flawson's seeming indifference, he knew. Rather, perhaps, the opposite; the complacent manner being merely the refuge sought by a man who, in the course of his grizzly business had seen too much. Careful to keep his tone even he pressed further. Flawson thought a moment.

'We-e-ll, zur, not being a physician, I can't rightly say. 'E's sufferin' from shock, o'course, but then, that's only to be expected. Pro-vided mortification don't set in – ?' he trailed off meaningfully.

Naseby decided to press no further.

Weary beyond belief and with his shoulder throbbing painfully he sought the sanctuary of the first lieutenant's quarters and some much needed sleep. With Mademoiselle Delacourt ensconced in the captain's cabin *Nemesis*'s commissioned officers had all had to shift one space along. In effect each returning to the berth which he had occupied prior to the untimely demise of Thomas Tewksbury.

Naseby's old cubby hole smelt stale and airless. His sea chest providing the sole furnishing in addition to the cot. Tugging off his boots (Walker was busy elsewhere) and without bothering to undress, save to divest himself of his coat and lay it neatly atop the sea chest, he stretched himself prone on the cot and within minutes was sound asleep.

The French frigate was waiting for them north of latitude forty (the Gulf of Lyons) on a bearing for Port Vendres. She was the *Montpelier* 44: veteran of a trio of blistering single ship actions, whose near legendary commander, frigate captain Andres Magon, had acquired a reputation for hard-headed tenacity in a score of raids carried out against the heavily guarded Baltic convoys some years back.

Nemesis was beating southward to clear Cape St Sebastian,

her larboard gunports awash as the *Montpelier* hove into view two points off the bow, the tricolour of France fluttering breezily at her stern as the big frigate swung to station herself across their path.

The afternoon watch had just been called and Naseby was leaning against the taffrail staring down at the creaming white waters being churned up in the ship's wake and keeping himself generally out of the way.

Midshipman Howarth panted up with the news of the Frenchman and the compliments of the first lieutenant.

'And – ' Howarth appeared to hesitate as if not wishing to give voice to the rest of the message.

'Well spit it out, damn your eyes!' rasped Naseby.

It worked; instantly the boy was himself again. 'The first lieutenant says she's *Montpelier*, sir! Forty-four guns. Says he saw her off the Texal, sir. Frigate captain Andres Magon!'

Minutes later, with the ruffle of the drums beating to quarters, *Nemesis* was clearing for action.

His heart pounding, Naseby turned his gaze forrad. Was there ever, he asked himself, a sight more exhilarating? To the staccato double-double-double beat of 'Heart of Oak', all of *Nemesis*'s officers, marines and seamen were being instantly galvanised into action. With a speed and agility to astound landlubbers, the frigate's topmen swarmed into the rigging, hardly needing to be urged on by the rope-wielding bo'sun's mates and rapidly climbing over a hundred feet into the upper shrouds. Their allotted task: to take in all but the ship's combat-necessary sails.

On the lower yards clouds of furling canvas were disappearing to lessen the risk of fire aloft. On deck seamen sprinted to their posts. Each task its man, and each man his place. A well-oiled machine of war turning with orchestral precision on the will of a single man – the all-powerful captain – on his will!

Along the gangways red-coated marines, their immaculately pipe-clayed cross-belts dazzling to the eye, took up positions at the hammock netting; others of their number hard at work setting up half-pounder swivel guns in the tops. From where a murderous hail of grapeshot could be directed down onto the deck below should an enemy succeed in boarding. There, too, would be stationed the sharp-shooters. Crack musketeers, who would strive to pick off opposing topmen and, should the opportunity present, easily identifiable officers on the other ship. Such it had been, on the French side, who had carried off Nelson on *Victory*'s blood-smeared quarterdeck.

Even now, the boarding nets were being hauled up, and chain slings rigged from the yards. Below, his, or rather Tewksbury's, furniture would at this moment be on its way to the orlop. Safe, unless the ship sunk. The carpenter and his mates at work striking bulkheads so as to make room for additional guns and also negate, to some extent, the greatest single cause of casualties aboard a ship in action – flying wood splinters.

On the starboard gangway Snelling was barking orders to his marines. Several being dispatched, bayonets fixed, to stand guard over the hatchways; lest the cowardly seek refuge below.

By the mainmast Manners was bawling lustily into his speaking trumpet to the men aloft. Sand was being sprayed on to the gundeck. Powder monkeys appeared from below. All over the ship, from the forward magazine where the master gunner and his mates, wearing felt list slippers against the risk of sparks, would be doling out the serge cartridges which the powder monkeys would tuck into their wood or leather 'salt boxes'; to Flawson down in the after-cockpit: all were engaged in transforming what was for many their floating home, into a lethal machine of destruction. A ship of war!

To Naseby as he watched, it seemed that each and every one of *Nemesis*'s people had been granted the luxury of having something with which to occupy the mind, now, as they sailed into action. Everyone, saving himself. For on his shoulders, and his alone, rested the heavy responsibility for these next hours, perhaps days, fraught with danger and rife with peril.

It was then that the feeling came upon him. That strange and oddly moving sense of things impending which often visited him. An awareness which touched his very being; stroking his soul with its melancholy breath. The action into which he was bound would be as none had been before in his life. Nor perhaps would be again. The hour had come. This would be the time of his testing. The moment for which he had been fore-arming himself all his days thus far. Grinning, he released a soft oath. Very well, and so be it. But the hour should not find him wanting!

Striding briskly forward, he rapped, 'We'll run up the colours, Mister Manners!'

'Ship cleared for action, guns loaded but not run out, sir!' reported Lieutenant Knowles, saluting.

'Very well,' replied Naseby, adding curtly, 'Eight minutes and fifty seconds, Mister Knowles. Well done!'

Knowles beamed and hurried off to his station forrad.

Walker appeared with his pistols and fighting sword, helping him wordlessly on with the wide shoulder belt and holding the double-barrelled pistols butt-forward for his inspection. Naseby took each in turn, checking its priming, drew the twin hammers to half cock and stuffed it snugly into his waistbelt. The shoulder was healing nicely, although it still felt like a red hot poker was being jabbed into the muscle every time he attempted to lift his right arm above the level of his breastbone.

The French frigate had run out her starboard battery, her guns appearing as foreshortened black figures pointing mockingly from their ports at the impudent English ship that had dared to show her colours in the presence of the immortal Andres Charles Magon. Naseby was not impressed.

'She's baring her teeth,' muttered Manners, grinning like a Cheshire cat.

'I do believe you're enjoying the prospect, Mister Manners,' Naseby returned amiably.

'Aye, aye, sir!' parodied the first lieutenant with a gleam in his eye.

This time he was taking *Nemesis* into action for real. No undefended seaport, this. But a sleek, red-hulled forty-four gunner commanded by a man who was probably the greatest frigate captain alive. In an hour, perhaps two, *Nemesis* might be a dismasted floating hulk. Her timbers scored by shot and half – perhaps three quarters – of her people dead or mutilated. Naseby himself might be dead and Sara a widow. Or perhaps worse: he might well survive as a helpless, legless cripple.

Another Jenks. One of those ghastly half human apparitions one could spot in any seaport.

The thought chilled him, but the effect was only momentary. For underlying all his quiet, natural apprehension, his humane concern for the frigate's people, even his fleeting thoughts of Sara, Naseby knew that he was relishing this moment; eagerly looking forward to it, as he had done almost every moment, waking or sleeping; since he had joined the service as a gangling boy of thirteen all those long years ago.

He was a man born to fight and a fight was in the offing. 'God help me!' he breathed, fervently, and then instantly shook off such morbid introspection. Braced himself upright and, with a glint in his eye, strode purposefully to the mizzen-shrouds, telescope tucked snugly underneath his good left armpit ...

XIII

Fates Anointed

'No captain can do very wrong if he places his ship alongside that of an enemy.'

Thus had spoken England's greatest naval strategist Horatio Nelson shortly before the battle of Trafalgar. Of course, the fiery little vice-admiral had been referring to the majestic ships-of-the-line and the scenario which he had been envisaging was admittedly a fleet action. Nonetheless, it was advice which Naseby intended to follow to the letter in his forthcoming duel with frigate captain Andres Magon.

Nemesis was laying over on the starboard tack, bearing swiftly down upon the *Montpelier*, whose captain showed no inclination to engage in any of the usual jockeying for position common to frigate actions.

'He's not even contesting the wind gauge,' commented Manners wonderingly.

It was true. *Montpelier* stood as if a terrier at a bolthole. Her long red hull beam-on to the advancing *Nemesis* – disdaining all contest of seamanship as if her battle-hardened commander had read the intent in his adversary's mind, and reading, was content to comply. And indeed, why not? mused Naseby silently. With the Strait at his back and a heavier gunned ship beneath his feet he was merely applying logic. Placing himself and his ship where the Englishman wished to go, it was as simple and as deadly as that.

'We'll lay her board to board, Mister Manners,' Naseby ordered, his features set and wooden as if hewn from the same oak as the vessel which he commanded. Manners cast him a reflective look before turning to bawl his orders.

Naseby was quietly conscious of the fact that he was

gambling the lives of everyone aboard his ship on the old and perhaps erroneous adage that every Englishman was worth two (or was it three?) Frenchmen. An absurd generalisation and a dangerous one should he be proved wrong. Against the *Montpelier*'s superior armament the *Nemesis* should by rights receive the worst of it in the coming broadside to broadside conflict. But that again was a somewhat naively applied rule of thumb, and one that missed the very real truth that engagements were fought with men and not inanimate walls of wood and cylinders of iron, however ingeniously put together, or imposing of appearance.

As *Nemesis*'s captain he was placing his trust in the proven ability and oft demonstrated superiority of British gun crews, whose rate of fire averaged out at three shots to every two of the enemy, when placed board to board – so close in fact that you could scent the enemy's bilge through his open gunports. When speed of reloading counted for more than accuracy of fire. A well drilled British gun crew could sponge out and reload in a time of two minutes flat.

Already the distance between the ships had closed to under half a mile. Notably the Frenchman had refrained from loosing off a broadside at long cannon shot, something the average Monsieur Crapaud was prone to do.

'He'll aim for our rigging with chain or bar-shot any time now,' forecast Manners grimly.

Naseby nodded; it was on the cards.

'You had our own guns double-shotted, Edward?' he asked conversationally. Already knowing the answer but using the brief informality to lighten the tension.

'Aye, and a charge of grape on top for good measure!' the first lieutenant supplied, grinning tightly. 'If we win you'll most likely get a knighthood.'

Naseby said nothing, nonetheless realising the blank truth of this simply made statement. For such had long been the customary reward for successfully fought single ship actions. 'Sir Philip Naseby'. It had a noble ring to it. Then, feeling that he should reciprocate in some way, offered, 'And yourself, Edward, they'll probably promote you commander.'

The first lieutenant smiled. 'Ah well, that makes no mind,

sir. I'm afraid I'm too old now for ambition. I've had my day, Philip!'

'Here it comes!' piped up Simmonds the master from his stance by the wheel.

A howling sheet of terror had erupted from the Frenchman's side. *Nemesis* seemed to check momentarily in the water, as if running head-on into an invisible hail of destruction. Naseby cast an anxious look aloft. The fore-t'gallant mast was hanging in its slings, hugely gaping holes appearing in both fore and main courses.

Impervious to the danger, he leapt for the weather shrouds. It was vital that he judge the moment perfectly. A cable and a half and closing fast. For one heart-stopping instant it seemed as if *Nemesis*, his beautiful frigate, were racing pell-mell to her doom. Doggedly he shook all thoughts of blazing ships and disembowelled men from his teeming brain.

Up forrad, Lieutenant Knowles had his boarding party told-off and ready: half pikes and tomahawks glinting brightly amongst the array of cutlasses, pistols and not a few muskets. Snelling had his marines, save for those posted at the hatchways, dispersed between the fighting tops, the nettings, and a reserve drawn up, bayonets gleaming, on the quarterdeck.

Nemesis was within a cable of her enemy now. From his precarious perch in the mizzen shrouds Naseby fancied that he could even pick out *Montpelier*'s captain on her rolling quarterdeck. Something about the braced stance and alert carriage of the man. Leaping to *Nemesis*'s quarterdeck, he snatched up the japanned speaking trumpet to bawl his orders.

Half a cable, and after that single murderous broadside, the Frenchman's guns had remained silent, both commanders grimly acknowledging the terrible inevitability of the slaughter which was to follow. Naseby raised the speaking trumpet to his lips.

'Quartermaster! Hard over! Back the mizzen top's'l! Open starboard gunports! Run out the guns! Quartermaster, lay her alongside!'

Heeling savagely, *Nemesis* lurched to obey the demands of helm and wind, her barefooted seamen hauling insanely at the braces while from up forrad Knowles' boarding party had started up with a rousing chorus of 'Portsmouth Lass'. Caught up in the spirit of the thing, a smattering of men on the gundeck had taken it up now, their lusty voices ringing along the length of the guncrews crouching beneath the gangways and being echoed by the sharpshooters in the tops.

In a gesture of melodramatic appeal to rival Nelson at his best, Naseby swept off his hat, jumped up onto a stubby thirty-two pound carronade and added his own tuneful baritone to the rendering. Despite the protest in his shoulder, waving urgently for Snelling and his men to do the same.

'Inspired. Bloody inspired,' applauded Manners, brandishing the speaking trumpet.

On the decks of the *Montpelier* men were also singing, although what tune, Naseby was never to know.

He had misjudged the moment to turn, leaving it late and not allowing sufficient searoom in which to swing. With a resounding crack, the like of a point blank pistol shot, *Nemesis*'s bowsprit snapped clean off, bringing down a goodly portion of her already damaged foretop in a tangle of cordage and slapping canvas. Seconds later the ship came to a traumatic standstill, her bow grinding sickeningly into the Frenchman's.

The enormous force of impact hurled Naseby from his perch, sending a vibrant shock wave the entire length of the hull. Screams and cries echoed everywhere. Picking himself dazedly off the deck, Naseby clawed out his sword, gazing about him until he located Manners in like case beside the binnacle box. Simmonds the master was staring stupidly at a spreading circle of red on the planking beside him. Evidence that the sharpshooters in the Frenchman's tops had already begun their deadly work. Moments later Simmonds was dead.

Up forrad the steadily growing roar of battle showed where Knowles and his boarders were already engaging the enemy. With a cry to Manners to remain aft, Naseby leapt nimbly to the starboard gangway, flourishing his sword like a clarion call as he raced its length to join the general mêlée that was taking place on the foredeck. Knowles' already bloodstained and hatless figure was caught up in a press of ferociously fighting men around the forehatch. Baring his teeth against the raw agony in his shoulder, Naseby hurled himself bodily into the fray: slashing, cutting, cleaving at the bare-chested swarm of insanely yelling Frenchmen who were surging like ants onto the frigate's foredeck.

A pistol banged almost in his face as a burly gun-captain cleared a swathe to him with a flailing hand spike.

'We must cut her loose!' Naseby bellowed at the man, gesturing with his sword at the tangle of cordage that was holding the two ships together. 'Use the guns! The guns!' he was shouting, attempting to relay that unless they could get broadside to broadside with the Frenchman they would be overwhelmed by her seemingly multifarious crew.

Fortunately the man had brains, and seeing the situation for himself, nodded quickly. Hacking to right and left, it took the pair a blood-drenched ten minutes to fight their way to where they could do some good with the wreckage. Young Knowles had seen them, and within several more minutes had fought his own way through, bringing with him a party of axemen.

Locked together as they were, neither ship could bring her guns to bear in any real way, save for the Frenchman's foremost starboard cannon. Which boomed out incessantly, shaking the deck beneath their feet as the impact of its twenty-four pound balls struck solidly home. Fervently Naseby hoped that its continuous onslaught would do its bit in driving the two ships apart.

They were drifting gently, like a pair of enraged stags whose sprouting headgear had become hopelessly enmeshed, leaving them with little choice but to sidestep together. Snelling had brought his marines up at last, their howling charge, bayonets levelled, doing more to clear *Nemesis*'s canting foredeck of milling Frenchmen than a canister of grape.

The marine lieutenant tossed him a gleeful look as he formed up his men for a second wave. Muskets were popping rhythmically from the Frenchman's fo'c'sle, spherical leaden hornets ploughing into the planking at their feet and spanging off the forward twelve pounders.

Suddenly they were free. But instead of drifting some small distance apart as he had hoped, *Nemesis* bumped jarringly along the length of the other ship; board to board, it was true, but also bulwark to bulwark. Or almost so; the only thing saving them from the worst of this unlooked for calamity being the shallow tumblehome of the two frigates.

As it was, how many of the jutting cannon were being dislodged and torn from their carriages on both ships was a matter for conjecture. What was infinitely worse was that the wily Frenchman, realising his advantage, had organised grappling irons; and above their heads nimble-footed enemy topmen were doing their best to lash the spars of the two ships fast together.

Naseby was vaguely conscious that he was yelling at the top of his lungs. Though to good effect, for already the cry had been taken up along the length of the frigate as a horde of voices roared, 'Fend her off! Fend her off!' It was to be hoped that somebody was actually doing something to put the order into effect – other than yelling.

Suiting action to the thought, Naseby grabbed a broken section of bowsprit, grunting hoarsely as his shoulder took the weight, and assisted by Snelling and some of the marines, drove the splintered end against the Frenchman's side. It seemed to him as he struggled with the length of spar that there was fighting everywhere; that the whole world had gone mad, and he alone grappling to bring some order into the confusion.

Nevertheless, inch by inch, then by a yard, they were succeeding. Screams rang shrilly as men, both friend and foe, tumbled helplessly to the brilliant blue waters between the inexorably separating ships. Many of *Montpelier*'s boarders, so triumphant but a short time ago, finding themselves trapped and being fast left behind by their countrymen, turned on their heels and leapt the steadily widening gap back to the safety of their own deck. Quite a few didn't make it, falling instead to their deaths – it being a strange irony that but few sailors could swim.

Witnessing this, a goodly number of Frenchmen threw down their weapons and surrendered. Naseby was beside himself; snarling like a rabid beast *Nemesis*'s captain cleared a path with the hilt of his heavy fighting sword through the throng of men on the starboard gangway, knocking aside English and French alike in his dread urgency to bring the frigate's broadside into action. Again the Frenchman beat him to it, *Nemesis* reeling drunkenly from a frightful barrage of roundshot and grape. 'A pox on the Frenchman!' Naseby found himself shouting. Andres Magon was living up to the legend that had grown up around him.

As if in answer to a prayer, a sudden ragged broadside blasted out from the guns beneath his feet. This time it was a pleasant sensation to feel the ship heeling as he watched the effect on the Frenchman of the frigate's double-shotted broadside. As if by a miracle that first ragged salvo, the first which *Nemesis* had fired thus far, had managed to bring down the enemy's mizzen; snapped off like a jagged toothpick, its stump sticking up a bare ten feet above her quarterdeck.

Wild with exhilaration, Naseby looked about for the ministering angel who had set the gun crews to their work. Manners! In the hectic furore of the past thirty minutes, he had quite forgotten the first lieutenant. There he was now, striding effortlessly below the gangway, barking orders in a stentorian voice to the diligently labouring gun crews.

'Stop yer vents! Sponge out! Properly there, do yer want ta lose yer arm! Reload! Lively, number six gun! Run out and fire when ready! Fire at will!'

Up forrad Knowles had joined in the gunnery, his harsh cries of 'Fire as your guns bear!' bringing a smile to Naseby's sweat-streaked face. Barely a dozen feet apart and board for board, it was hard to imagine a broadside gun that wouldn't bear.

On the quarterdeck the stubby thirty-two pound carronades were thundering out their lethal message. Courtesy of midshipman Soames, no doubt! That was Naseby's place. Sheathing his sword, and with a last quick look to check on the fact that the French prisoners were being satisfactorily herded below, he hurried aft to the quarterdeck.

Vast greasy brown coils of smoke overlaid all. Making it impossible to see the enemy with any degree of clarity and hard enough just to breathe. There was an almost continuous crescendo of weaponry from both ships now, the two frigates board and board and fighting it out like a pair of hundred-gun ships-of-the-line. *Nemesis* juddered and curtseyed as the weight of metal from the *Montpelier* slammed into her timbers, righted herself, and then heeled over again as her straining powder-stained gun crews sent Monsieur Crapaud his answer.

A violent wave of hot air slammed him in the back as a twenty-four pound roundshot tore across the quarterdeck, smashing through the feeble battlements provided by the rolled-up hammocks lashed to their nettings, and demolishing a bare-chested gunner on the way. A moment only he looked on the twitching red torso; as always when the battle was in and humanity out, totally unmoved by the sight. Seconds later a whole gun crew had joined the gory spectacle as a shot took one of the starboard carronades full in the muzzle. Wooden of aspect, Naseby stood as if a statue, feet firmly spaced apart, hands clasped beneath coat tails, his eye on the Frenchman. Someone was striving valiantly to raise a cheer, but with little result.

'All right, my lads,' he mouthed absently, 'save yer cheers. But see yer pepper that pox-ridden Frenchman.'

Hour upon hour the battle raged, and still *Nemesis*'s captain stood. Even when midshipman Soames took a musket ball in the belly and was carried screaming to the after cockpit, still he stood. Until all around him lay steeped in death and destruction. Yet still – impervious to ball and flying splinter, deafened by the roar of the guns and blinded by the fog of powdersmoke – yet still he stood, the single bullion epaulette showing dully on his shoulder and the determination fixed within him to be victorious or perish. And throughout all, amidst the clamour and the smoke, the danger and the dying, his brain worked coolly on.

Now was his moment of truth. Here was his chance for glory. If he lived he'd be a hero; while if he died – most like a fool. He had spied his fate, and spying, urged its coming. Gathering fate's fickle lady hotly to his bosom. If he fell, he fell in grace – the only grace which the fighting man can either know or understand. And if he stood? Untouched by all, shielded by chance. Why, then, he was by fate anointed – and fates anointed can know no terror!

As dusk began to cast her mercifully shielding mantle over the two protagonists, the Frenchman lost his foremast. By the time the quickly spreading darkness was full abroad, the *Nemesis* was a floating charnel-house.

Some time during the fray the frigate had lost her ensign. Lest the Frenchman think that he had struck, Naseby had unconsciously emulated several heros of the past, having his colours, the union flag, nailed to the mast. There to remain in plain sight for all who had the eyes and wits to read its tacit message: that there would be no surrendering that day. 'Victory or Westminster Abbey,' as Nelson had been wont to say, or something of that valorous flavour. In any event, Naseby heartily approved the sentiment.

Throughout the evening and far into the night the guns sounded. Until from sheer exhaustion the gun crews aboard both vessels fell limply across their red-hot charges; spent and ill from the horror and the din, and as if by mutual consent the conflict slowly abated and finally ceased.

Dawn Wednesday 27th May revealed a glossy expanse of calm blue sea, broken only by a faint morning breeze. Barely strong enough to lift the tiny catspaws that lapped gently against *Nemesis*'s battered hull as she drifted ever so slowly to leeward. Her captain sat hunched over a larboard carronade, doing his best to force down a few mouthfuls of cold salt pork as he grimly surveyed the havoc wreaked by the Frenchman's formidable weight of metal. Slowly his near vacant gaze took in the once beautiful frigate's shot-torn decks and splinter-riven bulwarks, lingering absently on the row upon row of canvas-draped mounds and the stinking human offal which seemed to everywhere abound.

Nemesis's foremast was a blackened stump, while her mizzen and maintops had long since ceased to exist. Struck to kindling or floating sorrowfully in the direction of Port Vendres, it mattered not.

There had been no time – or for that matter, thought – to cast astern the frigate's boats in her mad, glorious dash to come to grips with her enemy. Hence they had been smashed to matchwood, their indiscriminately flying splinters doubtless responsible for a large measure of the lethal work done on her bloodied decks. During the night the two ships had drifted some considerable distance apart; each in her own inanimate but somehow knowing way, retiring sadly away to lick her wounds and allow her flesh and blood helpers time to tend her hurts, before once again lifting all remaining canvas to the wind and limping resolutely back to begin the slaughter over.

Montpelier lay wallowing helplessly in the water, at perhaps three cables distance to starboard. A grotesque floating hulk; her once red hull a smoke-blackened ruin; the triple fangs of her previously majestic masts mere blistered stalks, sticking obscenely up against the luminescent brilliance of the sky. Only her limply drooping tricolour, hung from a spar affixed to the stump of her mainmast, showed her captain's mute defiance; evidenced the man's indomitable spirit and relentless will to fight. Naseby's heart went out to the man. The freely given but hard won respect of one warrior for another.

Lieutenants Manners and Knowles – the latter with a bloodstained rag encircling his head – stood together against the weather nettings, or rather, what remained of them. Getting unsteadily to his feet, Naseby paced resolutely across to join them, having to step over a tangle of cordage and an upended carronade on the way. At his approach Edward Manners, looking if anything even more elderly this morning, straightened himself to attention and ran a claw-like hand over his stubble of snowy white bristles. Without preamble, Naseby rapped out his orders.

An hour later *Nemesis*, all available canvas set, was inching slowly but inexorably towards the Frenchman, her stiff-backed captain intent on finishing the task upon which he had so willingly embarked.

Incredibly, it was to take another full hour to close to within pistol shot of the *Montpelier*. During which time the tiny black dots massed together on her upper deck and ravaged fo'c'sle grew steadily in stature. To become at last the smoke-grimed seamen and blue-coated soldiery of the Emperor Napoleon.

Neither ship had fired a shot. But the fact that they were ready to could be evidenced in the softly sputtering slow matches suspended over buckets of seawater and glimpsed on the resolute faces of the men. A proportion of the flintlock firing mechanisms on *Nemesis*'s guns were now defunct and would soon have need of linstock and slowmatch. No doubt the same story was true on *Montpelier*'s gun-carrying maindeck.

For a moment, as he watched the Frenchman, Naseby's mind went scurrying below. To the hellish pit of degradation that was the after cockpit. The bloodied domain of surgeon Flawson and his mates. The half-witted loblolly boys grinning foolishly at the severed limbs and pain-racked remains of brave English seamen. Someone, Naseby forgot who, had informed him that Mademoiselle Delacourt was there, helping to tend the wounded. Even assisting in the dread amputations. Naseby grunted aloud, eliciting an enquiring look from Manners at the rail beside him. Perhaps after all he had been a little hasty in his somewhat scathing mental summing up of the Frenchwoman's character.

At long last he was able to pick out the braced stance and erect bearing of the figure he had unconsciously sought: frigate captain Andres Magon standing aloof on his quarterdeck amid the wreckage and the ruin of his once invincible *Montpelier*. Even had he been amongst the crowd on the French maindeck, Naseby would have known him. Known him by the aura of almost mystic aloneness which surrounded him. It was almost like looking at himself, as he knew Magon was. A long moment they stood thus, silently regarding one another; kindred spirits in this Armageddon of war.

Then with a flourish the Frenchman lifted his hat, holding it steadily over his head as if acknowledging the imagined salute of cannon and the raucous blare of a band. The time-honoured salute of the old French Imperial Navy. Honoured, Naseby reciprocated, doffing his cocked hat and placing it across his broad chest. It was a final gesture, a last tribute.

Moments later the guns were speaking again. Roundshot thudding into timbers; seamen screaming in agony and the wild banshee howl of searching musket fire. Head bowed, Naseby took up his stance by the splintered quarterdeck rail. *Nemesis*'s people had fought bravely, valiantly, doing all that he had asked of them. It had been over; for all real purposes he had won. It had lain within his power to stand off, to bear away and, the wind permitting, bypass the stricken *Montpelier*. What was more, the thing would have been done in all honour. There was really no need for all to die because, because – Of what? His quest for a knighthood?

What would Magon have done were their situations reversed, he wondered dully. But he already knew the answer to that. Andres Magon would have done precisely as he was doing. 'Glorious victory or Westminster Abbey!' The famed rallying cry had a hollow ring to it now.

Montpelier's scuppers were awash with and spilling a steady stream of blood into the sea. Along the length of her smoke-wreathed hull large gaping holes had appeared between the gun ports, imparting an aspect of broken-toothed incongruity. *Nemesis*'s pumps had been working non-stop since almost the first broadside all those hours before, their dull clanking setting up a monotonous background to the thundering roar of the guns. A flying splinter grazed his thigh, cutting through the material of his breeches and breaking the skin. He didn't notice; his booted feet ('surgeons be bolluxed' he always preferred boots to shoes) planted firmly on the deck, now canting ever so slightly.

Montpelier was listing badly; such could be plainly evidenced, even through the smoke. Nonetheless the stabbing orange tongues of her broadside guns still bore vivid testament to her captain's indomitable fighting spirit. It could not last. Indeed, it seemed incredible that the two wooden-walled combatants were yet afloat. A pair of heedlessly drifting oak fortresses crammed with dead and dying men.

And two insane captains? Yes, Naseby had to admit that such was possible. For in truth, what else could account for such as this?

As the morning wore on, one by one the Frenchman's guns fell silent. Smashed asunder by *Nemesis*'s faster firing eighteen-pounders or merely lacking in able-bodied men to serve them. The result was now inevitable. And shortly after midday it came. Some unseen hand aboard *Montpelier*, Naseby was never to be able to find out who, deciding that enough was enough, struck down the valiant captain Magon and hauled down the tattered remnant of her tricolour. It was enough.

Montpelier had struck her colours.

'Cease fire! Cease fire all!' Naseby's hoarse-throated roar echoed and re-echoed in the sudden, eerie stillness ...

*

One whole week later, jury-rigged, the frigate *Nemesis*, her captive towing half a cable astern, limped triumphantly into the harbour at Gibraltar. On her quarterdeck her acting captain, Commander Philip Masterman Naseby, standing easily to attention to acknowledge the tribute of the fort's saluting cannon.

Nemesis's butcher's bill had been appalling. Fifty-four men dead, including midshipman Soames and also Marine Lieutenant Snelling; seventy more wounded, at least half of whom were not expected to live beyond a few days. On the French side the losses had been even more devastating: over ninety killed in action; a score above that figure wounded, a third of whom had expired shortly after, and perhaps thirty vanished overboard, leaving barely a skeleton crew to work the ship under *Nemesis*'s second, the rapidly maturing Lieutenant Knowles.

A scrap of canvas had been rigged from one of *Nemesis*'s few surviving spare spars, fished to *Montpelier*'s mainmast stump, following the solemn removal of her captain's improvised flag pole. Valiant Andres Magon had been sent to feed the fishes. A tardy end for such a brave man, Naseby had thought. But then, he was in good company. Altogether one hundred and ninety-seven men, from both ships, had gone sliding over the side, sewn up in their hammocks and with a roundshot at their feet to speed their going. 'A waste of good roundshot,' some lordly wag of a landlubber had once said ...

XIV

The People's Hero

Naseby's fame had preceded him. As the gunbrig *Vesper* hove-to in the Solent it seemed that the entire Channel fleet had turned out to honour him. At Gibraltar the Admiral commanding the Mediterranean station had snatched Naseby and his passenger, Mademoiselle Delacourt, unceremoniously out of the *Nemesis* and, with barely time, it seemed, in which to write his reports and dispatch them aboard the Falmouth-bound packet, had dumped them on board the gunbrig *Vesper*, the lieutenant of which – a bright spark named Mason – was taking her home for a refit. Two hours after landing on the wetly glistening cobblestones of the hard, Naseby and Mademoiselle Delacourt were aboard a racing post-chaise for London.

Before that, however, had come the long overdue informal chat with Cuthbert Collingwood. The Vice-Admiral was staying at The George, where he had taken a comfortable suite of rooms. It was late June and his lordship was cooling himself before a wide-flung upper floor window as Naseby entered the room. Turning, Collingwood treated his expected visitor to a warm smile, gesturing him towards a high-backed leather chair.

'We can dispense with all ceremony, Naseby,' the Admiral began at once, coming over to ease his growing bulk down into the chair opposite. A moment he fixed his visitor with a searching look. Then, apparently finding whatever it was that he sought, went on in a matter of fact voice, 'You've done well, my boy. Indeed, even better than I had anticipated. Absolutely justifying my – ' he laughed shortly, 'er, at times somewhat unpopular faith in you. For which I am well pleased!'

Flattered, if still a trifle perplexed, Naseby decided that it was high time to take the bull by the horns. Careful to keep his tone respectful, he said, 'You'll forgive me, m' lord – '

Collingwood waved an impatient hand in negation of the title.

Undeterred, Naseby resumed, 'Ah, hum, thank you, er, m' lord, but I trust that you'll forgive me if I ask – '

'The reason for my patronage of you?' The Admiral broke in shortly.

Naseby contented himself with a nod.

Collingwood leaned comfortably back in his chair. 'There's no mystery, Naseby. The plain fact is that England needs heroes. Needs them quite desperately at certain times.' His lordship's frank eyes glinted. 'And you, Naseby, are a hero.' Hastily he held up a forestalling hand. 'Oh, I don't mean now.' He laughed again, that same short, half reflective laugh that he had. 'Your, er, recent accomplishments and the resultant happy situation in which you accordingly find yourself, are, but, to put it plainly, er, the proof of the pudding! While the heroic Philip Naseby has long been a reality. A sort of hero-in-waiting, if you will.'

'In the making' would be a more appropriate phrase, Naseby thought, but allowed the Admiral to continue uninterrupted.

'You have the aura of it about you; plain as pease pudding, to those with eyes to see it.' He paused, a look of distant remembrance stealing into the almost sensual eyes. 'Nelson had it, too, you know. Kind of halo that grew up around him when sailing into action. "A cavalier riding to the sound of the guns," someone once termed it.'

Collingwood had fallen silent. Brooding in the glorious past. Tactfully and despite his growing embarrassment, Naseby recalled him to himself with a question.

'And you feel you see this, whatever it is, in me, sir?'

Collingwood answered brightly. 'Oh, not in the same way, perhaps. Different character altogether. Also I seriously doubt that you'll ever make a useful strategist. Although I'm willing to admit that I could be wrong; such a thing has been known to happen!' A moment his eyes twinkled, as if softening the words. 'No – but the leadership, the vainglorious bravery – that I see aplenty.'

Naseby didn't have anything to say which seemed suitable to the moment.

'So there you have it!' his lordship was saying. 'The people need heroes, and it's the task of those of us in a position so to do to, as it were, spot likely candidates and further, see to it that they receive their chance. You're an indifferent seaman, and by all accounts, a worse navigator. But when you leave this room, Philip Masterman Naseby, you leave it a post captain; you're to be gazetted within the week.' Collingwood considered him ironically. 'Do you live long enough and you'll be an admiral. But then, such is the quality of war. Whereas in peacetime – ' The implications of that were obvious, hence the Admiral didn't finish.

'I'd have ended my days as a lieutenant,' Naseby finished for him.

'Or perhaps a mere midshipman,' Collingwood countered mischievously. At once his manner tautened, becoming again all business. 'Go and be a hero for them, Naseby. The landed gentry will heap honours upon your head. While the herd will cheer themselves hoarse, and then promptly forget you the moment it's over and the danger past. But that, my plucky lad, is the lot of history's fighting men, and will ever be so until the dawning of some far distant day when such as we are no longer needed. And that day – ' he quietly appended taking up a long-stemmed clay pipe and stuffing it with tobacco from a wooden bowl – 'will not, I fancy, come in either your lifetime or mine. Good day to you, Captain Naseby.'

It was a clear statement, both of dismissal and of the fact that from this moment on in time post captain Philip Naseby's future career in the service resided entirely in his own two hands. To make or break as he so chose.

It was with somewhat mixed feelings that Naseby quietly drew the door closed on the contentedly puffing admiral.

*

London still stank of horseshit and the squalid maze of streets that inevitably seemed to wind back on themselves were as ever, ridiculously narrow for the incessant press of traffic, both vehicular as well as human. Nevertheless, it was the capital – a sprawling cesspit of violence, deprivation and, in certain quarters, genteel grace, easy living and privilege.

Philip Naseby loved it all as the stately black coach sped him swiftly beyond the city towards Surrey and a joyous reunion with his beloved Sara.

At first he had worried when his landing at Portsmouth had not found her waiting for him, being tremulously concerned for her health and well-being. He need not, however, have worried. As the letter written in her own fair hand and delivered to him, of all places, at the Admiralty had explained.

'Your devoted wife Sara,' the letter had read, ... accompanied by Sir Walter and Anne Perry, had been summoned to Hampton Court immediately news of his victorious exploits and imminent homecoming had reached England. Where they were presently ensconced as the favoured guests of His Majesty the King and the Prince of Wales. Who, as Sara had somewhat imprudently put in her letter, was, despite being a dread lecher and inveterate gambler, nonetheless for that, a quite jolly fat fellow!

Nemesis would in due course be returning to Plymouth and thence to Portsmouth where, following an extensive refit, she would lay up at Spithead awaiting the return to duty of her newly promoted captain.

Naseby allowed himself a smile of silent contemplation. In three years' time he should have acquired a second bullion-fringed epaulette for his now vacant left shoulder. Being then substantive in the rank and of equal standing with a colonel in His Majesty's army. He would be six months short of being twenty-seven. Nelson had made it earlier, but then, Nelson was dead. In twenty years, perhaps less, he could be an admiral!

His twenty-third birthday had passed unnoticed. Eclipsed by the sad death of William Perry. A man whom, had he lived, would surely have become a lifelong friend. The memory yet brought pain. For in truth, there were few enough such in the life of a man, to be so easily lost.

They were traversing Wimbledon Common now, favoured haunt of highwaymen these hundred and fifty years past. A fading breed; since the dawning of the nineteenth century there had yet been sufficient incidence of travellers upon the King's highway finding themselves waylaid by those self-styled 'gentlemen of the road' as to impart caution. Evidently the coachman up forrad agreed, for without doubt the horses were even now being urged on to greater efforts. The staccato crack of the driving whip ringing out crisp and clear above the racing hooves. A ragged series of distant pistol shots rolling wind-borne across the common.

Allowing his imagination free rein, Naseby smiled. It would be a bold highwayman indeed who dared stop a coach carrying a King's officer in full uniform and complete with sword and travelling pistol. Nevertheless, it was some wit amusing, as the speeding coach bore him momentarily nearer the eagerly awaited reunion with his beloved Sara and heaven knew what (should the unexpected summons to Hampton Court turn out to mean that which he hoped) to sit thus engaged in mental sport as will a child, and recall to mind some lines of verse, but long forgot.

The ballad concerned a highwayman purported to have operated along this stretch of road around 1720, whom the gentry had tagged with the evocative name of 'Moonlight', appending the honorific 'Captain' according to the custom of the day. Naseby could remember but portions of the thing, but knew that it went something like this:

His horse as black as midnight,
With hooves of burnished steel.
He rode abroad from dusk till dawn,
And lived but for to steal.

He stopped a coach on Kingston Hill,
His fortune for to make,
And cried 'Give me your money,
Or your life I'll surely take!'

With a final stanza that could, if one so desired, be utilised as a chorus throughout:

Ho! Stand and deliver!
Through the night his voice would ring;
Ho! Stand and deliver!
Like a phantom on the wing ...

There was a catchy little tune that went with it, too, but for the life of him he couldn't quite call it to mind.

Shocked back to reality by the larboard coach wheel bouncing over a rut in the road, he realised that the horses were slowing. He stuck his head out of the window. They were climbing Kingston Hill. In no time they would be at the palace. Over there, some five miles as the crow flew, lay Merton Place where Nelson had paced in his summer house, planning his tactics for the day when he should meet Villeneuve. The while responding to the coddling and solicitous nursing back to health which he had received from an adoring Lady Hamilton.

There also it had been that shortly before dawn on 2nd September Captain Henry Blackwood had arrived with the news that the Combined Fleet was in Cadiz, held under loose surveillance by Admiral Collingwood. 'Ripples in a stream,' someone had said, all 'ripples in a stream.' Pondering this had driven all thoughts of the long departed 'Captain Moonlight' from his mind. If indeed there had ever really been such a fellow – And when, raised from his reverie he again chose to look out of the window, the hill, its phantom horseman? and much else besides, had sped from view ...

Hampton Court, a royal residence since Henry VIII; partially rebuilt by Christopher Wren and originally the home of the bungling Cardinal Wolsey, presented an imposing enough sight, to be sure. Why, the grounds themselves were an education. All of which aside – however splendid and lofty his surroundings – at this precise moment His Majesty's newest post captain had eyes only for Sara. Surprised, stooping by the rose bushes, she yet remained still. Frozen in mid motion, neither kneeling nor yet upright. An essence of love emanated from her, what at other times could appear cool, green eyes, the like of which he should never in his entire lifetime have looked so to find directed at him.

A moment longer he was granted to wonder at the sun in her

hair; and then she was moving. Running happily to greet him. The roses forgotten, her basket fallen; all about them blithely receding. Only the radiant softness of her smile, the warmth of her tight in his arms, their first, silent embrace.

Sir Walter and a patently rejoicing Anne Perry came strolling across to join them in a while. The baronet was smiling, every wit the like of a proud father, touching Naseby deeply. Should the kindly old man's own son but have lived? But then, remember, 'ripples in a stream'. It were better he hold fast to that!

They dined that evening, not with the King, but alone, as a family, in the Perrys' apartments, Naseby having much to relate, all the while secretly awaiting the summons which he felt sure would come, and Sara and the Perrys ever eager to listen. Sara had appeared a wit perturbed upon his narrative having reached the part where he and a handful of *Nemesis*'s seamen had stormed the Fréjus gaol and rescued Mademoiselle Delacourt. Whether due the risk this entailed, or wholly natural feminine jealousy, he couldn't decide. All had been well, however, when, asked to describe Mademoiselle, he had adroitly side-stepped the issue, referring to her only as 'fat'.

'Fat like the Prince?' Anne Perry wanted to know.

Not having seen His Highness, Naseby was momentarily at a loss. Sir Walter came to the rescue. 'Did you then leave this Madame Delacourt at Whitehall?'

'Er, yes,' answered Naseby quickly. 'At the Admiralty. When I left she was closeted with the First Secretary and a couple of admirals.'

The dinner passed pleasantly and afterwards, with the ladies departed from the room, he and Sir Walter sat puffing contentedly on a pair of the new French cigars. Naseby had to admit that he found them much to his taste. His shoulder was now almost as good as new. There was a scar, of course, which he dreaded the thought of allowing Sara to see; having glossed over in recounting his adventures all but the briefest mention of the wound. Were he to attempt to relate the horrors of the cockpit, the instruments warming on the brazier, the –

Lieutenant Knowles, he knew, was being made commander and would be staying with the squadron at Gibraltar. Very pleasing and well deserved. Edward Manners was remaining in *Nemesis* and would doubtless be charged with the task of bringing her safe home. No promotion there. He had been sensibly careful when penning his reports that his words reflect equal credit on either man. With perhaps just an ounce more praise for his veteran first lieutenant, without whose able assistance he knew he should not now be sitting here.

Praise which in the event the Admiralty had chosen to ignore. Well, he reflected wryly, it wasn't after all the first time. Not that the reasoning behind same need be veiled in any great mystery. Their lordships having decided, doubtless with laudable expediency, that Knowles' obvious youth augured future usefulness. Whereas Manners' grey hairs did not. It was as simple as that. 'In the best interests of the service,' would be the official phrasing.

Which studied cynicism, however, didn't totally blind him to the fact that he could now count himself fortunate in having an exceedingly able and vastly experienced 'number one' with him on his and the *Nemesis*'s next voyage. Could that perhaps have been what their lordships had in mind? At any rate he would be returning to sea a … ?

*

The summons came at eight o'clock. And what a fine fat fellow he is indeed, mused Naseby patiently; as he stood in the partially open doorway of the little ante room on the second floor of the palace. Waiting to be presented to the reigning monarch King George III, and his heir apparent. For the occasion he had donned silk stockings and shoes with heavy gold buckles; the single epaulette, its swinging bullion fringe carefully untangled, struck reflections off the facing wall. His full dress coat was brand new and of the style and cut laid down in the dress regulations for captains of 1st June 1795. The sleeves slashed and edged in two rows of gold lace, two similar bands around each cuff, denoted his rank. His equally new cocked hat, splendid with tassles at either end, lace, button and black silk cockade, reposed importantly beneath his left arm. The plain fighting sword which had served him so well had been temporarily exchanged for its uniform counterpart, bearing the lion's head pommel.

The King was beckoning. At once a uniformed usher began to propel him forward, into the royal presence. The room was over-bright, forcing him to squint. He must make an effort to see and hear all. The exquisite clothing of the lords and ladies, the jewels; that for Anne and Sara, who of course had doubtless beheld its like already. The furnishings and exactly who had been there, for Sir Walter. While Gray for his part would be disappointed not to read in his letter a detailed recounting of the various distinctions and decorations which adorned the uniforms of those military personages present. Almost in desperation – a sea of faces, immaculate uniforms, and women in multifarious coloured gowns with pale cheeks and bare arms swimming before him – he strove valiantly to drink it all in.

Everywhere people stood about in attitudes of quiet deference; not a few sporting the blue ribbon of the Order of the Garter. One of their number stepped forth now to take his arm and introduce him to the Prince of Wales, who would present him formally to the King. A round-faced man with wide staring eyes and sensual lips and a jutting beak of a nose.

'Ah – Naseby, is't not? Fine fellow, fine fellow. But over here, my gallant captain, whilst I look at you.'

So saying His Highness moved back a pace, Naseby obediently following, bowing stiffly from the waist and doing his utmost to appear courtly. Unlike his father, the prince was heavy jowled and blotchy; liberal applications of a white face powder doing little to mask the untimely redness which a dissipated lifestyle had imparted. His hair, too, was thinning, and had the look of having been but recently dyed.

' 'Pon my word!' His Highness was beaming to some sycophant posturing gracelessly nearby. 'Methinks 'tis a fine figure of a fellow we see now before us, what?'

At last the great moment had arrived. Naseby kept his eyes firmly riveted on a strip of cracked plasterwork behind the royal shoulder.

'Well, come, come, then, let's at it, gentlemen,' rumbled the King. 'Captain Naseby, your sword. Kneel, if you please.'

Obsequious scurrying footmen had spread ready a narrow roll of carpet upon the mirror-polished floor. Three officials of the order he was about to receive hovered in attendance. Their ceremonial red cloaks lending solemnity to the proceedings. Someone else held a cushion bearing upon it the Order itself. It sparkled richly.

Trembling, and some wit in awe of the occasion, Naseby bent the knee. With his own sword bestowing the accolade and the formal words dubbing him a Knight, a ribbon was hung across his shoulder and a brightly glittering star pinned to his breast. Someone draped a cloak about him, red like the others, and he was bidden rise ...

Profoundly sensible of the moment, he repeated the vow, appended his signature when required so to do, and listened, his heart singing, as his new title was proclaimed loudly. He was now Captain Sir Philip Masterman Naseby, having duly been invested as a Knight of the Most Honourable Order of the Bath. The cloak was removed, and he was almost free to go his way.

'In due time, Captain, when once you attain seniority in your rank – ' The prince pointed with a stubby finger to his single bullion epaulette – 'It will please us greatly to appoint you one of our colonels of Marines! So do you look to your duty, Sir Philip. For now, fare you well.' Then to no one in particular: 'Damned fine fellow, what? Dammee if he isn't!'

Thus dismissed, his title and a royal promise ringing in his ears, the lad from Limehouse with a penchant for rough and tumble brawling, walked dazedly away. Back to the little ante room. Back to Sir Walter and Anne Perry, now fully confirmed in his affections as his family. Back to his very own beautiful wife Sara. A glittering career in prospect, more wealth than he could ever spend – and the frigate *Nemesis* soon returning, her snow white quarterdeck waiting anew the measured tread of her captain's pacing.

However, that was yet in the future. When once again his blood would rise and the need to be up and doing ensnare his dreams. For now there was some time to spend at home. His every ambition (at least for the moment) realised.

Dully he looked about him. He was back in the Perrys' apartments. His summons to court answered; as evidenced by his ribbon and star which he still wore, and at which Anne and

Sir Walter smiled knowingly. Privy from the outset to its bestowal upon him. Sara merely smiled.

'All this,' he mused softly. 'Not yet twenty-four and already all this, all this – !'